DARK
ENDING

C.L. BREES

Printed in the United States of America
First Printing: August 2017
Rostveit/Brees Media

ISBN-13 978-0-692-89502-3

To my amazing husband – thank you for always believing in me when I didn't always believe in myself and for always pushing me to be a better person.

"A sword never kills anybody; it is a tool in the killer's hand."
Lucius Annaeus Seneca

PROLOGUE

THE BRILLIANCE OF BLURRED fluorescent lights zipped by at frequent intervals and Alex slowly drifted back into awareness. He shifted his eyes from left to right at the unknown people surrounding him, each one with concerned facial expressions. Whispers originated from their lips but whatever they were saying made no sense to him.

He strained to fit together a sentence, but nothing would come out.

Where am I? What's going on?

He wanted so badly to reveal his puzzlement, but after numerous attempts he gave up, all he could manage was a grunt. A nurse shined a flashlight into his eyes and pointing out, "He's still with us."

"Alex, look at me, do you know where you are?" another voice inquired.

Alex shook his head ever so little, but a shooting pain ran down his backbone as he did.

What happened? Why am I here and in agony?

The gurney came to an abrupt stop beneath an overhead spotlight, which made Alex's already blurred vision even worse. He cocked his head to his left to avoid the blinding punishment.

He flickered his eyelids three or four times, trying to concentrate on the vague silhouette spread out on another stretcher only two feet apart. After a while, the figure of the body became visible, and he had to close his eyes and open them again to be confident.

I recognize him.

Alex was intimate with the person—it was the face he'd seen at a thousand times in his life, the very one he looked at each dawn when he woke up.

The man lying on one side to him was his fiancé, Mike.

Why's he all bloody, battered, and burned?

An immediate emotion of helplessness swept over him. The stretcher began racing down the corridor once again, and his brief encounter was over. He stared as long as possible as the face of his companion faded further into the background and eventually faded out of eyesight.

A strong masculine voice thundered, "This guy needs to go to surgery, stat."

He wasn't sure what was happening. Why did he need surgery? He fought to move his extremities, to stop the strangers and get some information—anything to ease his distress and aid him in assembling together the missing pieces of what happened. Every time he moved his arm, somebody would set it back down next to his side on the blood-soaked sheet. He tried forcing his feet, but they wouldn't move. There was a numb tingling sensation coursing through his whole body.

"What about the other cop down there?" a woman asked, and everyone became eerily quiet and tuned into her concern.

"Grab Dr. Williams and have him get prepped to take Officer Temple into surgery next."

Officer Temple—that was the last thing Alex picked up before he slipped back into unconsciousness once again.

ONE

Prospect Park, Brooklyn
November 16, 2005
5:47 A.M.

THE MID-NOVEMBER MORNING WAS BRISK and a moderate breeze swept through the sycamore trees of Prospect Park. Alex Jones shivered as he savored his large coffee. He tossed back the pick-me-up and stood towering over the ravaged corpse of another young woman. In the horizon, the sun cropped up, and Alex was glad it had arrived to further illuminate the crime scene. His anxiety grew more waiting for the sun to rise further, but he was also acutely aware that the longer he waited, the more evidence he was losing to the elements.

Another senseless killing. When will it stop?

This particular victim was the third young lady who turned up dead in the park in the previous thirty days. The massacres had the trademarks of a sadistic murderer. Was it even fathomable that a potential serial killer was executing the young women of Brooklyn?

Two points each woman had in common were their ages—they were in their early to mid-twenties—and they had their throats violently slashed. The only differentiation between them was their ethnic background.

There were two Caucasian and one Asian victims. In the first two crimes, the medical examiner concluded the knife used in the attacks as a nine-inch serrated hunting knife, more explicitly a Rambo MC-RB1.

Alex lifted his pant legs up as he knelt at her side, pulled out a clean set of latex gloves and slipped them on over his massive hands. He stripped back the white sheet that covered up the dead body. He took the chance to study her worn-out face. Her freshly cut shoulder-length brunette hair with blond undertones, polished nails, and skin tone all shown that she was a meticulous woman.

Alex built an inviting image of her from the prior night; with her hair fixed up nice, blowing free in the constant breeze that had prevailed over the megalopolis the preceding three days. He envisioned her laugh and celebrating with her acquaintances at a local dance club as the booze flowed. Now, reality set in, and it was a bitter contrast. Her once beautiful hair, now saturated with mud and waste from the earth where her attacker discarded her like yesterday's garbage.

Maybe she struggled with the attacker?

Alex inspected her fingernails. Her bright red nail polish twinkled as the beams of the sunlight burst over the skyline. Each nail was polished, contoured, and trimmed. They remained perfect, except for her right thumb and index finger.

She struggled — this might be the break I need.

Her eyes remained open, transfixed on the dreary sky above. Her lips, no longer a delicate shade of salmon, had a faint baby-blue tone. He fidgeted with his pants leg as a surge of emotions permeated through his muscular frame. All he could do was gawk at her and imagine the terror she must have endured as she breathed her last draw of oxygen. Shuffling a few inches to the left-hand side, he tried to shake off the anxiety from gruesome scene, but the sight of blood always made him squeamish. It took every ounce of strength for him to refocus his thought towards the irregular, gaping wound across her windpipe.

While this homicide victim wasn't his first, with each fresh victim, his heart only deadened more.

Something caught Alex's eye — he drifted in nearer to examine it. His nose was a mere inch from the wound when his colleague, Timothy Carr, interrupted him. Surprised, he fell back onto the damp ground. Carr shook his head, reached out his hand to assist him up.

Rubbing a droplet of perspiration from his temple, he stationed himself down near to Alex, "Sorry I was delayed, something happened at home. So, what have we here?"

"The third dead young woman this month — I'm beginning to see a pattern here, aren't you?"

"Hmm, not sure — you tell me. Aren't you the one with a forensic psych degree?" Carr replied, in a contemptuous tone.

"This is no laughing matter. Did you come across anybody from CSU on your hike here?"

"No one from the ME's office or Crime Scene Unit."

"So characteristic of them." Alex's Blackberry buzzed.

Carr shook his head and huffed.

"Before you answer that call, put a smile on your face."

Alex glanced down at his phone and watched his fiancé's name flash across the screen. "Ugh, thank God it's only you—how'd roll call go this morning?"

"All good at my precinct," Mike returned. "I was told you've got another dead young woman on your hands. Sorry I can't support you with this one."

"I don't believe you'd want to be here for this one — CSU is lost, and I haven't seen the ME yet either. Talk about a royal cluster. Anyhow, I'm happy you called—please, please don't forget we're having dinner with Amy and her current beau this evening."

"Oh right…. err, no, I haven't forgotten about it."

Alex rolled his eyes. "You forgot it, huh?"

"Shit — I hate how you can discover me in a lie even over the phone."

"Hey, I gotta go. Someone has to find the inept forensics team Maybe we could meet up for lunch," Alex suggested.

"All right, it's a date. I'll call you later."

Alex pressed the end button and placed the Blackberry back into the pocket of his black single-breasted wool jacket.

Detective Carr paced around, crisscrossing the space for added evidence. He pointed his pasty index finger towards the northeast. "Look at who agreed to show up."

Alex uncrossed his arms. "It's about freaking time."

Alex stepped towards the yellow crime scene tape that cordoned off the field. There he met up with a pleasant, young guy in his mid-twenties. The CSU investigator was decked out in the typical

NYPD attire. A dark blue windbreaker with the word Forensics spelled out in big letters, beige trousers, and a scuffed pair of black oxford shoes. The young man loomed somewhere between six-two and six-three with broad shoulders and a solid frame. In the man's right hand was a large toolbox—standard issue to the CSU unit.

The Detective, mesmerized by the young supervisors striking features, couldn't break his weakness for tall guys in uniforms. This bit played a huge part in him downplaying the CSU's tardiness to the scene.

"Well, normally I'd be a little more pissed that it took you so long. But now I understand why you were an hour late."

The man grimaced as Alex continued speaking.

"I suppose I should introduce myself; I'm Detective Jones, the lead investigator on this case. And you are?"

"Finch. Aaron Finch, I'm the new CSU Supervisor for this borough. Just started last week." Finch must have foreseen himself to receive an earful so he tried to still be as professional as possible.

"Makes sense now why you are late—got lost, didn't you?"

"Dispatch directed me to the boathouse instead of the picnic house. Same story just a different borough I guess," Finch explained. "I'm here now, so shall we get started?"

Alex beckoned with his pointer finger. "Follow me."

Raising the crime scene tape to permit the tech to move in, they walked side by side towards the corpse that remained beneath the cover. In the background, the landscape was humming with bystanders and reporters hoping to catch a peek. Alex shook his head. *These heathens are always so damn nosy.*

As the tech arrived at the body, he placed the case down on the soil and scoured for evidence. Without the medical examiner present, Alex was at an impasse. The crime scene tech took out a camera and snapped several mid-range photographs of the victim and the landscape. He dashed from one corner of the spot to the following without missing a beat.

"Hey, detectives—I don't believe the crime took place here."

Alex walked towards the supervisor and looked around the area as the Finch continued describing his observation.

"Look around. There isn't much blood here. When the carotid artery is slit you get a bloody mess—but that's not the case here. I'd put down money that this is only a secondary crime scene."

"Good observation, Finch."

"Thanks, Detective."

Alex came back to his feet just as two forensic investigators from the medical examiner's office appeared on the scene

Detective Carr glanced at Alex. "Suppose it's one of those days that everybody is late to the party."

"All right, Carr, that's enough. Can you sign them in?" Alex motioned his partner towards the two investigators standing at the cordon.

Alex walked back and forth in a limited circle.

The most recent victim confirmed his suspicion that a serial killer was emerging, but one thing about it pissed him off, and that was how could a recently promoted detective discern a correlation between the victims yet no one more experienced than he could? Most times he got ostracized because he was a junior, inexperienced, know-it-all detective straight out of college. Nothing could have been farther from the truth.

Alex was 21 when he started with the NYPD during his sophomore year in 2001. Once he graduated from the academy he spent the following two years working patrol out of the 73rd Precinct in Brooklyn—which was one of the seediest beats in the borough. Taking the position allowed him the opportunity to make a name for himself, and all the top people were paying attention.

He went on with his studies, and in spring 2005, he strolled across the stage of John Jay College with his Bachelors in Forensic Psychology in hand.

At the same time, a homicide detective from the 78th Precinct retired and Alex jumped at the chance to move up, so he flung his name into the candidate pool.

There was simply one minor problem at hand—his fiancé, Mike, worked at the 78th Precinct, and regulations prohibited the two from working together out of the same precinct. Mike, however, was supportive of his choice and sought to take a transfer to another district if it was necessary.

The time drew near, and Alex ended up getting the promotion, which meant that Mike would need to swap precincts with Alex. He remembered that bittersweet day vividly. He walked into the 78th precinct, his nerves on overdrive. But after a few hours of talking with the offices and detectives, they quietly subsided as he realized he already knew most of the officers there.

A small touch on his collar jolted him back to the present. He swung around, discovering Carr had moved back to his side. He smirked at him and refocused his concentration on the progress at the crime scene. Finch was now bent on one knee underneath a glorious sycamore tree. Alex looked past Finch towards the forensic investigators from the ME's office as they checked for vital signs.

Alex took his final sip of coffee. "Carr, who came across the victim?"

Carr flipped open his pocket-size notebook. "Anonymous 911 call. Male caller. The call originated around four-fifteen this morning, and a first responding officer showed up at 4:23 A.M."

"So, no indication who reported this?"

"It doesn't seem so."

"Is anything *actually* anonymous anymore?" Alex asked. "First thing we look at is who made that 911 call this morning. They may remember nothing, but it's still probable they saw the suspect and could cast information on the events."

"I can look into that."

"Thanks, Carr—I can look after everything else from here."

Carr retired from the scene, and Alex stayed with Finch as the ME investigators put the limp corpse of Jane Doe onto the stretcher.

"Finch, it's been a pleasure meeting you. Here's my card." The ME took out an oblong white business card from the inside pocket of his overcoat and handed it to the young CSU investigator. "Let me know if you can provide any further insight."

"You got it." answered Finch.

Alex marched towards the yellow crime scene tape that fluttered in the soft late autumn air and signed out from the crime scene.

TWO

Washington Avenue, Brooklyn
November 16, 2005
6:00 A.M.

AMY'S EYES FLUTTERED OPEN FROM THE SOUND of the alarm clock shrieking in her ear. Grouchily she flapped her hand about the nightstand until she made contact with the snooze button that subdued her foe. She rolled back onto her side and snuggled up with the warm body next to her.

Closing her eyes, she was eager for merely five more minutes of sleep. *That's all I need, only five more minutes.* Her eyes barely closed before a deep voice roused her.

"Good morning, beautiful."

Annoyed, Amy rolled onto her back, "Ugh, damn, Josh, I needed to fall back to sleep."

"That's so not the response I was expecting. Let's try that again. Good morning, beautiful."

She whispered back, "Very well, good morning to you as well."

"How did you sleep last night?" he asked.

"All right I suppose. I can't believe I finally convinced you to stay over."

"I was hoping we could snag a cappuccino and bagel on our way to the subway."

"Yeah, we can do that. Well, I suppose since I'm up, I should shower." Amy threw the white silk sheets from her nude body.

As she attempted to escape the bed, Josh quickly drew her back towards him and thrust his lips against hers. She pulled away in a slow fashion, their lips parting.

"Well, you could follow me in the shower, if you want." He batted his brilliant blue eyes at her.

"Why do you have to be so damn irresistible?"

"I'm Norwegian," he said in his Nordic accent.

They both slowly crawled from the bed as Josh mustered up a small amount of energy within himself and began chasing after her down the narrow corridor towards the bathroom.

Amy had been doing amazing things with her life since she left New York Institute of Technology. She was presently working as an architect for one of the city's most distinguished companies. She was also considering going back to NYIT for her master's degree in urban and regional design, but that plan was something that remained on the rear burner for the time being.

For the first time in her entire life, she was absolutely content. Glad to be in New York City where she was as far away as desirable from her deranged parents, grateful to have her best friend living just a few train stops away, and thrilled to have a remarkable guy in her life who accepted her eccentricities and still held fast to her nonetheless. He was nothing like the other guys that she blew through over the past three years.

The two stood in the crowded bathroom, bare, as the water from the shower changed from frigid to scalding in a matter of seconds. The light sprinkle of steam began taking over the room. They moved hastily into the deluge, simultaneously. The scorching water cascading off their bodies. Amy stood beneath the unbroken torrent of water that splattered across her breasts. Turning towards Josh, she drowned her scalp under the drenching water. Amy ran her fingers through her shoulder-length blond hair as it increasingly became soaked. She forced her eyes tightly closed as she felt Josh running his fingers over her hipbones.

Startled, she didn't object. Instead, she lay her palm on top of Josh's powerful hands and allowed him to carry on exploring her flesh and bones.

"I'm sorry for rudely waking you this morning, only wish there was some way I can make up for it," Josh softly breathed in her ear.

"How generous of you."

She twirled around, facing the reverse direction. She could feel Josh pulling her close into him. His wet, coarse chest hair rubbed against her behind. He caressed the back of her collar as she began working the shampoo into her hair.

"Now, now, we don't have time for a repeat performance if we want to grab that cappuccino and bagel."

"Screw it, I'd certainly blow my day off to spend it with you."

"I don't see love paying our bills, sadly."

"Maybe if I play my cards right, we can pick this up again this evening…"

"Has anyone ever told to you how cheesy you are?" she asked as she rinsed the shampoo from her hair.

"Only you so far."

"Well, just keep in mind that I fell for it."

They surfaced from the shower, the room feeling more humid than a day in south Florida. Amy picked up a large plush gray towel from the shelf and wrapped it around her breasts, sticking the free end in as she walked to a small window. She cracked it open slightly, liberating the steamy mist of fog into the environment. She stepped back to the tiny white pedestal sink and wiped her palm across the mirror. A few large drops of water tried to withstand gravity, but eventually dropped down and plopped into the basin.

Josh was behind her, running the towel over his wet, cut body. "I'm looking forward to getting together with your friends Alex and Mike this evening. It's about time I have the chance to get to know them." He folded his forearms around her midsection.

"I'll let them tell you the story about how we almost perished together back in Colorado."

He pulled back. "Wait, hold up—what? You nearly died? When? Where? How?"

"You're such a journalist. I'll let them fill you in; good things happen to those who wait."

"I just don't know how to turn off the reporter in me."

Amy hurried to her bedroom and opened her closet. It was about an eighth of the size of the one she had in Colorado. Space was sparse in the city that never sleeps. Nevertheless, with all the negatives that came with living in the city, she wouldn't trade any of it.

She rummaged through clothes organized by type and color and pulled out a white blouse, navy jacket and matching skirt. Setting them on the disheveled bed, she smiled as she recalled the steaminess of last evening.

Amy reached down and switched the clock radio on; a recognizable tune blared out. Cindi Lauper's "Girls Just Want to Have Fun." Her disposition switched from exhausted to pumped full of energy, and she began dancing wildly around her room.

Rounding the corner at the exact moment was Josh who very much cherished the sight of his girlfriend dancing in the buff.

"You are a free soul, aren't you?"

"Come on—this is the best song ever."

"Well, don't cease having fun on my behalf."

The song faded away as the radio announcer returned looking for the fourteenth caller to win a competition. Amy was soon out of breath as she skipped nonchalantly towards her chest.

Opening the top drawer, she picked out black lace panties and a pair of black pantyhose. She slammed the drawer closed and opened the one below it where she kept her bras. She sat down on the bed and glided her arms through and stretched the elastic band towards her back.

"Can you give me a hand with this, Josh?" she asked.

"Of course."

After a little more erotic touching, Amy went back to the bathroom where the fogginess had settled, but the air still felt damp. She glanced in the mirror, tussled her hair with a dollop of mousse and put on a sparse layer of foundation to her diamond-shaped face.

She turned off the light and sauntered towards the kitchen. Time was running out and she still hadn't made her lunch to take for the day. She'd have to hurry if she wanted to keep up with her goal of spending less and eating healthier for lunch.

After moving to New York City, she gave up smoking cigarettes, as it was difficult to afford smoking and living on her own—something had to go. She had also changed her diet and had lost over fifty pounds since she left Colorado. She was an utterly new person.

She snagged her cell phone off the kitchen counter where she regularly left it to charge. She squinted at the screen: a missed text from Alex.

> *Can't wait to meet your new beau tonight. Hoping this*
> *murder I'm working doesn't meddle.*

Amy clicked on reply and started punching out an answer to Alex.

Let's pray you don't have to cancel again. We'll catch
you tonight.

She smirked as she pushed the send key. She reached out for her handbag that rested on the high side table near to the front door. With bag in hand, she dropped her phone inside while simultaneously digging to the depths of the bag to find her keys.

Josh stood beside her as he bent in for a kiss.

"What was that for?"

"Just felt like it," he replied.

"Awe—we ready to go?"

"Let's move."

The two emerged onto the landing and Amy bolted the apartment door. She shimmied the door knob, assuring that it locked behind her. They wandered hand in hand down the three flights of steps to the foyer.

Josh walked out of the building first, holding the door for Amy. The sky was dark and unfriendly, and the wind whistled gently across her face.

"Wish I had remembered a heavier coat," she grumbled as she drew her jacket closer to her body.

"Do you need to go back upstairs and grab one? I can wait for you."

"I'll be fine; besides, the coffee should keep me warm."

They trudged along the footpath towards DeKalb Avenue. Just around the corner from her apartment was a quaint coffee café that she visited fairly often. They had the best bagels in the city, well Amy thought so at least. During the three years she'd lived in the community she'd become friends with the owner and a few of the baristas. It was completely conceivable that tidbit of knowledge caused her to be just a bit prejudiced.

They turned around the bend at DeKalb Avenue, and an icy blast of air rushed through the bare trees. She shuddered and pulled Josh closer to her.

"We actually should run back up and grab your coat. You're going to get a head cold, or worse, freeze to death out here," he said.

She shrugged. "No, honestly I'll be okay." "Damn woman, so ornery."

"And you're sometimes overbearing—so there, we're even."

As they drew near the glass and wood café frontage, the delicious aroma of freshly baked bread and coffee pervaded the atmosphere. Amy pulled the door open, and a shot of tepid air bolted towards her.

"This place smells heavenly this morning." "I'm shocked there isn't a line wrapped outside the entrance."

"It will get busy again in about ten minutes; that's why I hurried out of the house. I mean seriously, who chooses to wait in an endless line for coffee?"

They proceeded towards a spacious, white granite crowned counter where the barista welcomed them.

His name was Myles, and he and Amy had become friends over the past three years. He stood up behind the counter from his barstool. He was tall, stout, with an immaculately trimmed goatee. As his eyes fixed on her, he quickly displayed a wide, infectious smile which radiated from ear to ear. "Good morning, Amy. Your usual today?"

"Hey, Myles, I'm in dire need of some caffeine, so I'll go with a large skinny latte with two extra shots and a bagel with lox." she replied as she gestured towards Josh.

"Ah, a great choice," Myles commented as he rang up her order into the point of sale system, utterly disregarding the gesture she made to her companion.

Turning to Josh, she asked, "What are you going to have this morning, boo?"

His voice boomed and surprised Myles, "A large light roast and a toasted bagel with cream cheese and strawberry jam."

Myles stuttered, "Oh I'm so sorry, sir, I didn't know that you two were together."

"Oh, you're used to me showing up alone. Josh, this is Myles — Myles, this is my boyfriend, Josh."

Josh stretched his hand towards the gentlemen. "It's a pleasure to meet you."

"It's great to meet you as well. Amy, you hadn't mentioned you'd met someone—this is unexpected news." Myles shook Josh's hand.

"I guess it never came up. We've been seeing each other for about two months now, right?" Amy asked.

"That's about right," Josh replied as the front entrance of the café opened, and three new patrons entered.

"I hate to cut this short, but it's nearly time for the second morning rush. Again, congratulations to both of you. Should be a few minutes for your order," he said as they hustled towards the pick-up area.

"He appears to be a friendly fellow." Josh lightly stroked her arm.

"Oh, he is. I've accompanied him to some poetry readings. He's one of those guys you just feel relaxed around."

"Well, I hope I am too."

"I wouldn't be seeing you if I didn't feel that way."

The café filled rapidly until a line stretched outside the front door.

She glanced over at Josh who was going through his phone for emails. "See, I knew it would liven up in here."

He gazed up and smiled.

Their orders were delivered, so the two moved to the self-service stand near the front to dress up their drinks.

After dropping about a pound of sugar into his cappuccino, Josh snapped the top back on tight. The steam continued to surge from the vent hole.

As they left the café, he looked at the time on the wall clock; it was precisely fifteen minutes past eight. As Amy threw open the door, the brisk, sharp autumn air once again blasted them square in the face. The walk to the train was merely two blocks, but in the frigid wind, a few blocks seemed a daunting journey.

A shudder shot down Amy's spine. Noticing, Josh placed his arm around her shoulders and tugged her tight against him for warmth.

"I hope I'm not late," he eventually spoke up as Amy cocked her head towards him.

"We'll be okay."

After a five-minute trip, they ultimately reached the street stairs of the Clinton-Washington Avenue stop. They sped down the steps into the belly of underground Brooklyn. They went around the corner sharply and moved through the turnstile. The rumbling of the terrain beneath them indicated an express train was about to appear, so they raced towards the Queens-bound platform to catch the incoming train.

They made it in time the see a crowded platform of commuters flooding out of the subway cars as the doors slid open. Amy and Josh squeezed through the bodies pouring in just as the doors started to close.

"We did it," he enthusiastically exclaimed as she grabbed the stainless-steel bar above her head.

She acknowledged his remark, "Yeah, barely. Now don't forget, dinner with Alex and Mike this evening. We're meeting them at eight o'clock at Locanda Vini & Olii."

"I haven't forgotten. And I'll be on my best behavior," Josh joked as Amy flashed a grave face at him.

"I know full well you will — otherwise you'll be severely punished for it later," she warned as the subway pulled into the Flushing Avenue station.

"Have a wonderful day at work, and I can't wait for later this evening," he said as she reddened.

"You know the right things to say to a woman."

"My charm is the reason you care for me," he said.

The doors of the train car opened and Amy hopped out onto the platform and blew Josh a kiss as the train sped away from the station.

She raced along the platform towards the way out, her face gleaming, and a fresh skip in her stride. She was genuinely in love.

THREE

78th Precinct, Brooklyn
November 16, 2005
11:00 A.M.

ALEX SAT AT HIS LARGE METAL DESK amid a crowded stationhouse and glared out the floor-to-ceiling windows to his right. The murky sky allowed the smallest possible amount of daylight to penetrate the office, so Alex had to resort to dealing with the vivid glare of the fluorescent bulbs to light up his desk. The noise level on the second floor of the precinct continued to grow in intensity, as officers ushered the city's rowdiest individuals in and out. Alex found it harder and harder to focus on his task at hand.

He'd only turned a deaf ear to the intrusion just as his partner abruptly knocked on the corner of his desk.

"Wake up, Jones. Got the name of the individual who called in the anonymous report this morning," Carr muttered as he leaned in closer towards Alex.

"Excellent news! Happen to get an address to go with that name?" Alex reached his arm back for his black suit jacket.

"Boris Topol, 59 Prospect Park West," he said as he flipped his note pad to the next page.

"Well, what are we waiting for? Let's give Mr. Topol a brief visit and learn what he knows." Alex took out his 9mm Glock 19 from his locked top bureau drawer.

The two men left the station to meet with their witness. As Alex passed their vehicle parked out front, Detective Carr stood dead center in the walkway.

"Jones, the car is right here."

"It's hardly a twenty-minute walk over there. Could do us some good to get some fresh air. Lord knows I'm not getting any cooped up at my desk all day."

"Ugh, I hate walking."

"You'll live, Carr. Now get a move on so we can shut down this case before dinner tonight."

Carr grunted as he gave in to Alex's determination to get some exercise. They walked south on Sixth Avenue as the aroma of freshly baked pizza wafted from the eatery on the corner directly across from the precinct. Once they reached Flatbush Avenue, they hung a left down the diagonal street towards Prospect Park.

"I shouldn't have let you persuade me to walk. All these food smells are making me hungry," Carr admitted.

"Come on; a dead girl is lying flat on a slab at the morgue—let's stay fixated on the case and keep our fingers crossed that we find the psycho who carried out this appalling crime."

"I guess you're right."

As Alex predicted, the trek to Mr. Topol's residence took roughly twenty minutes. Just as they arrived at the steps that led to the house, an older gentleman shut the front door and hurried out onto the stoop.

"Excuse me, sir, we're searching for a Mr. Boris Topol. Do you know where we might find him?" Alex asked very calmly.

"Who's askin'?"

Pulling his shield from the breast pocket of his solid black Hugo Boss suit, Alex returned, "NYPD. Are you Mr. Topol or not?"

"You're here about that damned call I placed this morning, aren't you?"

"We are indeed, sir. Perhaps we can take up a few minutes of your day and spare you a trip down to the precinct?" Carr sarcastically said.

"Eh, look, I'm running late for a meeting — can we set up an appointment or something?"

"Do either of us seem like the kind of characters who set up appointments?" Alex continued staring stubbornly at the middle-aged man, but after a few seconds of stillness, gave the man an arrangement, "How about this — we all walk and talk at the same time. If I feel satisfied with your answers, then we'll leave you alone. We got an understanding?"

"Suppose I don't have any other choice — what'd you like to know?"

Alex took out his notepad and pen from his inner pocket as he started asking questions.

"What can you tell us about any circumstances that led up to the discovery you made this morning near the picnic house?"

"Not much to report. I was out walking my pup, and I stumbled across the dead body. Poor Penelope—that's my dog—made a break towards the body. Fortunately I jerked back on the leash just in time before she got any closer." Mr. Topol recalled as his eyes skimmed the cracked sidewalk beneath his feet.

He drew in a long, deep gasp and released it in the form of a sigh. He went on talking, "You understand I've watched enough cop shows to remember you don't disturb the scene. After I had gathered my thoughts, Penelope and I rushed back and called you guys to report it. Not certain what more information I can offer you, Detective, um, sorry, what did you say your name was again?"

"Jones. Detective Jones. Anything else you observed? An odor? Anything unusual or out of the ordinary? It could be anything as basic as a person who felt out of place."

"Hmm, now that you mention it, I did catch sight of a young woman casually walking towards me. But what's weird is that when she saw the dog and me, she picked up the pace dramatically. I just thought she was nervous being alone in the park that late at night and was only seeking to get somewhere better lit."

"Could you describe this woman? Was she tall, short, lean or overweight?"

"I didn't have a clear glimpse at her. All I can say is she was in between short and tall, she wasn't overweight, lankier more than anything." Topol sighed. "It was foggy, and with barely any light I can't be certain if she was black, white, Hispanic — just look at me, I'm not a spring chicken anymore, and my vision isn't the greatest, you know."

Carr chimed into the discussion once again. "What about hair color? Did you happen to see that?"

"No, she had a hoodie over her head. Listen, I only wanted to make certain it got reported—personally, I don't want any problem with the cops. That's why they term it 'anonymous.' Guess that doesn't mean anything, though — you still showed up at my doorstep."

Reaching into his pocket, Alex pulled out a white business card and gave it to Mr. Topol. "Well thank you for your time. If you can remember anything else, please give me a ring. I've written my cell number on the flip side."

"I'll do that," Mr. Topol said as he went on cruising along Union Street. He glanced back at the two detectives as they stood underneath a barren sycamore tree and hollered, "Have a safe day, gentlemen."

Alex smiled at the man and glanced back down at his notebook. He leaned back against a black wrought iron railing. He wanted to collect his impressions before he took another step.

A touch of deceit bounced around his brain. Alex stood in the bitter cold reflecting on the conversation that just occurred between the two. Carr squinted to protect his eyes from the icy wind that swirled in his face. All Alex could assume was either Mr. Topol was preoccupied to notice his surroundings, or worse still, he knew plenty more than he was admitting. Either way, Alex knew something about the man seemed off and that this wouldn't be the last time he'd come across Mr. Boris Topol.

Five minutes had passed by and Alex remained in a quiet, intense contemplation, staring at his notebook. The two investigators had barely uttered a word to each other in that period. Detective Carr was not a silent individual, constantly speaking about anything. He waited as Alex continued recording notes. Alex's lips went on moving, but no words came out. Carr, becoming more irritable by the second, turned away his head from the headwind and exclaimed.

"Damn it, Jones, let's go back to the office—we'll get further progress where it's heated."

"What, you got a hot date or something, Carr? Give me a frigging minute here," Alex hollered as his partner gave him a glance that was a blend of mortality and actual concern for his well-being. He had never seen Alex this immersed in thought before, so serious that he would lash out like he just now had. He saw Alex was becoming overly wrapped up in this case—*why was he was making it so personal?*

"Look, Jones, I'm going back to the station. I guess maybe I'll catch you sometime next week when you're capable of getting all of your observations down on record."

Alex merely waved, shooing him out of his sight.

He pushed on writing down his findings. It hardly took about twenty seconds before the guilt filled his thought. Alex glanced up from his notepad just in time to witness his partner turning the corner at Eighth Avenue. He scowled as he returned to his notes.

Why am I so bitchy today?

Extending his arm, he peeked at the huge stainless steel watch fastened to his right wrist. An ideal gift from Mike for his recent birthday. He exhaled as he saw the big hand click upon the fifty-eight-minute tick mark.

How could it already be two minutes before noon?

The dismal day was slipping by more swiftly than he expected.

His stomach let out a deafening rumble. *I better call Mike before he believes I'm standing him up once more—I should to be a better fiancé if I'm going to keep him.*

He pulled out his phone, skimmed through the recent call history and pressed send.

After only two rings a familiar voice addressed him. "About time. I was beginning to assume you'd stand me up once again. This case must be an interesting one."

"You don't know the half of it! You have a half hour to catch lunch? I'm starving, and I'll even meet you halfway this time."

"I suppose that depends on your idea of halfway. Where are you right now?"

"Union and Eighth. Where are you?" he asked.

"Eastern and Franklin. We could always meet up at Franny's on Flatbush," Mike offered.

"I like that plan. I'll meet with you there in about fifteen minutes."

"Sounds good, see you in a few."

Alex shut his notebook and closed his eyes so he could refocus on the grisly scene that had welcomed him so early that morning. The dead body, the blood, the expression of horror in the victim's eyes. He continually feared there was something he missed. His anxiety was periodically an advantage, but most of the time remained a burden he was powerless to shake.

The journal in his grasp, he stepped towards the corner and waited hungrily for the traffic signal to turn.

Both sides of the avenue were edged with brownstones, a typical Brooklyn residential streetscape. The cool breeze whistled through the half-barren trees above him. A few trees still holding fast to their crimson-and-yellow coats, which wouldn't exist very much longer with the stiff breeze and precipitation that was setting out towards the city that evening.

Franny's was one of their frequent meeting points for lunch. The service was prompt, and the crew went out of their way to guarantee a pleasant experience. Alex hoped his favorite server, Allison, was working the lunch shift today. Even though he was traveling along at a slacker speed he'd still be on time, and he couldn't wait to see the expression on Mike's face. He could imagine it clearly in his mind.

One of two things will occur: either Mike will be beaming at me, or he's going to have an expression of utter awe written across his face.

He made it, still two minutes to spare. No hint of Mike anywhere on the hectic thoroughfare. The piercing cold was definitely getting to him, and he moved into the establishment to get away from it. As he moved toward the hostess stand, a familiar face approached him.

"Always a pleasure to see you once again, Alex," the hostess exclaimed as her smile radiated from ear to ear.

"Likewise. I'm waiting for Mike to get here—you care if I just take my usual booth close to the window?"

"By all means, make yourself comfortable. Once Mike gets here I'll send him your way." She snatched two menus and started walking towards the two-top. "Can I grab you anything to drink while you wait?"

"Water with lemon and an Americano, one extra shot."

"You got it—oh and Allison will be right over," she said, walking towards Allison. Alex watched as she whispered something discreetly in her ear.

Allison rolled her head towards Alex and shown she realized he was there. Alex smiled as he gazed out the glass just in time to observe Mike hustling indoors. Alex smiled; his best friend in the whole universe was looking still more gorgeous than ever. Mike had hardly made it before he took off his navy blue jacket and tossed it across his forearm.

Alex rose as Mike walked up and casually folded his arms around his neck, "Aren't you touched that I arrived here on time for a change?"

"I am, seriously. I took my time because you're never early for anything whatsoever."

"Whatever, you know I'm trying to be more reliable." Alex grinned. Out of the corner of his eye, he could see Allison returning with a tall glass of tap water with two lemon wedges on the side and his Americano.

"Hey, boys, long time no see. Mike, something I can bring you to drink right now?"

"I'll just have a green tea with lemon and honey on the side, please."

She turned to Alex. "How about you, Alex? Anything else?"

"I'm all set for now, thanks," he said.

Allison walked away and Mike watched Alex take a drink of water. He took notice of the dark, puffy circles underneath his eyes. He cleared his throat as quietly as possible. "Wow, you seem worn out. You've been working too much recently, and we deserve a holiday."

"Oh, yeah, I couldn't agree with you more. Anywhere special you think we should visit?"

"Somewhere sunny. Is there any way I can persuade you to join me when I visit my parents in San Diego for Thanksgiving?"

"Doubtful." Alex emptied a little cream into his Americano. "This latest case might have a relation to something greater, I mean with the two previous murders and all — besides, you do realize your parents don't approve of me."

"What the hell? My parents ask me all the time when I'm going to introduce you. I mean, Jesus, if you don't want to go with me, then just tell me, stop making up stupid excuses. Why must you continually make things about work? Crime in Brooklyn isn't going to stop because you remain in New York."

"For fuck's sake, Mike. I don't want to go—okay?"

"Whatever. I didn't show up here to argue with you about meeting my parents. It was only an idea. I believe you actually do need to take a rest, badly. Have you glanced at yourself in the mirror recently? It's the same as when you were in school. You continually have to be number one, continually have to be the greatest at everything."

Mike sighed audibly. In a quieter, gentler tone, he changed the topic. "So, explain to me what you've learned about the latest victim."

Alex looked relieved that he'd switched the subject to something he could talk about. "Same as the last two: young woman, mid-twenties, throat cut from behind."

"And have you spoken to Captain Thompson about your impressions that you might be dealing with a serial killer?"

"I did and as he put it, 'Jones you seriously need to take a recess. No serial killer is running wild in Prospect Park.' But I believe he's wrong."

"Well, Thompson means well, but the truth will come out someday," Mike assured him as Allison came back to the table with his green tea.

She placed the teacup on the table. "Have we agreed on food yet?"

"We're going to split a medium three-meat pizza today," Alex replied as Mike nodded.

"Good decision. Should be up shortly." She picked up the menus and turned back towards the hostess stand.

As promised, the meal appeared in fewer than ten minutes. Between the two of them, the medium pizza didn't stand a chance of seeing a leftover box. The hostility from earlier had diminished; still Alex was quietly fuming about the concept of traveling all the way to San Diego for Thanksgiving.

Why would I choose to spend a holiday weekend with people I don't know and who surely don't care about me? Waste of my time.

The two finished their lunch, took care of the bill, and rose. Alex yanked his jacket from the end of the seat, throwing it around his back. While arranging his coat, he caught a look at Mike, who was drinking his last sip. Alex smiled. Even though they quarreled like an elderly married couple, he'd never trade him in for anybody else in the world, even if he could.

As they exited the restaurant onto the bustling avenue, a buzzing sound blared loudly. The two men patted their clothes.

"Damn, I wish this thing would offer me a break from time to time," Alex said as he took out the phone. He answered in his customary professional tone. "Jones."

He paused there, tapping his toes against the walkway with the telephone pressed against his elongated face. A minute went by as he often uttered the word *certainly*. He drew his notepad and started writing down a few remarks. Flipping his notebook closed, he rapidly switched which ear the phone was pressed to.

"Thanks. I'll be over there as soon as I can get a taxi." The call finished, Alex slipped the phone into his pants pocket this time.

"What was that all about?"

"ME's office. They finished the autopsy. I better get over there so I can call it an early night."

"I'll see you tonight. Just promise you won't get too engrossed with this case today. There's always tomorrow," Mike subtly reminded him as he stroked his finger.

Alex gently touched his finger back. "I can guarantee you I won't be late."

Mike disappeared around the bend, and Alex flagged down a cab.

Alex opened the rotted-out back passenger door and scooted to the midpoint of the back seat. The driver swung his head around and asked, "Where to, man?"

"599 Winthrop, the Office of the Chief Medical Examiner."

The scruffy-faced cabbie's character turned almost immediately as he responded, "All right. I'm sad for your loss."

"I'm an investigator; I'm only working a case."

"Oh—forget I ever mentioned anything at all."

The cabbie started the meter and flew off at a tremendous rate of speed heading southeast on Flatbush Avenue towards the Grand Army Plaza. After his blunder, the cab driver remained reserved and it caused an awkward, though peaceful trip for Alex. These days, silence was unusual in his life, and he cherished peace and quiet.

He slumped in the back seat, remembering back over the preceding two weeks. He thought of the appalling sight of the original victim, Rutchel Cox, which was yet current in his mind. He'd believed he'd seen it all, but that theory had quickly been dismissed. A week afterward, the second body turned up near where they came upon the first. The images would forever be etched in his memory.

Alex slouched even further back. This was only his second trip ever to the ME's office, as he typically forced Carr to tend to this part of the job.

There was something about the dead that scared the shit out of Alex, but with his partner MIA and him getting the call, it meant he was in for an unpleasant afternoon.

After ten minutes in the taxicab, he arrived at the destination. Alex stared up at the meter and slipped the driver a ten and a five.

He glanced both directions as he dashed across the two-way roadway. The trees that typically covered the frontal area of the glass and masonry structure had discarded their leaves recently, now leaving the front wide open to the public. He traversed the U-shaped drive and advanced on the double-sliding glass doors. He stepped up to a call box, searching through the index to buzz the reception counter.

A courteous, although stern voice came through the speaker. "How can I assist you?"

"I'm Detective Jones from the 78th precinct. I'm here to meet Dr. Callahan," he answered into the mouthpiece.

The doors buzzed open and Alex pushed through, and a warm burst of air exited the secured area. *What a welcome relief; finally, some warmer air.*

He hurried through the vestibule to the front desk. He assumed the unknown female voice from the speaker would meet him. Instead, the person at the counter was a man.

"Good day, I'm Detective Jones here to meet with Dr. Callahan," he repeated as he displayed his credentials.

"Ah, Detective, glad to see you. Here, sign in for me, and I'll give Dr. Callahan a buzz," the short, oval-faced gentlemen said as Alex leaned one elbow on top of the countertop.

The guy picked up the telephone handset and dialed the number. After Alex had flung aside the pen, the man passed him a visitor badge. "Place this on somewhere visible."

Alex clipped it on the front side of his jacket and studied the waiting area. *This place is more barren than my office on a dull day.*

All the area consisted of were four white-painted cinder-block walls with a semi-new glass counter that wound around one of the smaller walls.

He started feeling sticky, and he reached for his collar to alleviate the tightness. He peered up towards the ceiling. The lamps above his head were blazing brightly, like living on the sun with the mass amount of heat they were producing.

He drew in a sharp breath, and the faint scent of disinfectant attacked his senses.

Well at least it's sanitary.

He smiled softly to himself.

The smell always got to him every occasion he had to call on this building. His nose twitched as he reached into his slacks for a tiny jar of menthol-scented rub he kept on him, regardless of the season. Unscrewing the top, he dipped his pointer finger in the jelly, then spread it under his nose as thick as possible. He once again took a long whiff.

Ah, much better.

He resealed the jar, and the process caused him flashback to his police academy days.

Alex's mentor had shared this method with him back in 2002 *"If the stench of death troubles you just wipe a slight amount of this balm under your nose…it'll fool your senses and your nose will never again know death surrounds it."*

His fond memory was cut short by the attendant behind the counter. "Detective Jones, Dr. Callahan will be out in a minute. You're welcome to have a seat."

Alex looked disgustedly at the chair. "I'll just continue standing but I appreciate the offer."

He started walking in small circles in the waiting area—he was always an impatient person. Barely two minutes passed by when a lanky older gentleman burst through a set of double doors close to the counter.

The man stepped quickly towards Alex and reached out his hand. "You must be Detective Jones?"

"I am. You must be Dr. Callahan, it's a pleasure to meet with you, sir." He shook the doctor's hand.

"Come this way; I'll fill you in on what we've discovered."

Alex nodded and trailed behind the doctor, fearing the thought of having to return to the victim after seeing her state that morning. She could only look worse now that she had been cut up further. This ME's office was his least favorite element of the job and no matter how many times he was told, none of it ever made it any more appealing. The stench of death and decay that filled your senses. That no means known to man ever disappeared. It wasn't only the stench that disturbed him; it was the sense of fear and agony—when you got right down to it, it really was the unknown that terrified Alex the most.

When you were a beat cop, you regularly dealt principally with the living; domestic quarrels, robbery—a few days a year you'd make it to a death scene. In the homicide unit, you dealt mostly with those who couldn't share their story with you. Every time you dealt with darkness, it became you; it smoldered in your every thought. Each victim you came across, it was like your character died little-by-little each case you worked. Even though no one had ever mentioned that being a homicide detective would be comfortable, and even with his training and common sense, nothing had prepared Alex for the barrage of death that closed around him on a weekly basis. Although he'd prefer working with the living over the deceased, he felt deep down that he had to work for those who weren't capable of helping themselves anymore.

My mom would be proud of what I've become, and to me, that's all that's important.

The doctor touched his badge on a little black box along the wall. The thick portal swung inward slowly. Alex stepped through and immediately received a draft of chilly air combined with a strong, pungent aroma of disinfectant. The unpleasant odor struck him in the face as the doctor picked up his trot down the passageway. Oddly enough, the essence of mortality hadn't entirely found its course to him just yet… But he was sure of it arriving.

The ME completed autopsies early in the morning, around seven on the dot, and the processing area had been cleaned up and sanitized. Once in the room, the doctor reached into a package on a metal shelving unit and plucked out a white surgical mask and gloves.

"Here, you might want these—I've been told how you despise the smell." He stretched out his hand.

"I'll be all right; I'm beginning to grow accustomed to it."

"All right, if you say so. Me, I never become adapted to it."

"Right. So, you have some news for me regarding Jane Doe from this morning?"

"Okay, straight to business." He reached out for a metal clipboard that rested near a metal slab on casters. "Ah, perfect. CSU established the identity of the victim. Her fingerprints came back to a Marianne Bowman. 25-year-old Caucasian female."

"She had prints on file? She's been arrested previously?"

"Says here that she was in the system for an arrest, yes. However, no further details are provided."

"Okay."

"CSU also states they have a last known address, but you'll need to reach out to them to obtain it," Dr. Callahan said.

"Very good. Were you able to figure out the cause and manner of death?" Alex asked.

"Her manner of death was homicide. The cause of death was exsanguination." The doctor shut the cover of the clipboard.

"So she suffocated?"

"Yes, the slashing wound is not your cause of death. Bradburn mentioned to me that you were concerned this might have been a body dump due to a lack of blood at the scene," Dr. Callahan said.

"Yeah, CSU supervisor brought up that lack of artillery spray at the scene, which I'd expect in this type of attack."

"Well, you'll only get the spray when your victim is alive beforehand. But I can with complete certainty tell you that Ms. Bowman here died from suffocation, and the slashing was done after she had expired."

"Got you," Alex said as he jotted down the notes. "Could have a copy of your report before I leave?"

The doctor shook his head. "Detective Jones, I like you, and that might work with my subordinates, but you of all people understand a subpoena is needed for that."

Alex nodded, as he knew he couldn't bullshit his way through getting that court order.

"If you send me one over by tomorrow morning, I'll get it over to your office right away," the doctor promised. "So, if there's nothing else, Detective, I guess I'll head home for the day."

"That's all I have, much thanks, Dr. Callahan. I'll show myself out."

Alex couldn't leave soon enough to break away from the sickening stench that followed him as he passed down the hall. He pushed the exit button affixed to the wall and stood by waiting for them to open. He appeared back into the same lifeless place where his action packed afternoon began.

He unclipped his visitor badge from his jacket and returned it to the attendant. He smirked as he lightly tapped his hand on the ledge.

"Until next time," he scornfully said as the attendant smiled back up at him.

"There's invariably a next time in our profession."

Outside, Alex crouched down. *Fresh air.*

After several seconds of slow breathing, he pulled himself together and jumped up to his feet. He glanced around to see if anybody was watching him, and when he realized that no one had noticed him, he turned towards Winthrop Street.

It was closing in on three thirty. Two hours remained in his shift, so he headed back to the station.

While he admired the finer things in life, non-reimbursable taxi trips were starting to bite into his budget, so for this trip he'd be using the train.

The Winthrop Street station was an insignificant three blocks from the medical examiner's office. The good old number two subway was consistently reliable.

He stood quietly on the train platform, using a few moments out of his hectic day to take note of the living for a change. Individual lives, original stories each one possessed. He felt the floor beneath his feet rumble and twisted his head, squinting to scan down the tracks. He could see the headlights of the advancing train.

The doors of the subway car slid jerkily open and he moved on board. Alex was just happy to be on the train and returning to the office. His mood was already sour, but he also realized he was in New York City and somebody would either piss him off or knowing how criminals behaved, another corpse would shortly spring up, and his soul would experience further picking, more so than it already had.

He grabbed the chrome handrail as the train jerked away from Winthrop Street station. There was business that required his attention, and Alex groaned softly at the prospect of it.

FOUR

Locanda Vini & Olii, Brooklyn
November 16, 2005
7:55 P.M.

ALEX STOOD, BRACED UP AGAINST THE TRANSLUCENT GLASS window-front of the restaurant. The picturesque farm-to-table bistro wasn't a quick trip from his corner of Brooklyn—nevertheless this was Amy's favorite place so he'd offered no objections about hiking to her neighborhood.

Beside him, Mike was wiggling around like an antsy child to stay warm. Alex sensed something was bothering Mike and he suddenly stood very still.

The faint radiance from the street lamp fell gently on the right hand side of his face, and secretly all Alex could do was grin with joy.

Is this how true happiness should feel?

The sunlight had departed hours earlier, and the November air was growing colder by the minute. A sudden gust rushed past, and Alex drew up the collar of his wool jacket. The scratchy texture brushed against the back end of his nape as his body squirmed with tingles up and down his backbone. He pulled himself together, what did he care only as long as it prevented the unfriendly elements from biting him any further.

Alex had been so busy at work lately that he hadn't been out with friends for a while. Was it conceivable that just maybe, he was starting a new chapter in his life?

Since the abrupt death of his mother, the things he previously enjoyed didn't sound as pleasurable as they once did. He even felt guilty, like there was something he could have done differently, yet he felt deep down that he couldn't have changed anything that happened. He struggled every day to overcome his depression and gloomy outlook on life, and just when he was about to claw his way over the hump something would happen and it led him tumbling back down the mountainside to that familiar feeling he had developed a love-hate relationship with.

But he was becoming weary of holding onto the blame; he was beginning to run out of excuses to explain to himself. His psychiatrist at one point instructed him to seize the day—and after many years that passed since his last visit, today would be the beginning of that mission to break away from the past.

They kept on hanging outside, not exchanging words between each other. The silence caused Alex to think back to earlier in the evening.

He made it back to his condo around six fifteen, and the house was completely still. Mike was not anywhere in sight. He passed through the doorway to the laundry room and removed his clothes from his body. He exhaled as he could feel the burden of darkness, the scent, all the adverse energy leaving his soul. He threw the small pile of undergarments into the washing machine before the smell drifted through the rest of the condo. He tossed his suit into a sealed garment bag and decided to run it by the dry cleaners on the way to dinner.

I refuse to bring the stench of death into this home.

He shot across the living room and headed right for the shower. He sharply pushed the door forward as the serenity of the room hit him in the face. He cautiously moved his front foot forward and hurried faster towards the glass shower door.

After his fifteen-minute shower, the sound of rattling keys startled him. He swabbed his face as the sound of steps gradually became heavier. A light tap at the door appeared as expected.

"Alex, all right if I come in?"

"When have you ever asked? Door's unlocked," he said as he stepped out onto a soft, fluffy bath mat just as the door groaned open.

"No hurry, I just wanted to say hi. I'm impressed that you will be ready for me for a change."

"Ha, well, I'm finally taking everybody's input and making some changes to my life."

"Well, don't let me make you feel rushed—lots of time remaining," Mike grinned as he backed out into the hall, closing the door behind him.

Returning to the present, Alex felt the slight shake of his arm.

"I'm praying they arrive soon. Reservation was for eight o'clock—they're three minutes late." Mike flashed his wristwatch.

"Screw it—let's just go get checked in. I'm freezing out here."

"Thank God! She'll be here fashionably late as normal." Mike pulled open the massive oak door, letting Alex walk in first. The essence of sage and burning cedar occupied the space.

A gracious woman greeted them at the hostess stand. "Good evening, gentlemen. A table for two?"

"Good evening. We have a reservation for four at eight o'clock, under Jones, Alex Jones."

She took a moment to click the keys of her keyboard.

"I realize the other two haven't arrived yet, but it's freezing outside. Think it'd be possible to be seated while we wait for them?"

"Certainly. Right this way. I'll bring the remainder of your party over when they get here."

They followed her to a four-top reclaimed wood table set right near the picture window. Alex smiled broadly - sitting next to the window was his ideal spot to unwind. Secretly, he was a people watcher. The hostess placed their menus out at each place setting and gestured for them to have a seat.

"Should we sit across from each other or side by side?" Mike asked.

"I guess it's more appropriate to be seated across from each other. Amy can sit down beside me, and Josh can sit next to you—you're more of a people person than I am anyway."

They sat across from each other in the two chairs nearest the window. The establishment was crowded, full of energetic people with high levels of excitement. Alex reached discreetly across the dinner table and slightly touched the outer side of his hand against Mike's. Mike, who was gazing out the window, swung back and refocused his concentration on his fiancé.

Mike smiled. "How did the medical examiner's go? I know how much you dislike going there."

Alex sighed. "It doesn't matter how soon afterwards I get in the shower, I can never get that stink of death out of my nasal passages."

"You'll become adapted to it. Well, was the trip helpful? Was the ME able to cast further information on who your victim was or how she died?"

Alex glanced around the restaurant at all the happy people who didn't have to look at human suffering every day. It distressed him to have a conversation about such private, not to mention extremely sensitive material in a packed restaurant, subway, or grocery store. It concerned him that somebody would overhear them, and he didn't need to be the cause for destroying someone else's fun experience. "I love you very much, but let's not discuss work tonight, at least not here. I'll fill you in on our train ride back tonight. I think I better call Amy and see where she is."

Just as he reached into his jacket, he caught sight of her across the cramped room, arms linked with her new guy.

They rose and Alex raced around the table and wound his arms around Amy. He hugged her tightly. The preceding couple of weeks he hadn't seen as much of Amy as he used to. He leaned back, gazing into her eyes as she coyly smirked.

"Sorry, we're l—"

"Amy, don't stress about it—and this must be the elusive Josh." He reached out his hand.

"Josh, this is Alex and his fiancé, Mike."

"Good to finally meet you both! Amy does nothing but go on and on about you guys," Josh said.

"Well, she had better speak nonstop about us, as close as we are," Alex teased as he motioned for everybody to sit down.

They all sat, and the first few moments were awkward, uncomfortable enough to put off even the most sociable personality. Mike was the one who cut the stillness.

"So, Josh, Amy tells me you're a reporter with *The New York Times*?" Mike asked.

"I am. I'm actually an investigative journalist."

Humorously, Mike replied, "Ah, so you're the guy I constantly advise to back off at crime scenes, huh?"

"Yeah…probably so. So, you two are both detectives?"

"We'll, Alex is. I'm still just a mere patrol officer. Strangest thing, right, two gay guys becoming New York City officers?"

"Oh, wait, I didn't mean to imply that—I…"

Sensing panic about to occur, Amy jumped in. "Josh, honey, he's just screwing with you."

"Oh, thank God— I've been so anxious about being a jackass." He passed his fingers through his hair.

Mike patted the young man on the back. "Trust me, kiddo, you're fine. So I think we should settle on drinks before our server gets here. What sounds good to everyone?"

"Nothing too crazy—never know when my ass will receive a call out at four in the morning once again," Alex said, "so I suppose I'm only having a Pilsner or something."

"Well since lightweight over here isn't going to go all out, I think I'll have a Cosmo." Amy nudged Alex in the ribs. "Remember those afternoons you and I would come back from class and invade your mom's liquor cabinet."

"Ha, how could I forget…that was the first time I got sick from drinking whiskey."

"One time—you're such a drama queen. Besides, that day you drank *way* too much." She shook her head in amusement.

Changing the subject, Mike interlinked his fingers and glanced towards the fresh face at the dinner table. "So, Josh, I detect an accent…where are you from originally?"

"I moved here six years ago from Norway -- Oslo."

"No shit—we've always wanted to visit there—isn't that right, Alex?"

"Oh absolutely—from the pictures it seems like such a beautiful country. So, Josh… Tell us more about you."

"What d'you want to know?"

"Where did you attend college? I went to John Jay."

"New York University for my undergraduate, finished last year. I'm now taking a course in criminal justice—guess it can't hurt, seeing as how I'm an alleged investigative journalist and all. I'll probably go to grad school next fall."

Mike lightly touched his shoulder, "So how do you like working for *The New York Times*. I did understand that correctly, right?"

"Yup. I've been with them since I got out, so about a year. Wow, it's weird how you don't realize how much time has passed by when you love your career so much."

"You have to love what you do. Otherwise, you'll blow your whole adult life suffering. Who wants that?" Mike smiled as Josh nodded.

"Precisely. Fire away, hit me with all your questions."

"Do you plan to remain in the United States then?" Alex asked.

"I applied about a week ago for my permanent residency here in the United States."

"That's awesome!" Alex answered as their server approached the table.

The waiter stood at the table, getting everybody's drink orders, and the discussion carried on. The discomfort from earlier was all but a remote memory, even though Alex's thought floated in and out of the conversation through the course of the evening.

The only point he could concentrate on was the victims who lost their lives in the previous three weeks. Occasionally he'd zone back in and join in, have a belly laugh or two, even though the only thing he desired to do was peel himself apart from the celebration and concentrate on identifying a connection, something, large or small, that linked the victims so he could bring it to the captain.

Entrees arrived, and Alex went back to the small talk, but when they set down the plate of grilled Piedmontese Beef, he moved from hungry and hostile to overflowing with steam. Alex was so elated that he raised his bottle of Pilsner and proclaimed a toast.

"I just want to say thank you for turning up this evening. It's difficult to find such incredible people to enjoy life with, and I'm happy that I have all of you," he said as the entire table lifted their glasses, "and I further wish to welcome Josh to our small family."

"Alex, that is just so charming of you," Amy said. "For weeks now I've been doing nothing but worrying over you all meeting Josh. Thank you, both of you, for setting up this fun night."

Alex picked up the bottle, tilted it towards Amy, and then took a long swig. He was happy when he saw Amy was happy, and it appeared that she was—at least based on outward impressions. He, on the other hand, was conscious that his outward emotions never resembled the feelings he felt on the inside.

He'd been a nervous soul—hell, he amazed himself when he passed the psychological exam to become a police officer. In the most recent months, however, his thoughts were starting to dominate him stronger than normal. The nightmares, resulting in a clammy sweat each night. All he could think about—dream about—were the women who'd found their doom in the park. The expressions on their faces, the terror they must have suffered. Those thoughts took over his existence.

I can't become consumed with this case. I just can't. Look around you, Alex; people go on having fun, living active lives—your best friend finally met someone handsome, who isn't rude or a total wreck. Snap out of this depression.

When he reopened his eyes, he wasn't entirely certain how much time had lapsed, but he guessed it must have been a considerably amount of time. The look of dismay on Mike's face was unforgettable, and all Alex wished to do was crawl underneath the four-top and never emerge.

Instead of slinking away, he nervously grinned at Mike, who he could usually depend on to deflect the spotlight to anything else. It didn't work; it was too late. Not only was Mike staring at him…now Josh and Amy had followed. The only thing he could continue doing was the thing he succeeded at in these circumstances; he went on smiling.

With shakiness in his voice, he spoke up, "What are we waiting for? Let's eat."

He picked up his fork and knife and cut off a sliver of his steak. Soon enough the upsetting moment slipped by, and the others followed suit. It was back to stillness yet once more. However, this time around wasn't as unpleasant as being caught with his thoughts in the clouds.

The hyper-enhanced energy level in the restaurant was approaching a climax. The clinking of wineglasses, the roar of voices swirled around them. All the chatter made the atmosphere more pleasing for Alex, and shortly thereafter he felt more at peace.

Time was passing by more swiftly. Alex wasn't sure if it was because he was warming up to Josh or because he finally squelched his hunger.

Eventually, the scraping of silverware against the plates ended as everyone wrapped up their meals. But, unbeknownst to Alex the party was only getting started.

The waiter passed by the table and Amy flagged him down.

"Excuse me, sir. I'll have another Cosmo when you have an opportunity."

The waiter smiled. "Something else for anyone?"

"What the hell, make it another round for my new acquaintances," Josh said.

Alex, taken aback, slouched back in his chair. Josh flashed Alex a grin. Alex nodded amicably. He didn't need to be the reason that his friends didn't have an excellent time, even if he wasn't feeling very upbeat.

Amy turned Alex's way and grasped his hand. Being best friends for so many years, she was aware that he was putting on a show and that he wasn't having a great time. She leaned in towards him. "Don't worry, Alex. After this drink, I'll wrap things up—I can see something is on your mind and I don't want to keep you from it."

Is it that clear to everyone around me that I'm absorbed in my thoughts? I'm a mess...

"Amy, no, I'm fine. I just had an unpleasant day, that's all. I want to stick around for a little while longer. I'm sorry I'm reserved, but don't leave on my accord."

"If you're certain. I swear we won't linger past ten regardless. It is a work night, ya know."

"Deal," he said as she nodded. The confirmation instantly raised his mood further, and he rejoined the conversation.

They chatted, laughed, and wrapped up their second round of drinks. Amy stretched out her wrist, glanced down at her watch and observed that it was ten minutes past ten. The crowd was starting to diminish for the night, and Amy motioned for the check.

The waiter returned with the bill promptly, and Josh got out his billfold. "I wish to thank you all for such an amazing night—this meal is on me."

"Oh no, I insist…"

"Rubbish, you've both been so kind, and of course I sprung that second round on you guys…No, no, I'm picking this one up," Josh said. "If it makes you feel any better—next time I'll allow you return the favor."

"Well, I don't know what else to say but thank you." Alex smiled.

"And I know you're under some pressure right now, Alex, so don't stress about not being with us mentally tonight. Amy says you've had several murders take place in the last couple of weeks. Do you think it's a serial killer?"

"Josh, given what profession you're in, you understand I can't tell you—even if I wanted to, you know full well the policy about an open investigation. But, if it'll help, you can quote me on that."

"Fair enough. Don't be upset, Alex. I mean you can't fault me for trying, true?"

"Upset? Disappointed, but not upset." Alex lifted his pint glass and swigged down the last gulp of beer.

Sensing a scene about to possibly go down, Mike stood up quickly, snagged his coat from the rear of the chair, and shook Josh's hand.

"Well, it's been fun meeting you, Josh. But we need to head out."

"Completely understand. I'm so happy I ultimately met the two of you."

"Likewise, Josh." Alex said as he stuck his right arm through the sleeve of his jacket.

Alex turned and hugged Amy for the second time that evening before excusing himself outside to hunt down a taxi.

Mike pulled Amy and Josh aside, "Alex hasn't been the same since he lost his mother seven years ago. And for future reference, don't dredge up anything connected to his open cases. Anything but that."

"Got it, so his mother dying, is that tied to what Amy said about you all nearly dying in Colorado."

Mike looked at Amy. "You didn't tell him?"

Amy turned her head to watch Alex, who was attempting to flag down a taxi. "I told Josh we'd talk about it tonight over dinner, but then Alex seemed so distant, I didn't bring it up."

Mike looked back at Josh. "Make sure she fills you in on the whole story. The truth is stranger than fiction."

Mike hugged Amy and shook Josh's hand one final time before joining Alex in the back seat of a taxi.

The cab crept away from the edge of the curb and stopped at the red light. Alex leaned across Mike, glaring out the window as the new couple walked down Gates Avenue arm in arm.

"Cute couple, huh?" Mike said, making an effort to keep the discussion casual.

"If she's happy, that's all that's important to me."

"Seriously, what's with you tonight? I know you're pissed that he wanted to know about the crimes. Still, that doesn't excuse your mental absence this evening. Besides, I honestly want to find out how the Medical Examiners went."

"Oh, Mike you'll never figure out the things that move through my mind," Alex shook his head, irritated, "and my visit to the ME's office went all right. I truly don't believe this is another suitable place for this discussion."

"Whatever. For nine years now, I've been there for you. I rescued your ass when those psychotic girls abducted *and* nearly killed you; I was there when you buried your mom, and when you landed the promotion. For all those things, I stood by your side—and this is how I'm rewarded?"

"How dare you bring up my mother!"

"Deal with it. You're breaking down at the seams. All I can suggest is that you get some expert help or something—you have to come to terms with all that took place back in

Colorado. It's destroying you inside, and it's poisoning our relationship."

"What do you mean—poisoning our relationship? I believed everything between us was going amazing. Are you implying you're not content with me anymore?"

Mike threw his arms in the air. "Quite honestly, I don't remember the last time we were genuinely happy. You're not the same Alex I fell in love with ages ago. Now you've grown into a cruel, overworked investigator who's mad at the universe all the time. You can't even deal with your former life, how can I be certain that you can handle the future?"

"I've dealt with what occurred in those mountains, Mike. You're the only person who can't seem to let the matter rest."

"No, you haven't Alex, and until you deal with it—I—" Mike stopped, and considered the next words he said carefully. "I think I want some space for a while."

Mike let out a heavy sigh of relief; a burden had unloaded from his conscious. He rapped on the glass divider between the front and back seats. "Driver, drop me off at the next train station."

Anxiously, Alex laughed under his breath. "No, he's only kidding, he's not leaving."

"I am, Alex; I'm finished with this negative attitude. I do want some time to myself—I have a lot to think about. I can't deal with that with you around," he answered as the vehicle arrived at the Clinton-Washington Avenue station.

The back door of the taxi flung open.

"Don't do this to me," Alex cried in anguish, "Don't leave. I swear when we get back we'll talk." He took Mike's forearm, forbidding him to leave.

Mike hesitated. He glanced at the cabby and later at the masses standing outside the train stop. They all had noticed the commotion and watched the drama unfolding—complete strangers gawking at them. It was soon evident to Mike they were creating an enormous, unnecessary performance. In what appeared to be an eternity, he drew his right leg back inside the taxi and cautiously shut the door. Pouting, he crossed his arms as he typically did when he didn't have his way. It didn't matter what Alex did to him; he would continually give in to whatever he demanded.

The annoyed taxi driver screeched the wheels as he jerked back into traffic. They sat together in the back seat; the discomfort continued to mount as the cab had become completely quiet. Mike eventually got his anger in check and faced Alex.

Clearing his throat, he spoke softly. "You better be telling me the truth—we *will* discuss this when we get home."

"I swear, we'll talk. We both just need to settle down." Alex assured him as he got sight of the driver looking in the rearview mirror. Already pissed, Alex jumped on the driver. "Hey—eyes on the road, you didn't see anything happen here tonight."

FIVE

78th Precinct, Brooklyn
November 17, 2005
6:30 A.M.

ALEX EMERGED FROM THE BERGEN STREET STATION and walked the insignificant block to the precinct. The wind had improved overnight and the walk for once in the prior few days was pleasant. No more hurrying to retreat indoors. Passing by the taco stand on the corner, a haven for the street junkies, was no different this morning.

He squinted towards the entrance and like clockwork sat two of the regulars, hunched over. The woman had her head pressed against the man's shoulder; they huddled underneath the warmth of a feces-soiled blanket. *I don't have it as rough as I think…at least I have a roof over my head at bedtime and a warm bed to sleep in.*

The sky had begun showing traces of life as he turned the corner onto Sixth Avenue. The brilliance of the sun would soon

drown out the fear of the unknown that went with the pitch
darkness.

He approached the precinct and plodded onto the first tread. It
was a short flight of steps, six to be exact. Alex arrived at the
landing and tugged open the massive oak door and stepped in the
old structure and moved across the ivory tile and took off his
earmuffs. He wiped his sweaty fingers across his ears and started
up the staircase.

He ascended, his mind still spinning over the argument he and
Mike had the previous evening. He couldn't fathom what
happened—what should have been a happy, relaxed evening
transformed into something right out of the Dr. Phil playbook. It
was a fair statement to suggest that the evening didn't end the way
he wished it had.

After their quarrel in the taxi, it was a wonder that Mike let him
have any rest. They spoke for nearly three hours, all about
emotions, pet peeves, learning to accept the past and move on with
the future—you name it, there was an exchange. Alex realized he
had to deal with his frame of mind, but how? How could he let go
of all that happened back in Colorado? And how could he even
begin to know how to make the necessary adjustment?

Alex emerged onto the second-floor landing of the precinct.
Only a few people wandered around—all with the appearance of
people who urgently needed a mug or two of coffee. He touched
his desk, the first one on the right-hand side once you came in the
squad room. Alex's right eyebrow lifted and he cocked his head to
the side.

Odd—Carr's normally the first one here.

He waved off his observation and decided that it was plausible that he was getting his act together. He marched towards the coffeemaker situated atop an unsteady, timeworn cabinet, hoping for a steaming pot but all he found was an empty glass carafe with a trace of scorched coffee roasting away in the bottom. Annoyed, he brewed a fresh pot.

"I'll be damned! Jones got into the office before me for a change."

Swinging around abruptly, Alex frowned. "I couldn't sleep last night—thought I'd be better off here working to solve out what's going on in Prospect Park."

"Any word from the medical examiner on the name of our latest victim?" Carr asked.

"Oh, right—I didn't tell you. Crap. Sorry about that, Carr."

Alex stepped over to his side drawer, took out his keys, and unfastened the lock. He got out a bulky folder overflowing with recent case files. He paused there, sifting through, whispering names to himself. In due course, he yanked out the record he was looking for. Throwing the file folder back in his drawer and smashed it closed, he secured it with the lock.

He shuffled towards Carr's bureau, stopped close to him, and flipped the portfolio open. He had a taste for the melodramatic. On the initial sheet of the archive was a mugshot of the third victim from an arrest in 2002. Her eyes jumped off the page and hit him. How could he forget those eyes—they remained magnificent even if all life had faded from them. The set of eyes in the picture had a look of a happiness to them.

"Marianne Bowman, 25 years old. We picked her up in 2002 for shoplifting, she spent fewer than five hours in holding. Eventually the court let her off with a fine, and she's been clean ever since."

"Did you get a last known address for her?"

"Good question. I had Finch over in CSU checking into that as of yesterday afternoon, I have received nothing back yet. Let me give him a quick call and see if they turned up anything."

Carr readjusted himself in his out of style swivel chair as Alex returned to his desk to make the call. The precinct needed a revamp, but there was something about the grunginess of the building that made him appear at home. All of Alex's life he had the most recent and the best of—well, everything. Part of moving away to New York City and giving up his cushy life in Colorado was for him to part with those extravagances and attempt to be just an ordinary person.

Alex paced in circles while on hold to talk to his new contact at CSU—Aaron Finch. While he stood by, he flung the manila file on top of his desk. Alex looked in Carr's direction and resumed pacing. The older father of two was humming a tune to himself as he read *The New York Times*. With his cell phone glued to his ear, all Alex could do was shake his head.

So predictable of him.

Alex's nervous pacing came to a rest once he took in a familiar voice. "H-hello, Finch here."

"Ah, good morning, Finch...it's Detective Jones. We spoke last night about getting a last known address for our victim from

Prospect Park—Marianne Bowman. Any luck tracking that down for me?"

"Sorry, I didn't call sooner; I didn't want to wake you. Just bear with me a second—I have it here somewhere…"

"Ah, don't stress about it. Just phone me when you have anything, that's my job to be on call."

"Got it—it's 425 Fifth Avenue, corner of Fifth Avenue and Eighth Street, Brooklyn."

"You rock! Thanks for the information." Alex exclaimed.

"Anything I can do to help. Need anything else?" Aaron asked.

"Not yet, but you know that'll change. We'll work on obtaining a warrant and call you back to meet us once that's complete."

"I'll be on shift until noon today. Guess we'll chat again soon?"

"You know it."

Alex finished his call and thrust his cell back atop his desktop.

Carr lowered the newspaper. "So…what did you learn?"

"Got a home address. It looks like we should get ourselves a warrant but *you* get to call Finch once that task is done and have him meet us at her apartment. You imagine it's too early to hunt down a judge?"

"No, it's never too early, but for the love of god, why do I have to call that geek?"

"Because I'm dealing with all the heavy lifting here—and I picked up a hint of flirtation yesterday, you know, a connection of sorts. I don't need him to think I'm seeking reasons to call him."

"Well, are you?" Carr learned forward, a curious expression on his face.

"I'm involved with someone already."

"Evading the question … hmm."

Alex gave him a glance of utter disgust and swung around to carry on making his coffee. Carr recognized he was getting under his skin, and it made him smile. However, Carr also recognized that not all was perfect in paradise between his partner and Mike, and they hadn't been for quite a while. Carr didn't give a damn, he hated Mike. So, any chance Carr had to torment Alex, he did—and he enjoyed every moment of it.

Carr cleared his throat and sank back in his chair. "Move your skinny white ass up and let's get out there and catch a criminal."

Alex pressed the "brew" button. Carr stared at him while continuing to relax in his seat, and strumming his fingers on the desktop like a bored teenage girl waiting for her prom date to show up. He was a restless man. The only thing Alex could do anymore was to overlook it, write it off as one of his *many* quirks. Eventually, Carr picked up his phone and reached out to a judge. The appeal took fewer than two minutes, and he sprang to his feet.

"Found a judge to approve the warrant."

"Excellent!" Alex smiled.

"I'll write one up, and we'll be on our way to the courthouse," Carr said as he tapped at his keyboard.

"Okay good. I wrote up a warrant last night to get the autopsy results, so thanks for picking up the slack and getting this one."

Relaxation fell over Alex—perhaps once they discovered more about their victim, the closer they would be to catching her murderer.

Carr continued pecking away at the keys, which only drove Alex insane. The old man had his idiosyncrasies, and most people would express their frustration. Alex was the total opposite, he encouraged Carr to just be himself, which was something that the previous detectives who worked with Carr never did. Regardless, Alex realized that being matched up with him was perhaps the right place he needed to be at this moment in his career. Besides, having Carr as a partner wasn't all that bad. Underneath his harsh, bedraggled look, he was really an astute cop—something Alex wanted to be one day.

Alex popped the top of his travel mug and filled up the container to the brim. No milk, no sugar—just plain black was the way he loved his coffee.

Carr slid the warrant into a manila envelope and tossed it on Alex's desk as he reached for his police jacket, which read in tall white letters across the back "NYPD POLICE." Alex stuck the envelope between his teeth and slung on his black wool jacket.

The two plunged down the staircase towards the exit. For this mission, an automobile would be in necessary.

The heavy wood doors of the precinct flew open as they arrived outside. The sun had already passed the roofs of the neighboring structures.

Carr rushed for an awaiting detective vehicle parked out front. It was strange for Alex to be taking a vehicle as he never wanted to drive in the asphalt jungle. The traffic here was dissimilar from Ridgewood Hills, and dealing with idiotic drivers only made his anxiety worse. The ride to the courthouse was barely a ten-minute ride away, but it was more desirable than spending thirty in the drafty air.

Carr pulled the junker into the only empty parking spot along Schermerhorn Street. Once Carr put the gear shift in park, Alex pushed open the door and hurried out onto the pavement. He peered up at the massive building; the flags were wandering in the stiff breeze, which was already gathering in intensity. He moved towards the cast iron barrier, which rested there wide open to the public.

He paused to collect his thoughts.

"Jones, let's move—we don't have all day."

"Right. Mind drifted somewhere else for an instant."

Alex once again followed Carr through the entry as they moved toward the security checkpoint. The courthouse was just now stirring awake. A deputy greeted them. The guard seemed like he hadn't slept a wink in ages.

"Empty your pockets and place your items in the box," he instructed.

"NYPD, Detective Carr, and Jones," Carr said as he displayed his shield and pointed towards Alex.

"All right, proceed through," he answered with a grimace on his face.

The two went on through the metal detector, setting it off. They were on a mission and didn't try to stop and glance behind. There was one item on their mind, and that was to get the warrant signed and set off for Marianne Bowman's apartment.

They moved toward the elevator and pushed the switch to call it to the ground floor. It took forever to show up and when it did, the doors wobbled open. It lurched as they climbed inside, bobbing up and down. Alex reached over towards the keypad. Finding the correct key was a difficulty as the characters were barely visible anymore from generations of overwork. Alex pushed a button and it lit up a murky yellow.

Hope that's the right button.

He withdrew his arm and allowed it to fall back at his side. He inhaled deeply and was hopeful that it would take them to the fourth floor of the building. In truth, Alex didn't give a damn which floor it released him off on; all he demanded was to make it off the brittle thing alive.

After what appeared to take longer than it should, the doors shuttered open. He had pushed the right button, and Alex could make out the judge's office about a hundred yards down the hallway. He lost no time and briskly hopped out and away from the lift.

I'll take advantage of the stairs when we leave.

The two gentlemen strolled side-by-side down the dismal corridor towards the office. The fluorescent overhead lights must have been in power save mode as 50 percent of them were off, or more realistically burned out for all Alex knew.

At the doorway to Room 418 Carr raised his massive fist and pounded on the door and adjusted his windbreaker. He stood up straight, swelling out his chest. Alex mimicked the movements of his mentor. Twenty seconds passed before the doorway swung open and a pale white glow from the room illuminated the darkened corridor, making Alex squint his eyes.

A soaring older gentlemen with distinctive salt-and-pepper hair, chiseled jawline, and black framed spectacles pushed forward his designer frames and opened his mouth.

His voice reverberated as he spoke. "Can I assist you, gentlemen?"

Alex stood, mumbling under his breath, unable to put together a comprehensive sentence.

Carr stepped in, "Detectives Carr and Jones from the 78th Precinct. I phoned earlier about obtaining a signature on a warrant."

"Ah, Detective Carr, come on in," the magistrate replied as he threw open the door further, moving aside to permit the investigators to enter. "So you need the warrant to search a victim's residence, right?"

"That's correct, Your Honor. We're counting on finding some clues at her residence that might help us better understand the circumstances surrounding her murder," Carr answered.

"Grant me a couple minutes to review this, and I'll have you two on your way," Judge Howe said as he hunkered down in a leather executive chair that had known better days.

Alex glanced over at his partner who had made himself comfortable in an armchair that faced the judge's desk. Being a detective was all still new to Alex. When you're a beat cop working the dangerous streets you patrol, you arrest perps, bring them to booking, draft reports, and testify in court—that's it. But being a detective was more about schmoozing judges and demanding harder questions of the same perps. Alex nervously sat down.

I'm certain he's a friendly fellow, he just makes me so uneasy.

Alex eventually relaxed as he watched the judge read over the search warrant. The seat was hard and was beginning to irritate his ass as he wriggled in his chair.

The magistrate peered over the top of his black bifocals at Alex. He cleared his throat. "Well, all seems to be in order here." He picked up a pen from his desk and signed on the last sheet of the official paper.

Standing, Carr said, "Thank you so much, Your Honor."

"Anytime," he responded with an arrogant smirk on his face.

The investigators quickly withdrew from the judge's chamber and moved back to the lift. Alex poked his colleague in the back and pointed towards the staircase.

"You're insane if you think I'm going back on that thing."

"If you thought my big ass is walking down those stairs, you assumed wrong."

"Suit yourself, I'm going with the stairs this time."

Carr continued marching towards the elevator as Alex swiftly turned to the staircase around the corner. He moved so speedily that his boots squeaked across the recently waxed marble floor. He didn't care about the racket he was making; all Alex knew is that he'd better beat his partner downstairs or he'd never heard the last word about it.

He climbed down as the gentle buzzing from his cell vibrated against his rib cage. Reaching into his pocket, he answered the phone.

"Good morning," Alex said to his boyfriend.

"Is it true, Alex? The woman you found in the park yesterday was Marianne Bowman?"

"And once again, good morning, Mike. But, yes, the victim's name is Marianne Bowman. Odd that you're asking. Why do you sound so alarmed?"

Alex stood on the second-floor landing, waiting for a response. Mike sighed loudly.

"She's in my Tuesday and Thursday yoga group. I'm still in shock—I just spoke to her on Tuesday night."

"Where are you right now?" Alex asked with a touch of urgency in his voice.

"I'm standing at your desk. Where are you?"

"Courthouse. Carr and I just picked up a warrant to search Marianne's apartment."

"I have the address already—I'll meet you over there." Mike hung up.

Alex reached the phone away from his ear and looked at the display, astonished at what just now occurred between him and Mike.

The foregoing months, since his promotion, the image of their picture-perfect relationship started to weaken. It didn't take place overnight. Instead, it had built up gradually, like a tiny nick in the edge of a mirror. With sufficient force, the crack grew larger as time pushed on.

He didn't have the opportunity at this stage to dwell on his relationship spiraling out of control. No, there was a murderer on the loose who needed to be caught before he committed further violence against innocents.

Alex slid the phone back into his pocket and took a stride towards the final batch of steps.

Carr, perplexed at what the holdup was, shouted at Alex, "Jones, let's go! You're constantly taking your sweet ass time."

He arrived at the ground floor and kept on walking past his partner, not speaking a word to him as he neared the exit.

"Jones—STOP!" Carr ordered as Alex turned around, standing still.

"Yeah?"

"I don't understand what's going on with you recently, but you're beginning to terrify me a little with your bizarre actions."

"Carr, this isn't the time or place to talk about this. Mike's en route to Marianne's residence. He claims he knows her."

SIX

425 Fifth Avenue, Brooklyn
November 17, 2005
8:45 A.M.

DETECTIVES JONES AND CARR STEPPED OUT of their
unmarked cruiser and stood on the sidewalk, gazing up at the
victim's four-floor walk-up. A barren oak tree swayed in the
light breeze which blew across the property. Alex slammed the
rusted door shut and buttoned up his black wool jacket. Carr
loved to wear the navy-blue windbreaker, but for Alex it was all
about looking good. Vanity was his biggest downfall in life.

With the warrant in hand, Carr was the first to step towards
the building, his protégé close behind. Alex scanned the area;
Mike was nowhere in sight, and that simple fact worried Alex.

I hope he didn't break into the apartment—God, please tell me he
didn't do it.

The stairs were steep, but manageable by Brooklyn standards. Carr gripped the brass doorknob, which had seen better days. It turned with ease. He slowly turned his head over his shoulder and spoke in a lighthearted tone. "You ready for this, newbie?"

"Please stop with the newbie jabs already. I've been a detective for almost a year now; pretty sure I'm not considered green anymore."

Carr scoffed, "Still a newbie. When you get a few hundred homicides under your belt, we can revisit your nickname then."

"You're the most morbid person I've ever known, and I've known some real wackos," Alex muttered, only half joking.

They walked into the lobby of the building. The mosaic tile beneath their feet was worn away from many years of neglect and abuse; but what else could you expect with a structure of its age. Alex crossed the threshold last, his partner about four feet ahead of him. Alex casually released his hand from the door. At once, the spring jerked the door back and closed, slamming so hard the floor beneath their feet shook.

"For fuck's sake, Jones—you'll wake the whole building."

"Oops, my bad."

The two promptly ascended the stairs, rounding two landings before reaching the third floor. They stopped, each of them taking a moment to catch their breath before proceeding any further. Alex looked around; each side of the hallway contained two apartment doors.

Carr, still hunched over with both hands firmly planted on his knees, windily asked, "Which apartment is it again?"

"3B," Alex replied as he stepped forward towards the cream four-paneled door.

Alex forcefully knocked and harshly announced, "New York City police, we have a warrant to search the premises."

He listened, carefully, as the faint sound of rustling footsteps penetrated through it. He turned to his partner. "Someone's in there."

Carr, now fully recovered from the hike upstairs, reached for his sidearm from inside his jacket, drew it, and pulled the slide back. He motioned for Alex to move to the side as he cautiously approached. He formed a fist and thumped once again on the door—harder and more obvious this time.

Seconds ticked by; all either of them did was stare at one another. Just as Carr was preparing to bash the door in, it swung open without warning. Carr vaulted backward, almost knocking Alex to the ground.

Carr regained his bearings and there before him stood Mike Temple.

Alex stood there in complete disbelief; he couldn't believe his eyes. For once he thought that Mike actually listened to him, controlled himself. Yet, Alex was disappointed once again. No words needed to be exchanged at that moment, the scowl on Alex's face and his knife-like blue eyes piercing Mike's soul was just enough to get the point across.

Alex was pissed, and even though he was attempting to control his facial expression, each second that passed on proved that he was failing miserably at it.

Alex finally composed himself enough to speak. "What—the—hell, Mike. How'd you get in there? Better question, why are you here compromising our potential crime scene?"

"I told you, Alex, I knew her—we were good friends. I had a key to her apartment," he confessed, pulling a small silver key from his pocket. "Sometimes, while she was out of town, I'd come over here to check on her cat."

Alex puffed out his chest and folded his arms across it. He looked over towards Carr. "Go ahead and get started, Carr. I'll be in shortly."

Carr nodded and made his way towards the door. Mike's broad shoulders practically blocked the entire door frame, making it impossible for Carr to enter the residence. Mike stood a good foot taller than Carr and appeared intimidating; Carr knew better than that. Annoyed, Carr belted out, "Temple, get the hell out of my way and step out—don't make me report this incident to your sergeant."

Mike complied and stepped aside, allowing Carr to move into the apartment. As he brushed past Mike, the grumpy older detective knocked Mike in the ribs with his shoulder. Alex stood there, conspicuously unbothered; the only thing in that moment that concerned him was getting Mike out of the apartment before he tainted the scene any further.

Mike swaggered into the hallway, rubbing his right ribcage gingerly. After nine years together, Mike recognized all of Alex's facial expressions and knew exactly what each one signified. And the body language in that instant was one of disgust. Alex hung his head to gather his thoughts and shook it slightly. Mike stopped short of Alex by three feet, just in time to see him raised his head slowly while angrily biting his lower lip.

Alex inhaled deeply and exhaled slowly. "I'm not going to yell; I'm not even going to scold you; although you deserve both. I'm only going to ask you one question: what in the hell were you thinking going into that apartment like that?"

"I honestly don't know. I just let my emotions take over. I knocked a few times thinking she was going to answer the door and all of it was a big mistake. I blanked out, and the next thing I remember is being inside her apartment looking around."

"Oh, please, I don't believe a single word of that. Let's start this over, Mike. And please let's hear the truth; what were you doing inside the apartment of Marianne Bowman?"

"I'm telling you the God's honest truth! I was in a state of shock—disbelief. I thought she was in the shower and didn't hear me knocking. I figured I would walk in and she'd be there."

"I have to give an account of this incident in my official report."

"I know. You've never been one to sweep anything under the rug, not even for the love of your life," he said trying to be cute, "I just want it to go on record that I didn't touch anything inside the apartment; all I did was just look around."

"Noted. However, one huge thing you did do, Detective Temple, you touched the doorknob." Alex pointed at Mike's hands. "Where are your gloves?"

"Like I said, I wasn't thinking."

"That's the problem here, Mike. Now when CSU arrives and dusts for prints, guess whose they'll find—yours! Your prints are at a potential crime scene." Alex just couldn't stop himself from going into full-blown scolding mode, "You'll probably get suspended at a minimum."

Mike hung his head and rubbed his temples—all he wanted was for Alex to shut up. When Alex stopped, impatiently tapping his foot, Mike seized the moment to get his bottled-up words out. "I know I screwed up big time here, but I don't think this is the time nor the place for you to chew me out. I'll get plenty of that when I get back to the precinct."

Alex cocked his head to the side and sneered. "Just get out of here, Mike. I can't deal with this right now. I don't care where you go, just get away from me."

Mike emotions were running on overdrive, and his face was growing redder by the second. He sucked back the runny mucus from his nose and threw his hands in the air. "Fine—if you want me gone, I'm gone," he said as he approached the staircase.

Having to get the last word in, Alex said, "I'll see you at home."

"Whatever."

All Alex could do was watch Mike descend the stairs. Mike turned back to look one last time at Alex, but all he saw was Alex's unemotional scowl across his face as he continued to stand at the door frame of apartment 3B; his arms still folded coldly. Mike's eyes began to swell even more with tears—more now from the anger he felt towards himself. The anger towards Alex hadn't even hit him yet. He only stared at his lover a few seconds more before disappearing down the steep, unlit staircase.

Alex stopped for a moment to reflect on what just happened. He let out a huge sigh of relief. It was now becoming clear that a breaking point was near: not only in his relationship but with his entire life in general. He wasn't sure how much more he could take before everything would completely unravel.

How could I talk to him like a child? Sure, he's a fool, but he's still my fiancé.

In the past nine years, Alex not once ever spoke to Mike in the tone he just had. Alex was becoming cold and cruel and he truly didn't even know where to begin to change his downward spiral. After the blowup, there was one thing on his mind.

Where do things go from here?

He snapped back to reality; there was no more time to waste worrying about Mike. He had to keep his focus on the victim's apartment.

Pulling out a fresh pair of blue latex gloves from his pocket, he hustled inside, leaving the door slightly ajar as he entered the small foyer of apartment 3B. Once inside, he noticed the immaculate condition of the dwelling. Not a single clue to any struggle taking place. Everything looked to be in the proper place. He saw Carr standing in the kitchen area going through drawers.

"Anything you're looking for in particular?" Alex asked.

"Was hoping she had an address book or something. Damn kids these days keep everything on their fancy phones."

"Gotta keep up with the times, old man. I'll check out her bedroom and bathroom."

"Have fun."

Alex walked down the hallway towards the single bedroom in the apartment. The apartment, exactly like the building, was older, but the victim did her best to keep the place tidy—and as modern as possible. He extended his hand and turned the doorknob gradually.

As the door opened fully, complete darkness greeted him. He squinted his dark blue eyes, working hard to make out the outline of two large windows along the east wall of the bedroom. He felt the outer pockets of his jacket and grasped for the mini flashlight that was in his right pocket. He turned the light on and began cautiously working his way deeper into the room. He was worried about disturbing any potential evidence that might be strewn about.

He aimed his flashlight towards the bed and found a table lamp. The bright beam of the flashlight illuminated his path— nothing was blocking his direct route. He reached his hand beneath the lampshade and twisted the small knob—it clicked two times. Instantly, the room came to life.

Now able to see better, Alex's worry about disturbing any evidence subsided. He started his search in the nightstand beneath the lamp. It was strange searching someone else's belongings, but Alex figured that if he could find anything to help with finding her killer, Marianne wouldn't mind having her privacy invaded.

The nightstand turned up no clues, so he closed the drawer and stood up from his crouched position on the floor. Out of the corner of his eye, he spotted a six-drawer mahogany dresser just across the room.

There's gotta be something in there.

The room was weirdly silent; not even the distinctive street noise penetrated through the thick brick walls. Alex crossed the room; each step taken rumbled the floorboards beneath his feet. He pulled out the top left drawer; all undergarments. He stirred the clothes around, but nothing of importance stood out to him.

Alex continued searching the drawers from top to bottom, in a methodical manner. Finally, he opened the bottom right drawer and several things stood out to him immediately. The first thing: the address book they had so desperately been seeking. The second item that stood out was one tarot card.

One tarot card? Where's the rest of the deck?

Alex pulled the card and address book out and sealed each one separately in clear plastic bags. He studied the card, *The Fool* written beneath a photo of a man standing at the edge of a cliff. What did it all mean, Alex wondered.

Alex collected the two bags and turned around to find Aaron Finch standing behind him. Surprised, Alex jumped and reached for his heart.

"Scare the shit out of me, why don't you."

"Sorry, Jones. Carr said you needed my team to do fingerprint dusting and trace evidence collection."

"Ah right, I asked him to call you. So, I'm all done in here if you want to get them started." Alex motioned that the room was all his.

"Thanks, I'll let you know if my team finds anything," Finch said as Alex grinned and walked across the hallway into the bathroom.

Alex searched the bathroom, opening drawers and inspecting any items that felt out of place to him. After turning up no new clues he walked out into the hallway. He eyeballed the bedroom one final time and noticed Finch crouched down, one knee on the floor, dusting the nightstand. Alex stood there, fixated on how meticulous the young investigator was being. He twisted his neck sharply, a loud popping sound bounced off the walls. Finch unexpectedly stopped and turned around.

"Oh, it's just you," he exclaimed.

"Just a little payback," Alex said as he grinned.

"Well, you got me this time."

"Listen, how much longer will this take?" "Shouldn't take much longer. Maybe five more minutes in here."

"All right, sounds good. I'll go wait out in the kitchen with Carr."

"Sure, be out soon."

Alex returned to the main living area of the tiny apartment to find Carr leaning against the edge of the kitchen counter. The older man just stood there, gazing emotionless towards Alex.

"What's up?"

"Just waiting for your slow ass. Was a bust out here, did you find anything useful?"

"Found an address book and this lone tarot card." Alex handed Carr an evidence bag. "The card seems out of place. I've seen no signs that the victim was into anything pertaining to the occult."

"Hmm, may be substantial. Let's have Finch dusts this for prints," Carr said as he held the clear bag up to his eyes, examining the card in more detail.

"Sure, be right back," Alex said, snatching the bag away and walking back towards the bedroom.

Finch was zooming around the room snapping photos, and Alex cleared his throat to catch Finch's attention without startling him.

Finch lowered his camera and looked towards the doorway. "So I need a favor from you quick," Alex said as he emerged inside the room, holding the evidence bag in his left hand.

"What do you have there?" Finch asked, pointing to the bag.

"Right, so I found this in her dresser and was wondering if you could dust this for prints."

"Yeah, no problem. I assume you want to retain control of this?" Finch asked.

"I would like to, yes. However, if you find prints, you can take those with you."

Finch smirked as he took the bag from Alex. "I'd hate to wrestle you for the evidence."

Alex, dumbfounded by the comment thought to himself. *Wrestle me?*

Alex squinted at him, then looked away. "Just let me know if you find something."

Alex darted from the doorway and walked down the hall as Finch hollered out, "I'll let you know."

What just happened? Is he hitting on me?

He emerged back into the kitchen area to find Carr tapping his fingers across the countertop. "You look like you've seen a ghost."

"No, I'm fine. Finch is dusting the tarot card. He'll let me know if he finds anything."

"Um, okay. So once your friend finishes, we can get back to the precinct?"

"Yes, we need to figure out how the other two cases tie into this one," Alex said as Aaron Finch emerged from the hallway, his toolkit in hand.

"Bad news—no useful prints on the card you found," said Finch.

"Eh, worth a try. You all finished in here?" Alex asked.

"All finished. I'll let you know after we process everything if we found anything useful."

The team left the premises, turning all the lights off and closing the door behind them. Carr and Jones returned to the car and drove back towards the 78th precinct. Alex had submitted a subpoena the previous evening requesting the autopsy results, but his anxiety was building as he had yet to have them in his hand.

"Carr, let's take a detour before heading back."

"What? You need more coffee or something?"

"No, nothing like that. I still haven't seen the autopsy results for Ms. Bowman. I think a face-to-face visit is in order," Alex said.

"You're the lead on this case; we'll go wherever you need to go."

The car sped east along Parkside Avenue towards New York Avenue. Timothy Carr was serious about not wasting any more time then he had to. Thirty-six hours had passed since they discovered the body of Marianne Bowman in Prospect Park, and the two detectives were no closer to having any concrete evidence, let alone any clue as to her killer was.

From experience, Carr knew if they didn't locate a suspect within forty-eight hours, the case risked going cold and once that happened, finding a suspect diminished further.

The car skidded into the first available parking space just outside the ME's office, the force so great that the back of the car bounced a few feet into the air. Alex rushed from the car and towards the main entrance with Carr following behind. Alex approached the call box and pressed the buzzer. The unforgettable voice from yesterday responded.

"Can I help you?" the voice asked.

"Detective Jones and Carr from the 78th precinct," Alex replied.

A loud buzzing sound emanated from the door, and Carr reached down, grabbing the handle in his oversized hands. The door swung open, the two men entered the sterile corridor walking toward the lobby. A familiar face greeted them as they approached the desk.

"Oh, Detective Jones, great to see you again. Dr. Callahan left this for you," the young man behind the counter said as he handed over an interoffice folder.

"The autopsy report I was looking for. Tell Dr. Callahan I said thanks," Alex said as the man smiled.

"I'll relay the message. Have a good day."

The two retreated towards the door. In Alex's mind, he'd prepared himself to put up a fight to get the report. For once, things went as they should.

They arrived at the clunker, still parked crooked out front. Alex opened his door, sat on the ripped cloth seat, and before he even had his belt fastened Carr was hauling ass towards Winthrop Avenue. Alex flipped through the report as Carr boldly drove through traffic.

"Anything useful in there?" Carr asked.

"They found biological material under her fingernails, Finch had it sent off to the lab for analysis. We won't see results for a few weeks from that. Otherwise, nothing noteworthy that we didn't already know," Alex replied as Carr maneuvered in between slow-moving vehicles.

"Well let's get back and work. I'm positive you'll be staying late tonight after that blowup earlier," Carr said.

"Oh definitely! I have no interest in going home soon," Alex said as he stared out the window. "No interest at all."

SEVEN
Prospect Park, Brooklyn
November 20, 2005
3:36 A.M.

ALEX STOOD ONCE AGAIN OVER THE LIFELESS body of another young woman found brutally murdered on the grounds of the park. Alex kneeled beside the top end of the white sheet; the distinctive outline of a body lay beneath.

He took a sip of coffee, inhaled deeply, and peeled back the sheet; now confronting the horrific sight of the mutilated victim. Alex coughed, softly, as he shuffled over to his left. The surroundings had been badly lit when he arrived, but quickly the area came alive with the bright white light of the flood lamps.

Jesus that's bright.

Alex finished his thought, and his partner rounded the corner. Alex tugged the sheet back over the victim's face.

"Jones, please tell me you've gone home within the past three days?" Carr asked.

"Been to pick up a few things; I've been staying at a hotel down from the precinct. I can't go home, I don't want to face Mike," Alex matter-of-factly said.

"You must see him at some point; anyway, enough about your sensational life, who do we have here?"

"Jane Doe for now; the style of this slaughter fits the pattern of the past three. The only variance is race," explained Alex.

Alex rolled his eyes, "I find it astonishing how I'm always the first on the scene these days."

Carr shook his head. "There's a reason for that; you have no life."

Carr walked over towards the sheet, pulled it back, and fell backward; he looked like he had seen a ghost. He scampered away from the body. Alex, dumbfounded, followed his partner's erratic actions and moved towards him.

"The hell has gotten into you?" Alex asked.

"I-I ah…" Carr mumbled, incapable of forming a sentence.

Alex squatted down beside Carr, who was sitting on the moist ground. "No, seriously, what is wrong with you?"

Carr inhaled, trying hard to collect his thoughts. It took a few seconds, but he blurted out, "I recognize her."

Those three words were all he could muster up. Alex flagged an officer to come over while he sat there with his partner. Alex tried to console him the best he could, but Alex wasn't the most compassionate person in the world.

"How do you know her?" Alex asked.

"She's, um, the victim—um, she's my daughter's best friend. Her name's Afiza Aziz. She and my daughter went to high school together, and now they attend Brooklyn College."

Alex's heart sank, and he became fully in tune with Carr's inner emotions, which he hid so well with his gruff exterior. "Wow—man, I don't know what to say. It's awful you had to be here for this."

Alex placed his palm against Carr's back as another officer walked past on his way to the entry point.

"Excuse me, officer," Alex said, "do you mind taking Carr back to his car?"

"No! I'm okay; I'll stay and help," Carr said. "I know you're the lead on this case, but I refuse to leave."

"All right, you can stay, but under one condition: I want you to wait over there alongside those officers," Alex said, pointing over towards the entrance point.

"Yeah, okay," said Carr as he walked towards the flapping yellow tape.

"Also, under no circumstances are you to get near the body again," Alex hollered.

Once Carr was far enough removed from the scene, Alex refocused his attention back to the victim. Just like the previous murders, evidence was sparse at the scene, and Alex stood around waiting the medical examiner team to arrive. He returned to a crouched position next to the body and just waited patiently.

He glanced over his shoulder towards Carr. It was then Alex experienced a deep, gnawing pain in his stomach. The one he got when something didn't add up.

What's going on here? First, Mike was friends with Marianne—now Carr knows the latest victim. What am I missing?

He pulled the sheet back once again, scrutinizing the gaping wound across the victim's neck. The faint scent of roasted coffee mixed with the pungent smell of iron wafted from the victim's body. He inhaled deeply, the aroma of citrus and smokiness lingered in the air.

I get a hint of light roast coffee.

He looked back up in time to see two forensic investigators from the ME's office arriving on the scene. He replaced the white sheet again and stood to his feet.

His phone rang suddenly.

"Crap," he said as he recognized the number displayed. "Jones here."

"Detective Jones, it's Aaron Finch. I'm on my way to the scene, can you give me a location?"

"Near Sled Hill, right off East Drive."

"Give me five minutes."

Alex hung up the phone and slid it back in his pocket. The two investigators from the ME's office arrived and stopped side-by-side. Alex hadn't looked up yet as a familiar voice echoed from a few feet away.

"Hey, Jones," said the taller investigator.

"Oh, Bradburn, good morning."

"Got anything, in particular, you want us to look for, or should we process this scene like usual?"

"I've got nothing. Counting on you guys to have better luck," Alex said. "Hey, do you think Callahan would care if I came for the entire autopsy this time?"

"You? Seriously?"

"Let's keep the sarcasm to a minimum. Things aren't adding up, and I have to be there for this one since Carr can't. Is it cool or not if I come?"

"Yeah, it's cool. Damn, Jones, I'm gonna need you to calm down, all right? Remember I'm not the enemy here."

"Sorry, I don't mean to snap at you—it's just been, well, an interesting few days," Alex said as Bradburn pointed towards Carr.

"Why's Carr lazing around over there?"

"Actually, for once he's not. Carr can't have any access to the body—his daughter is best friends with the victim."

"Oh. That's messed up! Not to sound callous, but if he knows the victim, why's he still hanging around?" Bradburn probed.

"He won't leave. I informed him he could stay, but with one stipulation; he had to remain on the other side of the police line."

CSU Supervisor Finch ducked underneath the yellow tape, and Bradburn nudged Alex in the shoulder. "Looks like your new boyfriend is here."

"For your information, Mike is likely at home reveling in the fact that he has found himself suspended for two weeks without pay. So don't start any unwanted drama."

"Temple's suspended? The hell did he do? Wait a minute, is he the beat cop who entered a victim's apartment without a warrant?"

"Yes, that's him. Now do me a favor and don't go spreading gossip around the medical examiner's office. It's bad enough I haven't been home in three days, and if he finds out I told you, I'll never hear the end of it."

Bradburn nodded before rejoining his partner. Alex grinned as Finch stood before him. The young CSU investigator set his toolbox on the ground and extended his hand.

As he released his grip, Finch said, "Sorry we have to meet under these circumstances once again."

"Yeah, me too," said Alex, breaking eye contact.

"Well, I'm always happy to see you, regardless of the reason. However, no more small talk, I gotta get to work so Bradburn can take our victim to the ME."

"If you need me I'll be over at the entrance speaking with my partner."

Alex approached his partner, who was standing with two other officers, trying his best to keep his mind off the haunting sight he witnessed. Alex took his time, walking at a slow pace. He wasn't sure where to even begin with his partner.

Alex cleared his throat before speaking. "Carr, do you feel up for questions now?"

"Yeah, I'm okay now. Fire away."

"Okay, do you know where the victim lives?"

"With her parents in a four-floor walk-up at Sixth Avenue and 13th." Carr wiped a tear from his cheek. "If you don't mind, I think I should be the one to notify them."

"I think that's a good idea. Just a couple more questions and I'll send you on your way."

"Okay."

"You said she's friends with your daughter, right?"

"She is."

"Is there a chance that your daughter might be in danger? Have you heard from her?" Alex asked.

"I talked to her around eleven last night. Do you think I should go home and check on her?"

"I can't think of any place better for you to be right now," Alex said.

Carr cracked a half smirk and nodded, then shook Alex's hand and signed out with the officer in charge. Alex stayed at the entry point until Carr disappeared into the darkness of night.

The two forensic investigators finished zipping closed the black body bag. Alex waited as they lifted the body onto the stretcher and wheeled her from the scene.

Bradburn stopped and looked at Alex. "We'll still see you at the office, right?"

"I'd be there—give me like an hour so I can finish up here."

"I'll believe it when I see it," Bradburn said while the other investigator snickered under his breath.

What have I agreed to?

Alex shook his head and walked over to Finch, who was standing next to an oak tree, writing on a plastic evidence bag. Alex hung back and watched him finish, doing his best to not interrupt.

Alex approached the young man. "Hey, you about done? I have to get over to the medical examiner's office."

"Yeah, I need to finish logging this evidence. Maybe need another two minutes," said Finch. "To be honest, I'm stunned that you'll watch the postmortem."

"I'm a little stunned myself. I need to get over my fear at some point," said Alex.

"True enough. You can't live your life scared all the time of dead bodies and work in homicide—the two don't go together."

The guy was right. Alex stepped aside to allow Finch to finish logging his evidence. Aaron picked up a large paper bag, sealed it closed with evidence tape, and lifted it from the ground.

"All set?" Finch asked.

"Let's get out of here."

The two walked away from the crime scene and back towards their cars. Alex peered over at Finch and scanned him with his blue eyes. Alex was still in awe at his sheet height. The four inches and more muscular body frame intimidated the young detective.

Alex cleared his throat. "So, when did you start with the department?"

"Almost five years ago now. I'm doing the job I love to do."

"Exciting. I'll have been with NYPD for four years in January."

Finch smiled. "It's surprising we've never worked together."

"Well, I used to work in patrol until a few months ago. Doubt our paths would have crossed."

"True, especially if you were at a different precinct," Finch replied, "but I'm glad I get to work with you now."

"Yeah, I'm glad too. You're a smart guy, which is rare these days."

"Couldn't agree more. And ditto on the smart guy thing - you got a good head on your shoulders, which is probably why they gave you the promotion."

Alex smiled, and was the first to arrive at his vehicle. "So, I'll look forward to hearing from you about what you found here."

"You'll be the first person I call," Finch said as he extended his hand.

There seemed to be a chemistry between Alex and his newfound colleague, but figuring out what the interest was, well, that proved a tad more difficult. The two shook hands, and Alex partially opened his car door. He stood there, his forearm propped against the frame of the vehicle as he looked out over the expansive park. With the crime scene van parked a few hundred feet down the lane, Alex wanted to ensure Finch arrived there safely with the critical evidence he'd collected.

Once the man was out of sight, Alex leapt into the driver's seat to escape the brutal cold. He tried to warm himself by rubbing his hands together and blowing on his hands. It did the trick and he turned over the engine. He sat in the same spot for five minutes, struggling internally over facing his fear of the autopsy. He took a deep breath and moved the driveshaft downward, putting the car into drive.

He approached the intersection of Flatbush Avenue and Lincoln Road as the light changed to red. Alex removed his cell from his pocket, looked at the screen to check for any missed calls. There were none.

His obsessive thoughts fixated on Mike again. They hadn't seen or uttered a single word in three days. On day one, Mike phoned five times an hour, but as the days went on, those calls and texts slowed and ultimately stopped by day three.

I miss Mike—I should go home and check on him after the autopsy.

The light changed to green, and the car sped off down Flatbush Avenue. The drive took only a few minutes at five o'clock in the morning, and before he noticed, he was sitting inside the car outside the ME's office. He sat there frozen as the expected uneasiness washed over him. His hands became clammy, and he took a deep breath; all he could do was wipe his sweaty palms on his dress pants.

"You can do this. Suck it up and get it over."

He turned the engine off and removed the keys from the ignition. His breaths were getting deeper and deeper with every passing second. He reached across the center console and grabbed his jacket off the passenger seat, opened the car door, and stepped out onto the blacktop.

EIGHT

Office of Chief Medical Examiner, Brooklyn
November 20, 2005
5:48 A.M.

ALEX STOOD AT THE MAIN DOOR OF THE ME'S OFFICE.
He followed the same protocols as he had that last time; Alex
pressed the button, someone answered, and he entered the
building. This time was different though—this would be the
first real-time autopsy he had witnessed in his entire career. This
part of the job had always been Carr's responsibility—until
now.

He walked into the same sterile white waiting area, the
pungent stink of ammonia slapped him in the face as he
approached the main desk. The only difference this time was
the person behind the counter who greeted him.

"Detective Jones, I presume," the cheery older woman behind the desk said.

"Morning. I'm here for the autopsy of Afiya Aziz. Bradburn brought her in a little while ago."

"He sure did—do me a favor, hon, and sign in for me," she said as she reached for a visitor badge.

Alex did as he instructed, placing the pen atop of the sign-in sheet when he finished. The friendly woman grinned and handed him his credentials. He clipped the badge with a big red V onto his jacket as she stood to her feet.

She walked around to the front of the desk, still cheerful as ever. "Follow me."

She guided him towards the set of secured double doors, tapping her badge to gain access. The doors slowly opened wide, exposing the same long, white, sterile hallway that was now all too familiar.

She took a few steps in and extended her right arm outward. "Autopsy room is down the hall, the last door on your left. Dr. Callahan is expecting you."

"Thanks."

Alex scanned the empty hallway for any signs of life. All was quiet. He quickly reached into his pocket and took out his tin of mentholated petroleum jelly. After unscrewing the cap, Alex dipped his right index finger in and scooped up a large glob. He continued his journey down the corridor, rubbing it under his nostrils.

A moment later he found himself positioned at a set of automatic glass doors that led into the autopsy room. He looked inside; the brilliance of the fluorescent lights shimmered off the few empty stainless steel slabs. Alex stepped forward a few inches to get a better look as the doors slid open.

Shit.

The sickly smell of formaldehyde seeped from every corner of the room; he glanced around the room, his eyes scrutinizing its contents more closely than he had before.

Eighteen slabs.

Of the eighteen metal table tops, fifteen held the nude bodies of the suspicious deaths from the earlier night. He paid close attention to the emotionless souls, some mangled beyond recognition while others were in a perfect untouched state. In the far corner of the room, he discovered Dr. Callahan writing something in a chart over the body of Afiya Aziz.

"Ah, Detective Jones. I was beginning to wonder if you'd show. Come in closer, she isn't going to bite," Callahan said.

Alex grabbed a surgical mask and pair of gloves from the metal rack next to the door and stood paralyzed for a few moments before he eventually stepped closer.

He felt that sense of fear creeping from the back of his mind. It was the same feeling he experienced after his last visit to the slab lab. Alex looked at her body, lying there with her eyes wide open. He shuddered as he thought about her last moments on this earth.

"I must admit that I'm impressed you made it here."

"You and the rest of your team," Alex said.

"Well, I already started the Y-incision, so that much is over, so shall we get started?" the doctor asked.

"I suppose so, I'm as ready as ever."

For the next twenty minutes Alex stood by, watching as Dr. Callahan removed organs, one after another. The doctor spoke as he worked, rattling off random thoughts. Alex was trying his best to take this newfound role in stride, but, with every slice and crack, he winced in disgust.

The doctor pried open her mouth to look. He reached for a long pair of tweezers sitting next to him on a silver tray.

"What do we have here," he said, sticking them inside her mouth and pulling out a folded cardboard card.

"The hell is that?"

"Not sure yet, I'll send it over to trace, and they'll let you know," the doctor said.

It was all over. The doctor threw his gloves into a biohazard bag and motioned for Alex to follow him to the sink area. "Well, I can tell you that this young lady met the same tragic end as your previous three victims."

"Are you sure? I need to know you're 100 percent sure," Alex said.

"It's okay, relax—and please take that stupid mask off and inhale a little non-recycled air for a minute."

Alex cautiously removed the mask and took a deep breath. The smell of eucalyptus flooded his nose, and he was a little more relaxed. He exhaled slowly.

"So you're positive that Afiya died the same way as my other three victims did?"

"With 110 percent certainty," the doctor replied as Alex reached for his notepad.

Alex nodded and saw the unwavering look in Dr. Callahan's eyes. "So, I'm glad to hear you're certain. I believe all these murders were committed by the same assailant."

"You've mentioned that before. And quite honestly, I'm also beginning to see a pattern here."

"I'm glad you have my back on this. Last question, were you able to retrieve any trace or biological evidence?" Alex asked.

"There weren't any signs of sexual assault, but we did retrieve some skin cells from underneath your victim's fingernails. It appears your killer is becoming careless."

"This is possibly the break I'm looking for."

"Also, I can say with definite certainty that the weapon used was the same from the three previous murders: a Rambo MC-RB1," Dr. Callahan said.

"So these killings are personal. It's hard to just slash someone's throat—so this killer must know the victims enough they trust them," Alex mumbled aloud.

"You're the one with a degree in forensic psychology."

"Touché. Anything else, doctor?"

"I've pretty much conveyed my main points. Again, I'll send this paper I found over to trace, and I'm sure they'll have more news for you, soon," Callahan said.

Alex nodded and walked back towards the automatic doors, tossing his mask and gloves into a biohazard bin on his way out. The time was closing in on seven o'clock in the morning, and all Alex had on his mind was taking a few moments to check on Mike.

He dropped his visitor's badge at the main desk and stepped outside into the crisp fall air. The sun was cresting the horizon, and it marked another day of hunting down a psychopath.

Alex opened his car door and plopped into the driver's seat lined with years of grime. He planned his day quickly in his head.

Check on Mike, check on Carr, get to the office and hunt down this S.O.B.

The tires screeched as the car pulled out of the parking lot and onto Winthrop Street. Alex was on a tight schedule but wanted to make sure he attempted to make up with Mike. He drove along Parkside Avenue, catching every traffic light green along the way for a change. His condo was only a twenty-minute drive on a good day.

He arrived, swerving the car into the lane for the parking garage underneath the building. Alex could feel the tension building up as he stepped from the car and towards the elevator. In the nine years, they had been together, this was one of the few time Alex had grown so angry that he cut off every means of communication. These times were far and few between though.

The elevator opened, and he stepped in, pressing the button for the ninth floor. It sped toward the top of the building, making no stops along the way, as Alex leaned against the icy metal-coated siding. It lost steam and stopped on the tenth floor. The door slid open and he stepped out into the colorful lit hallway. His condo was just three down and to the left from the elevator.

He stood at his front door; an uneasiness poured over him as he huffed and slid his key into the deadbolt. He walked inside, the blinds cracked partially, allowing for the beams of sunlight to flow in. It was eerily quiet; no television or radio playing. The only thing he could hear was the tick from the cheap plastic clock on the wall. With each second that passed, another annoying *tick...tick* occurred in a rhythmic pattern.

He moved deeper into their condo, taking notice of the surroundings. It was in order, almost a little too in order. On the kitchen island sat one white rose and an envelope with his name written across the front. Alex sensed the worst news imaginable scribbled on a piece of scratch paper crammed inside it. He trembled, undecided if he wished to know what Mike had left for him.

What else could he do?

He walked towards the counter and lifted the rose; sniffing it before setting it back down. He picked up the card and opened it.

> Alex,
>
> Where do I begin this letter? So many emotions are swirling around my brain all at the same time. If we're being honest, our relationship is in serious jeopardy. It's an extremely dark place for us to be, and I never thought we'd end up here. All I know

is things can't go on like this, not if we want our relationship to grow stronger. But right now, it's crumbling away right before our eyes. I know I don't want to allow this to happen, so something, *ANYTHING* must change.

I've left for San Diego to stay with my parents for a few weeks or at least until you can decide what's more important to you; me or the job.

I'm sorry to leave you like this, but you haven't been here, I'm suspended until God only knows when and the emptiness of this condo is driving me to insanity because you're not here to comfort me like a husband-to-be should.

I'll be in touch soon. In the meantime, do me a favor and at least take the time to smell the roses and get some rest.

-Love, Mike

Placing the note on the counter he pulled out a barstool and plopped down on it. His hands placed firmly on his thighs, he leaned forward. How had he and Mike come to be at this point in their lives? How could the love of his life just up and leave him? Emotions never came easy, Alex could always keep a straight face during just about every situation, be it funny or serious. But this time his eyes filled up with tears, and no matter how much he tried to stop them from flowing, nothing worked.

He gave up trying and sat there and cried until he couldn't cry any longer. After about ten minutes, he wiped the salty tears from his face, sucked up the runny mucus, and stood. Other things needed his attention more at that moment than this spat he was having with Mike.

He reached for his cell phone, 11 percent battery left. He dialed Carr and leaned against the large floor-to-ceiling window that overlooked the Hudson River. The phone rang twice before a familiar grumpy voice greeted him.

"Hey," Carr answered.

"Hey to you too. How'd it go with Afiya's parents?"

"How do you think they went?" Carr angrily answered.

"I'd assume how it always goes—lots of crying and questions. Where are you?"

"Prospect Park. I need to clear my head before going into the office," he said.

"Good idea," Alex said.

"Oh, how did your first autopsy go?"

"I guess better than I expected. And I know this will be a huge shock to you, but I didn't rush home to shower right away either," Alex said as his eyes homed in on the bathroom across the apartment.

"So I guess I'll see you at the office in a little while. We need to get started on putting together a profile of our victims and suspects; suppose that means you can use that fancy degree for a change."

Alex paced around the kitchen. "I use that degree every day. I'll see you soon."

Alex hung up the phone and plugged it in, then went into the bedroom. He sniffed his shirt and wrinkled his nose in disgust. Alex unbuttoned the white dress shirt, crumpled it up, and threw it onto the floor. He walked towards his closet and slid the door open.

His wardrobe was extremely boring with an unwavering demand for consistency. Ten suits, dress shirts, and pants. He tried to stay as conservative as he could with work clothes. He'd seen older detectives wearing out-of-style suits, and even worse were the ones who insisted on wearing those nineties pimpish wide pinstripes. Alex didn't want that type of attention; no one wants to be on the nominated for worst-dressed detective; he'd prefer to blend in with the rest of 'em.

He finished changing and skipped the shower. He walked back into the kitchen to grab his cell phone from the charger; twenty-two percent.

Better bring this with me today.

Before he headed towards the door, he again looked at the rose and note that sat in the exact spot that Mike left them. All he could do was let out a sigh. The moment was short-lived, and he turned back towards the front door and made his way to the office.

NINE

78th Precinct, Brooklyn
November 20, 2005
9:45 A.M.

ALEX ROLLED UP AND SLID INTO A PARKING SPOT
RIGHT OUT FRONT. The precinct was buzzing with activity.
Two patrol officers were wrestling with a drunken man, who
continuously spouted off at the top of his lungs about the end
of the world coming. They fought the man to the ground in an
attempt to get his compliance with their orders. All Alex could
do was stand by and watch the free entertainment. He shook his
head, laughing softly to himself.

"Oh, another beautiful day in Brooklyn."

He ascended the stairs and rushed to the second floor where
he discovered his partner waiting motionless at his desk; he
looked disheveled and taken aback. He walked by their desks,

which were pushed together, and greeted him. The fresh smell of coffee lingered gently in the air, and Alex just couldn't resist the temptation for another cup. Alex kept moving towards the scent.

Carr lifted his head just as Alex arrived at the coffee machine. "You look like shit, man."

"I guess I could say the same about you, old man."

Alex filled up his travel mug to the top and moved back, reaching for his rickety chair. He sat down, staring Carr directly in the face. The old man continued to be dazed and in deep thought. Alex just sat there, staring at him as he took his first sip of black coffee. His gaze never broke.

He couldn't take the calmness any longer and decided to break the silence. "So…where you want to start?"

Carr snapped back to reality and pondered the question put to him. "Let's just assume you're correct, and we are dealing with a serial killer here—I think the best place for us to begin is by comparing victim characteristics."

Slowly Alex set his travel mug down on the desk and stood. In front of him sat a yellow folder full of pictures and documents. Across the top read "PROSPECT PARK SLASHER." He pushed the chair out of his way and walked towards a large dry erase board. He pulled several large photographs of each victim and began taping them across the top of the board.

With each photo he hung up, the face of the innocent victims made him wonder what in each of their lives made them happy? Each still image projected a smiling face full of vitality. He struggled to continue his task, because all he could think about was that burning, haunting question still stuck in the back of his mind.

"Good point," Alex agreed, "Let's start with the race of our victims. Our first was Rutchel Cox, and she's Asian. Victim two, Veronica Park was white, as was Marianne Bowman. Our latest victim, Afiya Aziz was Middle Eastern; I'm not seeing a pattern dealing with race, are you?"

"I think we can rule out race and ethnicity as a commonality," Carr said, "First one down. How about age?"

"Youngest victim is twenty, oldest is twenty-eight." Alex wrote the ages of the victims alongside their photos.

"How about this, and I know you'll laugh, but hear me out, okay? Did you or anyone you're acquainted with be acquainted with victims one and two?"

"No, how about you?" asked Alex.

"I didn't, and I don't know of anyone else who did. However, victim three was a friend of Mike's, and victim four was a family friend of mine." Carr paused. "Just saying it might be worth noting this just in case a trend continues."

"I could say it's just a coincidence, but I don't believe in them. Good call." Alex wrote the link next to Marianne's and Afiya's profiles. Just then another officer interrupted them.

"Hey, guys, sorry to interrupt! I got those documents you requested yesterday, sir," the tall, burly officer said as he passed over an envelope to Carr.

"Thanks," Carr replied.

The officer smiled, nodded, turned and walked away. Alex, always being nosy, flung the marker on top of his desk and stepped beside Carr.

"Whatcha got there?" he asked.

"I had Cyber run financials on the first three victims. I also asked Afiya's parents if they could provide me with a copy of her most recent bank statement; which they did." Carr opened the envelope. "Always been my saying: Follow the money."

"Smart move. Hopefully, the cyber unit found a connection," Alex said.

Carr's eyes moved back and forth as he read. "Bingo!"

"What?"

"Looks like they did find one common thread tying the first three together," Carr excitedly said as he pushed papers around his desk.

"Sharing is caring, ya know."

"Just a second. I'm looking for Afiya's bank statement before I get my hopes up."

He continued shuffling through the mounds of paperwork on top of his desk. He yanked up a blue folder, quickly flipping through its contents.

His lips continued moving as he whispered to himself; the scanning of each line item of her bank statement was taking him some time. He adjusted his wire-rimmed glasses and slammed the paper down on the desk.

"Ah-ha. Found it! They all visited the same coffee shop in Clinton Park within the past two weeks."

"Interesting." Alex said. "That's where my best friend Amy lives: Clinton Park."

"Amy, Amy—the one from Colorado?" Carr asked.

"Yup, that's her; don't think you two have ever met, have you?" Alex asked.

"Don't think so. We really need to focus on this right now though." Carr steered the conversation back to the cases at hand.

"Right, sorry—continue."

"Anyway, the name of the coffee shop is Sip, it's on St. James Place," Carr said.

"Damn, that's right around the corner from her apartment. Matter of fact, she goes there every morning before work," Alex said.

The conversation trailed off once again, and Carr began clicking away at his keyboard. Alex observed the older detective peck away at the keys as he took another sip of his coffee. Eventually, the impatience kicked in, and Alex walked back to the dry erase board and continued writing out the traits of each victim.

Carr called out. "When you're done with your cute little board I think we should head over to Sip and ask some questions, don't you think?"

Alex rested the black marker on the bottom lip of the board and turned around to face his partner. "Um, yeah—clever idea."

Carr finished jotting down something on a scrap piece of paper and yanked his jacket from the back of his chair. Alex followed suit, and the two descended the stairs back outside into the blustery conditions.

TEN

Sip Coffeehouse & Bookstore
St. James Place, Brooklyn
November 20, 2005
11:15 A.M.

CARR CUT OFF THE ENGINE. They sat there, gazing out the grungy windows of their unmarked cruiser towards the coffeehouse. It was obvious to the detectives that they arrived during the height of the busy lunch hour in the quaint enclave of Clinton Park. Not wanting to waste more time, they each clutched their jackets and bundled up before exiting the vehicle.

Alex stepped out first and onto the curb, slamming the dusty door closed. He pulled his scarf tighter around his lower face, doing his best to block out the freezing wind that blew hard through the narrow cut between the buildings. Carr moved up behind him, and the two walked towards the business.

The popular coffeehouse was a constant staple in the neighborhood, with a few people visiting many days a week.

Alex tugged on the door handle, pulling the massive wooden door open towards him. He gestured for his partner to pass through first. He soon followed.

From the outside, the place looked small. Once indoors, Alex, and Carr glanced around the vast landscape of tables, bookcases, and espresso machines in awe. Even at eleven o'clock in the morning, every table was full of either Generation X'ers typing away on laptops or people drowning out the world by cramming a book in their face. They ventured closer to the counter, and a cheerful man greeted them.

"Welcome to Sip, how can I help you today, gentlemen?" the barista asked.

"Um, hi. I'm Detective Jones, and this guy here's my partner, Detective Carr—wondered if you had a few minutes you could spare—ah, Myles. We have a few questions?"

"Oh, yeah," Myles said as he hollered towards the backroom, "Rose, can you take over for a few minutes?"

He untied his apron and threw it underneath the counter. Myles slipped behind a swinging door and returned with a large black jacket in hand. He stepped around the counter and into the lobby.

"Hope you don't care if I use this as an opportunity to take a smoke break," Myles said.

"Doesn't bother me," Alex said as Carr pulled the door outward and allowed the two men to step outdoors.

The three moved around the corner and into a narrow alleyway between the coffee bar and a florist. Alex cleared his throat and pulled out a yellow folder. Though this folder wasn't the same one labeled with the crude name that Alex used to name the killer.

Pulling out the first photo of Rutchel Cox, Alex he held it up a few feet from Myles's face. "Have you ever seen this young woman at the coffee shop?"

"That's Rutchel, yeah, she's a regular here. Haven't seen her in a few weeks though, figured she was out of town. But since two detectives are standing in front of me, I suspect the worst now."

"I hate to tell you this, but we found Rutchel murdered two weeks ago. Haven't you seen this on the news? Read it in the newspaper?" Alex asked.

"I've been so busy working and studying for finals these past three weeks I haven't turned on the television or even read the newspaper."

Carr pulled out a photo of the second victim, Veronica Park. "Do you know her?"

"Shit, man—tha-that's Veronica. She gets a medium mocha, no whip, only soy milk because of her lactose intolerance. You're telling me she's dead too?" Myles asked, visibly shaken.

"Yes, she's one of our homicide victims."

Myles hung his head in shock. It sank in that several of his regulars were dead, and he seemed flustered by the news. Carr didn't handle emotions well—and the only thing he could do was keep his stern facial expression as he faced the poor kid, who now was in tears.

Carr pulled out the next photo, held it up like before. The barista kept answering yes to every picture. He took a long drag from his cigarette and exhaled slowly before speaking again.

"Well, thanks for ruining the rest of my day. If there's nothing further you need my help with, I should get back inside," Myles said.

"What can you tell us about them? And before you begin, something besides their drink orders. Do you hang out with any of them outside the coffee house?" Alex asked as he flipped open his notepad.

"I've never *hung out* with any of them. Seen them around the neighborhood, though. Oh, and Afiya and I had a film class together last year," he recalled.

Alex wrote on his notebook as Carr stepped up to the plate. "So you didn't know none of the victims very well?"

"Like I said, we weren't like best friends. I remember that Veronica just moved in with her boyfriend, and that Marianne's cat ran away. You know, random things that people blurt out."

"Did you ever see any customers with a weird vibe? Maybe a guy who seemed to hang out and watch the female customers a little too closely?" Alex glanced up from scribbling.

"Well-l-l…"

"Spit it out, man," the older detective said.

"Rutchel. I remember a guy, he hung out here too much, in my opinion. One night he got some psychotic thought to follow her home and stand outside her apartment, staring into her apartment window."

"Think she ever reported this?" Carr asked.

"I don't recall—he left, and she never mentioned him again," the barista replied.

Alex finished scratching his responses in his notebook and after crossing his last T, he shut the cover. He reached into his jacket pocket and pulled out a business card.

"Thanks for your help, Myles. Here's my card. If you think of anything, and I mean anything, please call," Alex said as he flipped it over, pointing out his writing. "I also wrote my cell number for you in case anything else comes to mind."

"All right, thanks," he said as he took another cigarette out of the pack and lit it. "I'll ask around for you; someone may have more information than I do."

Carr and Alex returned to their car. Alex opened the passenger side door and slipped into the seat. He yawned and rubbed his eyes, the undersides of which were turning a light shade of charcoal and become puffy from the lack of sleep in the earlier three days.

"I can't go much longer without sleep," Alex blurted.

"Jesus, yeah you need to get rest. You should get out of that hotel and go home. Have you two lovebirds made up yet?"

"He's gone," Alex uttered, "I stopped by this morning for fresh clothes and, well—he left a note saying he's gone to San Diego to clear his head."

"Man, you screwed that one up. Is he coming back?"

"No, he screwed up—I did what I had to do."

"If you say so. Keep telling yourself that," Carr replied.

After their unpleasant exchange, Alex stared out the window, eyeing the swarms of people straggling along Atlantic

Avenue, bundled from head to toe. He was happy, for once, to be in a warm vehicle.

The silence soon broke as his famous deafening ringtone blasted from Alex lap.

He fumbled with the phone, nearly dropping it between his legs onto the floorboard.

"Jones," he answered.

"Detective, it's Samantha from the trace lab. Finch asked me to call you about the evidence recovered this morning at Afiya Aziz postmortem," she said.

"Yes, thanks for the quick response, Sam. So, what can you tell me about the item the ME found in her throat?"

"Strangest thing; it was a tarot card."

"A what? That's a new one for me. Which one?"

"The seven of swords. If I'm not mistaken, didn't we work another tarot card you found at Marianne Bowman's residence?" Samantha asked.

"You did. The Fool card."

"We found no traces of biological or organic material on either card though. Sorry to call with unfavorable news," Samantha said.

"I don't think it's bad, just unfortunate; I think you may have helped more than you know. Thanks for the call," Alex said as they ended their conversation.

Alex dropped his phone into his lap and ran his fingers through his hair. He yawned again, but this time it lasted much longer. Alex slouched back in the seat, resting his head against the head support. As he did, he closed his eyes but tried not to pass out.

He could hear Carr speaking to him. "I'm taking you home; you're no good this tired."

Alex didn't reply; he sat there with his eyes closed and a frown on his face.

"Jones, are you listening?" Carr shouted.

Alex jumped, awakening from his semi-slumber. "What? Yes, I'm listening."

"I'm taking you home," he repeated.

"No, everything is all right—trust me. My mind just drifted."

"If you think I'm going to let you keep going, then we're both going to need something stronger than coffee to keep us on pace," Carr said as he pulled the car into an empty spot outside a bodega.

The pit stop lasted a few moments and out walked Carr with a bag full of drinks and snacks. He jumped back in the running car and handed over the bag to Alex.

"Drink one so we can get busy catching this SOB," Carr demanded.

Alex snapped the metal tab back, and the carbonation fizzed from the can. He pressed the can to his lips and flung his head back. He gulped the energy drink for a few seconds longer before he had to come up for air.

"Delicious," said Alex.

ELEVEN

78th Precinct, Brooklyn
November 20, 2005
1:08 P.M.

THEY RETURNED TO THE PRECINCT and went straight
back to work. Alex sat at his computer tapping his pen on top
of the desktop. He reached for his mouse and opened his
search browser. He couldn't shake the discovery of two tarot
cards found at the most recent crime scenes. He typed in the
short phrase:

Tarot Card Meanings.

Within seconds a multitude of search results popped up.
Alex clicked on the first hyperlink which instantly sent him to a
page describing the meaning of each card in a complete set of
tarot cards.

The Fool.

A new screen opened, and he scanned the page for its meaning. Just as he was halfway finished reading the page, Carr stepped around his desk and crouched down beside him.

"Find something useful?" he asked.

"These tarot cards have some meaning, I just have a hunch that I can't shake," Alex replied as he tried to continue reading.

"Wait, I was so focused on getting you some energy I didn't even ask what the phone call was about." Carr said.

"It was Samantha from the trace unit. During the autopsy this morning Dr. Callahan found a tarot card lodged in Afiya's throat," Alex said.

Carr's face turned bright red, "This killer is sick."

"So I thought, you know, maybe the killer is leaving these cards behind as some sort of message; taunting us, perhaps," Alex said.

Carr leaned in closer to the computer monitor and began reading.

> The Fool card, in general, signifies
> a new beginning, but it also stands for
> an end to something in your old life.
> The Fool card shows significant
> decisions lie ahead for you which may
> not be painless to make and each time
> involves an aspect of risk.

"What in the hell does that mean?" Carr asked.

"I know exactly what this means; take a seat, I have a lot to fill you in on," Alex ordered.

For the next twenty minutes, Alex and his partner sat while Alex explained in further detail about his past in Colorado and everything that went down that fateful night in the snowy mountains outside of Denver.

When he finally expressed how emotional the event was to his partner, a weight lifted from his soul. Carr sat beside him with a bewildered expression on his face. Alex reached out and patted his partner on the shoulder.

"So, let me get this straight, so I am up to speed. Your father locked some mob guys up, they murdered him, you went into witness protection when you were what, like seven?" Carr asked.

"Yes."

"And your new identity was blown and these Russian mob people tried to kill you in Colorado and you think they are back now still trying to kill you?"

"That about sums it up," Alex said. "Why else would they be making this message so personal?"

"I believe you, I just don't even know where to start searching for the person who's after you," said Carr as he cracked his knuckles. "What about the second card, the one you found this morning; what does it mean?

Alex returned to the computer and searched for the seven of swords card.

The source may be aware of you
and is deliberately sabotaging you.

This card also represents failure, theft,
and unknown opponents.

"Yeah, that sounds personal," Alex replied.

"So, from the sounds of it, this isn't over," said Carr.

"Doesn't appear so. And if you put together the messages with the simple fact that the last two victims knew people I know, I think we must accept the fact that they want my attention. Well, now they got it."

"You should go home for the rest of the day and rest, Jones. We can pick this back up tomorrow morning after we're both rested."

"Doubt I'll get any sleep, but you're right—tomorrow we kick it up a notch," Alex said as he closed out his browser and reached for his jacket.

TWELVE

Prospect Park Well House, Brooklyn
December 2, 2005
5:29 A.M.

TWELVE DAYS HAD PASSED, and the two detectives were no closer to locating a suspect than they were when they discovered the first victim. It was a chilly early December morning, and Alex was curled up, sound asleep. His tranquil dream was rudely interrupted by the shrieking sound of his cell phone ringing on the nightstand.

"He—hello," he murmured. He patiently listened to the voice on the other end of the line before he interjected. "Okay, okay, I got it. I'll be there soon."

As usual of late, it was another call informing him of another homicide in Prospect Park. Alex was becoming annoyed with the killer; he hated these early hour call-outs.

He flung his phone onto the nightstand and swung his feet onto the floor. He planted them firmly there while he sat at the edge of the bed, rubbing his eyes. He squinted his eyes in the darkness and looked towards the spot where Mike would typically be tossing and turning, trying to fall back asleep after a call like this; but that side sat empty.

Damn, I need him back.

After a few moments of gathering his thoughts, he clicked the switch on the lamp, twice, and made his way towards the bathroom to get ready.

Alex arrived at the latest crime scene in about forty minutes, still half asleep, to find Carr standing with Aaron Finch over another body covered in a white sheet.

Alex approached the two men just as the exact moment a bright flash from an SLR camera illuminated the dark atmosphere, blinding him in the process.

"Same as last time?" Alex asked.

"To the T," Carr said as he knelt, lifting the sheet from the latest casualty's face.

"Damnit!" Alex exclaimed as he paced in a small circle.

Finch interrupted, "Detective, I found something over here you should see." The young investigator guided the way.

Alex and Carr followed behind carefully through the densely packed trees. The sound of rotted tree branches crunched beneath their feet as they stumbled in the dimly lit forest. After a few hundred feet, they soon found themselves standing in a clearing. Finch raised his hand and pointed onward towards a lone oak tree.

"The killer left you another message. Go have a look," Finch said. The two men cautiously walked in its direction.

"How much you want to wager he's left behind another card," Carr said.

"No need to wager anything, I'm damn certain that's *exactly* what we're going to find there."

The darkness was making it impossible to make out anything noteworthy. Alex couldn't take straining his eyes any longer and pulled a flashlight from his right pocket, shining the beam of bright light on the tree. The blue glow revealed what he expected to find.

They moved even closer. There it was: The Judgement card, stapled upside down to the trunk of the tree.

Alex hollered back at Finch, "You got photos of this, right?"

"I did. I figured you'd want to be the one to collect this," Finch answered.

"Yes, indeed I did. Thanks, Finch."

Alex reached into his left pocket and pulled out a fresh pair of latex gloves and a small evidence bag. He studied the card before disturbing it. He waved the flashlight around the entire card, and there it was, a dried blood stain on the upper right-hand corner.

Got you now, you sick son of a bitch.

Alex plucked the card from the tree, keeping the staple attached. He bagged it, sealed it, and walked back across the clearing to where Finch was standing. He handed the evidence bag over to him.

"I want this prioritized," he demanded, pointing out the dried blood on the corner.

"You got it."

The three returned to the body to find the medical examiner investigators had arrived. The same faces Alex had grown accustomed to greeted him with a smile.

"Jones! Heard you made it through your first autopsy like a champ the other day," Bradburn called out.

"Um, yeah, like a champ," Alex wearily said.

"Looks like your serial killer is back at it again," Bradburn said.

"That's what I'm told," Alex said.

"Well if it's any comfort, she would have bled out in a matter of seconds," said Bradburn.

"Not comforting at all."

"Nothing is comforting about death, Jones. We're all set to go unless there's anything you need from us?"

"Nah, go ahead. I'll be over as soon as I'm finished here. Let Callahan know," Alex said.

"Oh, check you out, going for another round," the investigator said.

"Ugh, just go, and I'll almost guarantee I'll see you soon."

The investigators hoisted the black body bag on top of the stretcher; it made a loud thud as they let go of it. He looked on as they wheeled another unknowing soul from yet one more horrific scene. Bradburn stopped as he passed by, patting Alex on the back.

Alex had so many pressing things on his mind, and now this psychopath continued to add more innocent victims to his body count.

Finch picked up his toolbox and stood. "I'm all finished here; I'll let you know if anything substantial comes from our analysis."

"Thanks," Alex sighed. "We have to stop meeting this way, you know."

"You're telling me. Hey listen, this is going to sound so unprofessional, but my buddy's band is playing tonight at this bar in the Village. I know this is very last minute, but think you'd be interested in tagging along?" Finch asked.

"Um," Alex said as Carr stood by, tapping his watch. "Yeah, where and what time?"

Finch provided Alex with the details, and they parted ways. Alex caught up with Carr, who impatiently took off towards the car.

It's not cheating—it's just a relaxing night out.

Carr smiled at Alex. "So…did I overhear you making a date with the young investigator."

"You know it's not like that! Besides, I haven't heard anything from Mike since our fight at Marianne's apartment. That was almost two weeks ago. I need a night out."

"Oh please, the two of you keep giving each other looks, it doesn't take a rocket scientist to see that he's trying to sample the goods," Carr joked.

Alex rolled his eyes. "Only you would think that; such a perv."

THIRTEEN

Office of the Chief Medical Examiner, Brooklyn
December 2, 2005
6:43 A.M.

ALEX AND HIS PARTNER STOOD AROUND the metal slab
and watched as Dr. Callahan unzipped the body bag. This
would be Alex's first time attending the entire post-mortem,
beginning to end. The area was silent, more so than usual. Alex
glanced around the room, his head slowly turning to the right.
This morning, all slabs were used up by the overflow of bodies
and even more waited along the hallway outside the chamber.

Dr. Callahan cleared his throat and began the autopsy by
cutting the blood-stained clothing off the victim. He started at
the bottom, running the scissors along the creases of each pant
leg of her jeans. Then Callahan pulled them off and placed them
into a brown paper bag. The process continued, cutting away at

each piece of fabric; her top, panties, and her bra. Once he cut the strap of the bra, a plastic card fell out, making a clinking sound as it hit the metal table.

"What do we have here?" the doctor asked as he picked up the plastic card.

"Looked like a license," Carr said as the doctor held up the object.

"Well, that was lucky."

The doctor handed the ID card over to Alex.

> Juliette Cochran
> 1667 11th Avenue
> New York, NY 11215

"Don't you recognize the name?"

"Should I? Jesus, don't tell me you know her too," Alex said.

"I don't know her 'personally,' but I know she's a journalist," Carr said. "She's the one who wrote that story last year that unearthed that NYPD scandal. You know, the officers who were smuggling weapons in from New Jersey—I know you remember that. It was the story of the year."

"I remember. So, you're saying this is the same person?"

"Well, I think it is," Carr replied.

"Which news agency does she work for?"

"*The New York Times*," Carr said.

Alex remembered back to a few weeks earlier and his meeting with Amy's new boyfriend, Josh. "Um, I'll be right back."

Carr watched Alex dash out of the autopsy room and into the corridor, his cell phone in hand. Dr. Callahan commented, "Boy, he left in a hurry."

Outside in the hallway, Alex searched through his contact list and dialed Amy. The phone rang three times, and the muffled voice of his best friend answered.

"Alex—what in God's name are you calling me for so early? Everything all right?"

"Sorry to wake you, is Josh with you?"

"Yeah, he's here. Do you need him?" Amy asked.

"Yeah, for a moment. Then I'll let you two lovebirds go back to sleep."

"Okay, hold on."

Alex waited for about thirty seconds, and a deep voice returned to the line, "Alex, hey."

"Hey, I hate to wake you up, but this couldn't wait. I need to ask about one of your colleagues," Alex said.

"Okay, which one?"

"A Juliette Cochran. Do you know her by chance?"

"Yeah, everyone knows Juliette. You don't?" Josh asked.

"Apparently, I'm the only one in New York City who doesn't," Alex said, "Can you describe her?"

"Sure, she's like twenty-six, brunette, tall. Oh, she has a small mole on her left cheek. Why are you asking me about Juliette? Has something happened to her?"

"Well, I hate to be the one to tell you this. We found her body in Prospect Park this morning."

The line went quiet; the only sound Alex could hear was Josh's slight breathing that resonated through the phone. Eventually, he responded, "It's that killer that's going around slashing people, isn't it?"

"It looks that way," Alex said.

"I got a feeling the other day that this moment would come," Josh said, "She was working on a case, a massive case. I have something that might help you out, but we should meet in person. Can't be 100 percent sure this line is secure. Can you meet me this evening after work?"

"Christ, what have you guys over at *The New York Times* gotten into now?" Alex asked.

"Look, I'll tell you what I know, but tonight. What time?"

"Um, okay, I could do six-thirty. Just name the place," Alex said.

"Alexander's at St. Marks and Fifth."

"Okay, I'll see you—" Alex said before the phone line went dead "—there."

Alex slipped his phone back into his pocket and walked back towards the autopsy room. The doors slid open, and he rejoined his partner.

"What the hell was that about, Jones?"

"So, I know a guy who works at *The New York Times*. I called him to verify that this was *the* Juliette Cochran."

"And?" Carr dragged out his word.

"It is her. This guy wants to meet me in person tonight to talk—whatever it is, it sounds like it has him nervous," Alex said as Dr. Callahan rolled the victim onto her side.

It was at that moment that a disturbing image appeared in Alex's line of sight. "Wait, don't move the body."

Callahan stopped rolling the victim as Alex approached the table. He remained standing, for a few seconds, in total disbelief. Carr walked over to look. His jaw dropped.

"What, what is it?" Callahan asked.

"They've carved a message into her back," Carr at last said.

> Give us back what your family
> stole.

"The hell does that mean?" asked Carr.

"It's started again, I... I need to go." Alex took off towards the door.

Confused, Carr rushed out the door to follow his partner. Carr never got the complete story of what happened back in Colorado. All he knew about was Alex's father's assassination, the witness protection; he was in the dark about the death threats and Alex's own attempted murder.

Carr sped down the long corridor, catching up with Alex.

"Stop! Was that a message directed at you?"

"Yes. It's a long story, I don't want to get into it here," Alex replied.

"No. We're not going anywhere until you tell me what's going on here," Carr demanded as Alex continued walking towards the lobby.

"Leave it be. I knew this wasn't over."

"What isn't over? Talk, Jones," Carr demanded as he grabbed Alex's forearm, swinging him around.

Alex stood there, folding his arms across his chest. He inhaled and exhaled. He didn't even know where to begin the story. "Let's talk in the waiting room."

The two men exited through the double doors and walked towards a corner of the lobby where they could speak in private.

"Okay, so I'll skip everything you already know," Alex began. "Remember those guys who kidnapped Amy and me years ago?"

"Yeah, I knew you, Temple, and your friend got abducted years ago, but that's all I ever heard of it."

Alex covered his mouth with both hands. "Well, what I didn't tell you is they tried to kill me, Amy, and Mike. They say my family took something that belongs to them."

Carr nodded, trying to pay close attention to what Alex was describing to him.

"I don't know what they think I have," Alex continued.

"Maybe your father took drugs, or worse, money from them?"

"I've yet to find any convincing evidence that my dad took anything from their organization."

"I've known you for a good year now, and I know you're a good kid. Whoever this person is that's killing these women is trying to get your attention," Carr said, "And not only do they have yours, but they also got mine now."

FOURTEEN

Alexander's Bar, Brooklyn
December 2, 2005
6:28 P.M.

A LIGHT SNOW HAD BEGUN FALLING OVER THE CITY as
Alex approached the entrance to the bar. Face after face passed
by, that all too familiar exhausted look written across each of
their faces. He opened the door and was greeted by a soft pop
song playing quietly in the foreground and a sparsely filled,
dimly lit neighborhood bar.

He walked farther into the place, scanning the room until he
caught a glimpse of Josh sitting alone in a corner booth, far
away from the local crowd who were drowning their sorrows in
a glass of whiskey.

He removed his jacket as he inched closer to the booth.

"Thanks for agreeing to meet me here," Josh said. The two men shook hands.

"Sure, anytime. Mind if I grab a beer before we get started?"

"Go for it."

Alex wandered towards the bar, where a tall, handsome bartender took his order. Alex stood, nervously tapping his fingers on the countertop as he glanced back towards Josh and smiled.

The barkeep returned, and Alex flung a five dollar bill onto the counter, smiled, and drifted back to the booth, his drink grasped firmly in his hand.

"So, yeah, where were we?" Alex asked as he took a sip of his pale ale.

"So first off, let me just say this straight out—Amy's told me all about your past; you know, the Russian mobsters who tried to have you all killed."

"Well, yeah, I sort of figured she'd tell you all about it at some point," Alex said. "This why you asked me here today?"

"Sort of. You see, Juliette was working on a huge story. She had—well, has—an informant who was feeding her information about the Prospect Park Slasher, as you all call him." Josh took a long gulp of his Chardonnay.

"Wait? How do you know that's what we call him?"

"I just do, okay?"

"Okay, we'll leave it at that. What did she discover about the slasher? Did she find out who it was?"

"She was close. All I know from our conversations is that the person she was talking to always met her at Sip; you know, the same one that Amy goes to every morning," Josh replied.

"Interesting. Yeah, I know the place. Was just there earlier today," Alex said as he took another sip of beer.

In situations like this, Alex never probed for more information, he always just let the talker do what they did best: talk. Josh carried on divulging various amounts of information, pulling papers and pictures from his messenger bag which he kept secured to his side. Most of the information he provided was irrelevant, but one thing stood out.

"Hold up a second." Alex grabbed a paper with chicken scratch written across it with lots of question marks. He scanned it for a few seconds before speaking again. "How did she even know about the tarot cards? That wasn't released to the public."

"All of this information came from her informant; that's all I know—I swear." Josh raised his right hand, just like he was in a courtroom.

Alex just shook his head. He was in complete disbelief that such vital information was leaked—or was it? Was it possible that Juliette Cochran had really met with the actual killer?

Who else would have this kind of information besides CSU, Carr and myself? She had to have met with the slasher.

"Josh, is it possible that Juliette was actually meeting with the Prospect Park Slasher?"

"Like I said, I have no idea who the informant is; she just referred to him as 'M.J.' See for yourself." Josh flipped the planner around and pointed to the December 1st entry.

Alex took a larger gulp of his beer and set it back down forcefully on the table. He sifted through Juliette's notes, photos, and day planner. A large stack of photos sat just to his right, and he picked up the pile and fanned them out across the table.

As he sorted through, one photo stood out above the rest, and he plucked it out of the array. He held the picture gently with his index finger and thumb pinched together on the upper right corner. He studied it; his eyes squinted as he pulled it closer to his face. A familiar face stood out in the crowd.

Mr. Topol—that lying sack of shit; he was at the second crime scene as well.

Alex set the photo back down on the table and lifted his head, staring penetratingly at Josh, who was sitting back watching Alex.

"You look perplexed," Josh eventually said after a moment of awkwardness.

"Listen, I know that all of this belongs to Juliette, and I'm sure she's passed it on to you in the event something happened to her. But—" Alex swallowed hard "—I need this photo, just this one photo."

Josh sank against the backrest of the booth and cleared his throat. "Why that picture? Off the record, I swear."

"Look, I like you, you're smart—so as long as this is off the record," Alex said, and Josh nodded. "Someone of interest is in it."

Josh grinned and interlocked his fingers together. He sat forward and his eyes stared into Alex's. "If it helps find her killer, take it."

Alex reached around the back of the chair, the feeling of soft wool brushing against the back of his hand. He pulled the jacket forward, sliding the rectangular photo into the inner pocket of his coat.

He looked at the half empty glass of beer in front of him and then at his watch. His arm extended out as he grasped the handle of the stein, lifting it up to his thin lips.

Josh sat back in the plush booth seat and scanned the room. He was acting paranoid, and it was growing more and more evident to Alex.

"Why do you keep scanning the room? Is someone following you? Did someone threaten you?" Alex asked.

"What, no, er, everything is all right," he said unsurely.

"I can see right through that lie a mile away." "Alright, alright—I'm worried. Actually, *apprehensive* is a better way to describe how I feel," Josh confessed.

"What are you so worried about?" Alex leaned forward so they could talk a little more privately.

"I got a strange call last night around midnight from an unknown number. The caller was a female. She—she stated that Juliette and I should mind our own business if we know what's good for us."

"And you didn't think to tell me this earlier? Like when I called this morning?" Alex inquired, his brow raising slightly.

"Didn't think anything of it—not until now."

Alex sat in the chair, motionless. He wanted to speak, but the little voice inside his head insisted he keep his mouth closed for once in his life. Alex was never any good at keeping his opinions to himself, but in this instance, he didn't want to rile up Josh's nerves any more than they already were.

Alex glanced at his watch again; 7:05 in the evening. He grabbed his glass one last time and chugged the rest of his beer. "Hey, I have to get going, I have another engagement in about thirty minutes. You sure you're going to be all right?"

"Of course, of course! I'm Josh Karlsen, no one can stop me," Josh joked. "Besides, I'll be staying with Amy tonight; safety in numbers they always say, right?"

"Call me if anything seems out of the ordinary."

"You don't have to worry; we're going to be fine."

Alex nodded, shook his hand, and walked back through the row of gloomy patrons that occupied the barstools at the wooden bar. He had about twenty minutes to make his way to Greenwich Village to meet up with Finch, and given his meeting ran over with Josh due to an extraordinary find, he was pretty sure that he'd be late making it to the party; but what else was new. He hustled along towards the subway station and descended into the dark abyss below.

FIFTEEN

The Flux, Greenwich Village
December 2, 2005
7:49 P.M.

ALEX MADE IT TO THE CLUB AND WAS HELD UP at the entrance by the bouncer. He drew out his badge and flashed it as the young security guard, who himself was an off-duty NYPD officer, grinned and motioned him past. He stepped through the metal detector, shocked that he didn't set off any alarms.

It had been at least two years since Alex had the chance to have a night out like this. Those were the great days of being a college student.

Now, late nights parties were replaced with relaxing baths, date nights, and curling up on the sofa together.

As he walked in the club, he could hear the band on stage warming up.

Made it just in time.

The club was pumped up, and the number of people easily surpassed the allotted limit set by the fire marshal. However, Alex wasn't here tonight to be a prude, he was here to let loose and enjoy a nice night out with a colleague. That's the only thing that interested him at that point.

He gazed around, scanning the room for a recognizable face in an expanse of well-dressed people, but that chore was turning out to be more trying than he presumed it would be. He shoved a path through a crowd of youthful girls snickering at some college-aged guy dancing erratically.

He eventually worked his way to the bar and waved down a barkeep who indicated he'd be over shortly. Alex leaned on the counter, swinging his head from left-to-right watching the lively, shit-faced kids bouncing around him.

What am I dealing with here? Finch owes me.

Just as he finished his observation, somebody touched him on the arm from behind. He immediately turned his head around, all set to confront some rebellious teenager and put them in their place. Surprisingly, it was Finch. Alex was astonished; he looked so different out of his NYPD issue crime scene get-up. He smiled and shook his hand.

"God, I'm so glad to see you; these juveniles are beginning to annoy me," Alex said as Finch smiled.

"Yeah, my bad—I should have told you. My buddy's band possesses a—oh, how do I say this tactfully? —a fairly immature following," he explained.

"Well, glad you ran into me. I was beginning to doubt you'd show," Alex said as the bartender arrived.

The two placed their drink orders. Alex another pale ale, and Finch a Knob Creek neat. Alex grinned and turned to face him.

"Wow, kicking it up a notch, huh?"

"Man, I love bourbon. You ever had it?" Finch asked.

"I've only ever had whiskey, and to be honest, it isn't quite my thing. Long story," Alex said.

"Hey, we have all night," Finch said as he patted Alex on the shoulder, "So why is it that you hate whiskey?"

"Fine, fine. I'll tell you. Can we find someplace to relax and hang out?" Alex suggested.

Finch pushed a pair of ditzy girls out of his way and made a path for Alex to break away from the foolishness. Alex caught sight of a deserted area where the two could sit down and talk, undisturbed.

Alex plopped down in a fuchsia colored chair and Finch sat across from him on a firm brown upholstered sofa. Alex made himself comfortable as he explained his embarrassing story of why he hated whiskey, and before he finished speaking, the band had finally reached the stage.

They kicked off their set with a sped-up cover of "Nothing Compares 2 U," and Alex could tell that the crowd was intensely getting into the song. As he turned back around to face Finch, he was busy buying another round of drinks for them.

"Jones, I appreciate you showing up tonight. I genuinely do," Finch said as Alex grinned.

"Yeah, and thanks for encouraging me to come out. Everything with Mike has literally thrown my life out of whack, so, I was in need of this."

"Oh, right—I was informed of the rumor, but I didn't want to bring it up. I can't imagine your fiancé just up and leaving you like that. Have you heard from him?" Finch leaned in closer.

"No. Not even a text message. I'm sort of concerned about Mike at this moment. But screw him, he'll call me when he's ready," Alex said.

A fresh round of drinks arrived at the table.

"How'd you convince them to bring the drinks to us?"

"Pays to appreciate people. And a massive tip doesn't hurt either," Finch said as he winked.

The two grabbed their drinks and stood up. Finch snatched Alex by the hand and ushered him towards the stage, forcing him to deal with the immature brats who had no common sense. The place was dynamic, and the band was very enjoyable, once you got past the clientele.

The night carried on, and the drinks kept flowing, and after about an hour of jamming out to the music the two went back to relaxing. Alex mildly staggered towards the bench, and Finch walked beside him, slightly more inebriated than Alex.

"I'm so messed up," Finch announced as he plopped down close to Alex on the bench.

"I've got a pretty good buzz going myself. Here's to hoping that psychopath doesn't decide to slaughter someone tonight." Alex and Finch clanked glasses, and each took a huge swig.

"Absolutely!" Finch hollered over the music. "Can I ask you an intimate question?"

"Um, yeah—sure."

"Do you enjoy working as a detective?" asked Finch.

"Well…" Alex hesitated. "I love the feeling I have when I lock somebody's ass away, but otherwise, no. The job's gritty, chaotic, and downright too emotional for me most of the time. What about you? Do you enjoy being a crime scene supervisor?"

"Absolutely!"

The discussion went on, with Finch doing most of the talking. He was a talker for sure, but even with the lively environment, all Alex could reminisce about was Mike and how he wanted him to be there with him. Alex yanked out his phone to check for any missed calls or texts; still nothing. At that instant he was more alone than he ever had been, although he was surrounded by hundreds of people all appreciating life.

He turned to Finch, who was in mid-sentence and just looked at him. He made an effort to appear interested in the conversation, but the beer was beginning to pass faster through his veins, and he was growing more exhausted.

The handsome CSU supervisor stopped talking and laid his hand on Alex's chest. Alex remained there, not interrupting him. And suddenly it occurred; Finch leaned in and thrust his full-shaped lips onto Alex's.

Alex, in a state of confusion, just allowed it to keep going on for several seconds longer. When Alex finally understood what was happening, he pushed Finch from him and sat up, bewildered.

"Finch, what the hell was that?" Alex asked.

Finch looked flustered. "I'm, uh, Alex, I'm very sorry. I don't know what came over me," he attempted to explain.

"Man, seriously? I know Mike's away right now and our relationship situation is—well, I don't know what it is at this point—but I can't cheat on him."

"I know, I just got carried away. Please accept my apology."

"You're forgiven, Aaron," Alex said glancing at his timepiece, "but on that note, it's nearly eleven now; I have to run." Alex stood up.

Alex hugged the younger man, said goodnight, and bolted for the exit.

It wasn't like Alex to just up and run away in such a frenzy. In this situation, he was so distraught about what had just occurred between them, he just had to get outside for some fresh air.

Alex shoved the glass door, and the frigid night air hit him square in the face. He dashed towards the curb, trying to flag down a taxi, his breathing so quick that the fog billowed out of his mouth like a car exhaust.

Just then, the door swung open, and Finch emerged. "Alex, seriously—allow me get you get home."

"I'm okay, Aaron. Thanks, anyway."

"All right, I won't trouble you," Finch said as he backed away.

A taxicab pulled up promptly, and Alex threw the rear door open, jumping inside. He stared out the window at Finch pacing slowly on the sidewalk where he left him with a mix of embarrassment and fear across his handsome face. The taxi pulled away and back out onto the slush-covered road. Alex couldn't take his eyes off of Finch, and he kept him in view until he was no longer in clear sight.

Finally, he was alone to assemble his thoughts, and all he could do was shake his head in disappointment. How was he going to ever face Finch again at work?

I've once again destroyed another friendship.

SIXTEEN

Bridge Park Drive, Brooklyn
December 3, 2005
8:45 A.M.

THE SCREECHING OF HIS ALARM CLOCK WOKE ALEX from a less than stellar sleep. He reached over and slammed his hand down on the snooze button, groaned, and rolled over onto his stomach. He buried his face deep into the pillow, trying his best to block out any light. Alex dozed back to sleep.

Eight minutes later the alarm went off again. Alex was becoming annoyed, and instead turned it off and sat up in bed, his back pressed against the pillow. His cupped his head in his hands. He was woozy, and his body felt achy and worn out. He took a deep breath, the smell of alcohol bled from his pores, and he shook his head.

I'm a mess. That's the last time I get trashed.

Garnering enough strength to fling the sheets from his body he staggered his way towards the bathroom, moaning with each step he took. He flipped the light switch on and walked towards the shower. He pulled his gray night shirt off over his head and slipped his sweatpants and underwear off and stepped into the shower. The initial shock of the warm water rolling off of his body sent shivers down his spine. All he wanted to do was stand there, motionless and allow the warmth to wash away the stench of alcohol from his pores.

Alex finished his shower, his fingers were shriveled, as he ran his fingers through his medium length brown hair, wiping away the excess water. He reached for a towel and stood in the shower, rubbing it across his face and upper body.

His head felt a little clearer after the rejuvenating shower, and he stepped out onto the bathmat to finish drying the rest of his lower body.

He cracked the bathroom door to allow some of the steam to escape. As he opened it, he heard a rustling sound coming from the front door. Alarmed, he wrapped the white bath towel around his waist and slipped out towards the bedroom.

The noise only amplified in strength, and he opened his nightstand drawer and pulled out his loaded service weapon. He pulled back on the slide and tiptoed towards the bedroom door. He kept his back pressed tightly against the wall as he moved ever so guardedly. He heard the front door burst open with force and the distinctive sound of jingling keys.

Someone was in the house. With every breath he took, his heart beat faster and faster. He could hear the pronounced footsteps coming closer to the bedroom door, and he pivoted around through the door with his gun aimed straight ahead, and yelled, "Stop!"

It all happened so fast, and then it registered that it was his fiancé who stood before him, holding his hand up like an ordinary criminal.

"Jesus Christ, Alex, put the gun down! It's just me."

"Scare the shit out of me, why don't you," Alex said as he lowered his weapon. "What are you doing here?"

"I wanted to surprise you. Well—surprise!" Mike said as Alex tightened the towel around his waist.

"Damn, a phone call or at least a text would have been helpful, just to let me know you were coming home. I thought you were *them*," Alex confessed.

"Them? Them, who?"

"Those psychos—the ones from Colorado—they're back," Alex said as he walked up to Mike and wrapped his arms around his neck.

"What do you mean? They are dead, remember? Dead people don't resurrect. This isn't *Night of the Living Dead*," Mike joked.

"You don't understand. I'm not talking about Brandy, Heather, or their cronies; I'm not that out of touch with reality, yet. No, someone new is after me," Alex insisted as he and Mike sat down on the couch.

"First thing I have to get off my chest before I miss the opportunity—I've missed you, and I'm sorry for everything that happened at Marianne's crime scene," Mike said.

"Oh, right, sorry—I've missed you too, you don't know how lonely I've been the past few weeks. And I forgive you for what happened that day, I shouldn't have gone off like a lunatic. I was wrong also to be such an asshole."

They hugged, and Mike kissed Alex softly on the forehead. The two spent the next ten minutes catching up on everything that happened during Mike's extended getaway, but Alex became cold and stood. "I'm freezing. I'll finish getting ready."

"Sure, so now we're caught up on everything, I want to hear more about why you think the Russian mobsters are after you again," Mike said.

He followed Alex into the bedroom.

"While you were visiting your family, two additional murders occurred. The first one was a family friend of Carr's and the second was a high-profile investigative journalist from *The New York Times*, Juliette Cochran."

"Wait, you mean the Juliette Cochran is dead? When did this happen?" Mike's face turned from joyful to panicked.

"We found her body yesterday morning in the park," Alex said.

"She worked with Josh, am I right?" inquired Mike.

"Yeah, I met with Josh last night, and he knew a lot about the slasher case; he knew more than we do."

"A leak within the NYPD?" Mike asked.

"I don't believe so. I believe Juliette was meeting with the slasher. At her autopsy yesterday there was a message carved into her back. 'Give us back what your family stole.'"

"I'm lost. How is this message directed towards you? Could it be that she stole something, and the killer was just sending a warning?"

"Doubtful," Alex said as he slipped on a white undershirt and a pair of black Calvin Klein boxer briefs.

"Alex, now I'm worried for you. If they've sent someone new to hunt you down, ugh." Mike raised his voice and ran his hands across his face. "I don't know how to say this politely, but I demand you stop investigating this case."

"Absolutely not. Back in Colorado, I was just a kid in high school who had no power. Times have changed, and now I'm a detective, working with one of the largest police forces in the world. Not a chance in hell I'm quitting this case. I will find this person, and we'll end this madness once and for all!" he shouted.

Mike fell onto the end of the bed and looked up at Alex. "I see having some distance didn't change you one bit."

"Jesus, Mike, what do you want from me? Nothing I say or do ever makes you happy anymore. I've told you I missed you. I tell you I love you—what more can I say or do to prove that to you?"

"You want our lives to go back to normal, quit this case. You will wind up getting yourself killed if you keep going; I don't want that to happen," Mike confessed as his eyes swelled with tears. "I almost lost you seven years ago, and I'll be damned if we will go through that again."

He rolled his eyes as he stood towering over Mike, who was now almost in full emotional breakdown mode. He sat down next to him at the foot of the bed and wrapped his arms around his chest.

Alex realized Mike was watching out for him. He had almost lost him seven years earlier. But Mike also failed to understand that it wasn't his battle to fight. These thugs wouldn't disappear, and Alex seemed to associate the craziness ending with it being on his terms.

"Mike, look—I promise I will not go insane and I promise you I will not die. You will be there with me to get through this, just like last time," Alex said as he ran his finger across Mike's cheek, wiping away a teardrop.

"Wish I could say I felt better about this, Alex. I don't. I have a strange feeling this won't end like last time." Mike wiped the palms of his hands across his face.

"Nothing will happen."

"I hope not because—well, because I love you, damn it. But I also know how you are: stubborn. So, if you demand to continue on this suicide mission; well, I won't stand in your way," Mike said.

Alex sat up straight, turning to look Mike in the eye. He knew Mike was becoming tired of arguing with him every day and Alex was tired of having the same conversations over and over. If they hoped to regain that healthy relationship, one of them would have to let go of the past. Otherwise, everything the two had built over the past nine years was worthless.

Alex glanced away, smiled, and then looked back to Mike. "You hungry? I thought we could grab breakfast down the street at our favorite brunch place."

"Best offer I've had all morning, just let me change out of these stinky clothes I wore on the plane," Mike said as he unfastened his button-down shirt.

Alex watched Mike remove his shirt and grinned. "Actually, I think I have an even better idea," he teased as he pushed Mike down onto the bed.

Mike smirked, his face lit up with life. "I think I like this idea better than getting food."

A couple hours passed and they remained stretched across the mattress. Mike cuddled Alex in his arms. Alex savored the moment and was happy to finally receive some intimacy.

Mike was putting off so much heat that Alex became overheated. Alex slid out of Mike's arms and rolled over onto his side, flinging the white cotton sheets from his body.

"What's wrong?" Mike asked.

"Oh, just burning up is all. Besides, it's closing in on 11:30," Alex replied, "I don't know about you, but I'm famished."

Mike looked over at the alarm clock on the nightstand. "Oh shit, I lost track of time. We had better get our asses in gear."

"I have one small favor to ask though; I promise it won't take too long. You remember that guy, Boris Topol?"

"The creepy witness you told me about from the third crime scene, right?"

"The one and only; turns out he was also at the second crime scene," Alex said. "I found a photo in with Juliette Cochran's notes."

"So, it sounds like the favor you want to ask is if I'm all right with you going to question him." Mike's right brow arched.

"It puzzles me why he failed to mention it when we talked before. But look, this is our day; just say the word, and I'll go another day." Alex said as he slipped on a pair of dark jeans.

"Are you kidding me? What if he's the killer? I can't let you go alone. Count me in." Mike pulled a gray V-neck undershirt over his head.

The two finished getting dressed, and Alex checked his hair and put some moisturizing lotion on his face. He looked in the mirror and smiled; his face lit up with happiness.

While he waited in the kitchen for Mike to finish, he looked upon the city. The bright sun beaming down on the earth was deceiving for anyone who didn't know it was cold outside.

Mike stepped into the kitchen, slipping his jacket on. "Ready to go? You're right, I didn't even realize how hungry I am— damn jet lag."

SEVENTEEN

Home of Boris Topol
59 Prospect Park West, Brooklyn
December 3, 2005
1:17 P.M.

ALEX AND MIKE STOOD ON THE OVERSIZED brick staircase in front of the home. The wind was calm, and the warmth of the sun hitting against Alex's back made him feel at ease.

Grabbing the door knocker shaped like a lion, Alex swung the metal ring back and forth; a loud clanking sound followed with each strike against the sturdy wooden door. Alex stood there, waiting patiently for the man to answer; but after waiting a few minutes, there was no stirring from within the brownstone.

"Looks like we're shit out of luck," Mike replied.

"I'll find him, don't you worry about that."

The two stepped down the stairs. Alex turned his head and looked back at the house, the residence sat there eerily silent. Alex returned his thoughts to getting back home and having an enjoyable rest of his day. As they began walking back along the leafless tree lined street towards the subway station a buzzing sound radiated from Alex's front pocket.

He pulled his phone out of his jeans pocket and quickly glanced at the caller ID. It was Amy.

"Amy, it's been a while," Alex joked.

"I just talked to you yesterday."

"I know, just a joke. What's up?"

"Was just seeing if you wanted to go out with Josh and I this evening. You must be terribly lonely without Mike," Amy said.

"Matter of fact, he's back. We're walking along the park right now about to head home. What did you have in mind?"

"Was going to have you guys over to my place, a little cozier and we can just relax and chat—sound like a good plan?"

"Let me check with Mike." Alex pulled the phone away from his face and turned to Mike, who was all smiles at the thought. Alex returned to the phone. "So, yeah, what time?"

"Let's try early; you just never know when you'll get called out. How does six o'clock work?" she asked.

"Perfect. See you around six."

Alex hung up the phone and slid it back into his jeans. Mike smiled, and Alex returned the smile back at him.

"Was sweet of them to think of you—I guess it is a shock that I came back without warning, huh?" Mike joked.

"That's an understatement—scared the living shit out of me this morning; but I've forgiven you. Let's just have an enjoyable rest of our day."

EIGHTEEN

Quaker Cemetery, Brooklyn
December 14, 2005
5:45 A.M.

**A FRESH SNOW HAD FALLEN OVERNIGHT IN
BROOKLYN.** The terrain and trees shimmered as the bright
light of the street lamps hit them. The air was still and silent,
and Alex trudged along the snow-covered cobblestone pathway
to the site of the latest homicide victim, moving slowly along
the icy stones, trying his best not to slip. With each step he
took, the snow and ice beneath his feet crunched.

In the distance, he could make out the outline of his partner
and Finch talking to one another at the entrance to the Quaker
Cemetery. When Alex spotted Finch standing there, he
immediately grew uneasy. Neither of them had seen or spoken
to one another since the incident at Flux two weeks ago.
However, Alex knew he had to disconnect his personal life
from the job and keep things as professional as he could.

You catch more flies with honey.

There was no way that Alex would ever allow a personal incident to derail a crime scene. These days, you just never knew who was watching or eavesdropping, as he recently discovered searching through Juliette's photos.

As Alex approached his colleagues he shouted out, "Heard a rumor that my friend has returned; and just before Christmas, now isn't that a damn shame."

"Well, we're not quite sure yet if it's the slasher. It appears to be the work of the slasher," Carr said as he lifted the crime scene tape allowing Alex to duck underneath. "However, this one's a bit different."

"How?" Alex asked.

"Walk this way, I'll show you what I mean." Carr trotted off deeper into the cemetery.

Alex ran his hands down the front of his jacket to sweep off the clumps of snow that stuck to him. Carr led the way and was doing a majority of the talking. Alex and Finch hung a few feet back, the unnerving stares from Finch were creeping out Alex. As the seconds passed on, Alex could feel the tension building more and more with each step they took. Alex promised himself that if he got a free minute, his first task would be to clear up the mess before the situation got any more thorny than it already was.

Alex interrupted Carr as he rambled on. "You both seem a little on edge, is it really that bad?"

Finch looked over at Alex and spoke up, "It's, well—how do I put this—it's a bloodbath, sir."

Sir? Why is he calling me sir? What's his deal?

"*Bloodbath*? That doesn't sound like our killer at all. He's never left blood at the scene before," Alex recalled.

"Yeah, hence why Carr said it's different this time," Finch sarcastically replied.

Damn, now he's getting sassy.

"Did we find any tarot cards at this scene?" Alex calmly said as they arrived at the body."

"None yet, sir," Finch replied.

Alex cringed. He hated being called sir; it made him feel like an old man.

The conversation went silent as Alex took a moment to take in his surroundings. The most noteworthy difference in this scene was the substantial amount of blood, which was spewed all over in an almost perfect pattern. He took notice of the ordinarily pristine white sheet used to cover victims, which was drenched in bright red blood. He closed his eyes and took in a deep breath. The overpowering stench of iron filled the area around him. The scent was so overwhelming that he slightly coughed as he reopened his eyes.

He moved his left foot forward and shined his flashlight from one place to another in the vicinity of the body. The blood trail didn't just stop at the victim, it was sprayed across nearby headstones, a tree, and the virgin snowfall was soiled in blood. He sighed, a feeling of dread washing over him. What was he going to discover when he lifted the sheet? He hated to admit it, but Finch was right, though—there was no other way to describe this scene other than a bloodbath.

Alex cautiously knelt down beside the body. He patted the outside of his jacket pockets for a pair of latex gloves. "Hey, I forgot gloves; have a couple to spare?"

Finch crouched down and pulled a sterile pair from his kit and handed them over to Alex.

"Thanks."

Alex stretched the gloves over his large hands and slowly lifted the sheet, folding it down to just below her breasts. He soundlessly gasped, a reaction that he had never experienced in any of the crime scenes he had ever worked before. He took a moment and hung his head, paying his last respects to the latest victim.

He pivoted to his right, starting his examination near her torso. His first observation was her once-white blouse soaked through with blood, and the three large knife wounds which cut through the fabric. The bottom of the shirt had been ripped.

He moved upwards towards her wrists and arms. Several lacerations on her left arm and defensive wounds on her hands told Alex that she had put up a fight with her attacker. On her left wrist, the outline of four fingers was visible from the sheer force the assailant used to control her.

Alex finally examined her face and neck. It was the same signature as the previous four; her throat was slit from behind, but Alex assumed that the attacker was thrown off-guard by the victim's willingness to live that they used overkill on this victim. The gaping neck wound was so deep that the pinkness of the muscle and ligaments was exposed to the winter air.

The only thing Alex knew for sure was that she was a dark blonde. Otherwise, all of her other identifiable features were now gone. He would have to wait for the medical examiner's office to arrive before he would be able to know if she had any identification on her.

The one thing he did know for certain was that this killer was escalating. Each crime scene was becoming more violent than the previous one. And now with the substantial amount of blood, this killer was sending a message. But what exactly was this supposed to mean?

He pulled the sheet back over her face and stood. Turning towards his partner and Finch, he shook his head in disbelief.

"This guy really did a number on her," Alex commented.

"How do we know it's a he?" Finch asked.

"You know any woman who has the kind of strength to do this sort of carnage?"

"I'm just saying, don't assume it's a man," Finch said as he crossed his arms across his chest.

Alex scoffed, pulled the latex gloves from his hands, and threw them into an evidence bag that Finch was holding out for him. "Finch, before you leave we need to have a chat."

Finch rolled his eyes. "Whatever you say. You know where to find me."

Alex stepped away, motioning for Carr to join him. The two stopped a safe distance from Finch.

"Any witnesses?" Alex asked.

"Actually, it's our lucky day. See that older lady over there?" Carr pointed. "She was walking past when she heard a woman screaming. Lady says she crept over and says she saw the entire murder take place. You want to talk with her now?"

Alex looked over towards the bloody sheet. "Not much more I can do with her at this point, so yeah, let me talk to our witness."

"Hey, what's up with you and Finch? Something I missed?" Carr asked.

"It's a long story—remind me to fill you in later," Alex said.

Carr grinned. "I bet it's good, too."

Alex walked away from his partner towards an older grey-haired lady who was talking with a beat officer across the cemetery. She was fidgety, moving her legs up and down as she grew impatient talking with the policeman. Alex could tell that whatever she saw scared her to the core.

He advanced, and she glanced over in his direction. She slowly calmed down and stopped being restless. He scoped her out; she appeared to be in her late sixties. She was short and a little heavyset. Alex gallantly smiled as he got closer, hoping that his soft spokenenss would put her mind at ease.

"Thanks, Officer, can you give me a minute," Alex said as the officer closed his notepad and stepped back, "Ma'am, I'm Detective Alex Jones. I heard you may have seen something this morning?"

The woman nervously looked around, "I–I–I—" she stuttered, "think I saw that poor woman being murdered."

"Take your time, ma'am. I know this is scary and you're worried; how about we start small. May I ask your name?"

"Phyllis Peterson. I live just down the block."

Alex jotted down her name. "Now what do you think you saw?"

"Well, I was walking through the park to clear my head," she began. "I'm a writer, so I always walk late at night when my writer's block kicks in, anyway, as I was walking past the cemetery, I heard a god-awful shrill coming from inside. So naturally, I walked over to see what was going on."

"Okay, by the way, you're doing great," Alex encouraged her as he continued writing down what she said.

"Now I was a good distance away, and my eyesight isn't what it used to be. But I saw a body lying on the ground, and there was this tall hooded figure standing over the body with something metal in their hand," Ms. Peterson recalled as her hand began trembling again.

"Go on," Alex said.

"The attacker just kept swinging and bashing the person lying on the ground. But they were tall, as I said earlier, really tall; I'd say maybe six foot four."

"Ms. Peterson, were you able to tell if the attacker was a male or female?"

"I didn't see a face; it was obscured by the hood over their head," she said as she nervously rubbed her hands together, "but I have to assume that the attacker was a man. I don't know any woman that tall."

"That's an excellent deduction," Alex said as he handed her a business card. "Ms. Peterson, you've been very helpful. If you remember anything, please give me a call, day or night."

She took the card in her trembling hands and tried her best to smile, but failed miserably at it. "Thank you, detective. I will surely call if I remember anything."

Alex nodded, flipped his notepad closed, and walked back towards Carr and Finch, who were patiently waiting nearby. He was maybe ten feet away from the witness when she suddenly had an epiphany.

"Detective, wait," she hollered, "I remember something else."

Alex hurriedly swung around and walked back to her, removing his notepad again. "Go on."

"It was the hood the attacker was wearing. Like I said it was black, but there was an enormous white skull and bones on the back of the jacket, and I'm no language expert, but it had something written in what I thought was Russian just below the picture."

"Russian?" Alex jotted the notes down. "What made you believe the writing was Russian?"

"There were a few letters from the Russian alphabet that I remember, and I distinctly remember seeing a backward N, and the only time I've ever seen that is when I took Russian many years ago," she said.

"Yes, that's critical information, Ms. Peterson," Alex said. "Anything else other than the backward N you can remember in the lettering?"

She closed her eyes and took a few moments to recall. Her lips and fingers moved around when suddenly her eyes fluttered open. "It started with a C, then there was a backward N somewhere in the middle, and the letters H-O-B were at the end. I'm sorry, but that's all I can remember."

"Wow, I'm really impressed. You have no idea how helpful that is, Ms. Peterson," Alex said as he motioned for an officer. "This officer here will see to it that you get home safely."

He slipped the notepad back into his jacket and again walked away. Off to his left several reporters and cameramen from every newspaper and TV station in New York lined the police tape trying hard to get information about the scene. It took all he had to not pay them any attention. He wanted to get the word out about the serial killer, but the bosses weren't as eager to panic the general public just yet.

The bright lights and flashes from the photojournalist's cameras blinded him; all he could do was hang his head as he walked by the shouting masses.

He lifted his head briefly to scan the area for Carr and Finch, who were standing about forty yards straight ahead doing anything they could to avoid the chaos of the media. Alex and Finch's eyes locked and he made a beeline towards them.

"Looks like you're a bit of a celebrity these days," Carr joked. "Learn anything from Grandma Moses over there?"

"Totally not appropriate," Alex scolded, "and to answer your questions, yes, she was actually very helpful. She gave me a few interesting details."

"Jones, you've got to learn to take it a little easier; I was just joking," Carr said. "What did you learn from her?"

"So, the attacker was tall, around six four, and wore a black jacket with a white skull and bones plastered across the back," Alex said. "She also stated there was a Russian word embroidered beneath the picture."

"Pretty good recall for someone her age," Finch replied in a more pleasant tone than earlier.

"That's all I was able to get from her, but we'll see if it's of any use," Alex said.

The investigators from the ME's office had finally arrived on the scene. They were making better progress, being only thirty minutes late this time. The two men approached.

"Jones, we have to stop meeting like this," Bradburn joked.

"Why is everyone a comedian today?" Alex asked with a scowl on his face.

Carr stood behind Alex, waving his hands in a criss-cross fashion, alerting Bradburn to calm down.

"Oh, sorry, Jones, I see you once again got up on the wrong side of the bed. We'll be over there tending to the victim if you need us," Bradburn said as he and the new investigator wheeled the gurney away.

"You're getting a bad reputation for being an asshole, Jones," Finch said.

"That's it—you, me, we need to talk," Alex said angrily.

Finch was thrown off by Alex's uncharacteristic demeanor. Finch nodded guardedly as the two men disappeared into a more private area within the cemetery.

Alex stopped in a dimly lit corner, far enough away from Carr and the media. "Look, you're acting like a big baby. You know I have a fiancé, and what happened between us should have never happened," Alex said as he began pacing back and forth, "and it happened because of alcohol."

"You're absolutely right, and I'm sorry for being such a jerk. I guess—well, I like you," Finch blurted out.

"Finch, I'm getting married. You can't 'like' me in a romantic way."

The young man sighed. "I know, but that doesn't stop the fact that I am interested," Finch said as Alex stopped pacing and looked at him.

"You better not do anything to jeopardize my relationship. We won't discuss this again," Alex said firmly.

"I got your message loud and clear. I won't ruin anything for you, and I'll try to keep our relationship strictly professional."

"All right, then. Now, can we get back to the tragedy at hand here, and catch this son of a bitch before he kills someone else."

Finch only nodded, agreeing to the terms, before he slunk away towards the scene. Finch wasn't the first, and probably wouldn't be the last to try to come between him and Mike. Last year it was a fellow beat officer, the year before that was a lab tech. Alex always found himself in these situations.

Alex remained behind, gathering his composure. He closed his eyes and counted while inhaling and exhaling slowly.

One, Two, Three...

He had almost gotten to four when he was disrupted by a tap on the shoulder. He jumped forward slightly and swung around. It was Bradburn, standing there alone.

"Damn it, Bradburn. Scare me to death; no pun intended," Alex said.

"Couldn't help but overhear your little squabble with Finch. Want me to take care of anything for you?"

"Christ—how much did you hear?"

"Basically the whole thing. I know people who could take care of the problem," he offered.

"No. Enough about my personal issues, are you guys finished with the body?" Alex asked.

"Yeah, my partner is wheeling her off now. This one's disturbing, Jones, like really one of the worst scenes I've seen. The attacker even took the time to cut off most of her fingerprints."

"Seriously?"

"I realize I joke a lot, but I'm not this time," Bradburn said. Alex ran his hands across his face.

"Okay, thanks. You said *most* of her fingerprints. You think there's enough left to possibly get an identity of our victim?"

"Might be, we'll have to wait and see what the doc can do once we get her cleaned up," said Bradburn.

"Okay; I'll send Carr for this one, I have to pay someone a visit," Alex said as Bradburn grasped his shoulder.

"Remember what I said, though. If you need help with this problem, I'm your guy." Bradburn released his grip and walked away.

Alex closed his eyes again and started over with his counting and breathing.

One, Two, Three…

He finished and opened his eyes to find that the scene was winding down. He trekked back towards the entrance to the cemetery and ran into Carr. The senior detective was standing outside the crime scene tape, smoking a Newport cigarette.

"I told you to stop that shit," Alex said.

"Yeah, yeah—you love to annoy me with your health crap. Bradburn caught up with you?" Carr took another drag.

"Yeah, looks like this one's pretty bad," Alex said, and Carr nodded. "Do me a favor, can you go to the autopsy? I need to pay our little friend Mr. Topol a visit. He's been avoiding me, and I think the best time to catch up with him is early."

"Topol? What's he got to do with anything?"

"He left out a few crucial details; like why he was at the second crime scene and didn't mention it," Alex revealed.

"Thanks for sharing that information with your partner." Carr threw his cigarette butt on the ground and squished it with his glossy black shoes.

"I totally forgot to tell you—I'm slowly losing my mind," Alex admitted as the sky slowly began filling with light.

"All right, go see Topol, I'll head over to the ME's office. I'll call you if they find anything."

Carr rushed away towards the unmarked cruiser, and Alex stayed behind, taking one last look at the scene where Finch was working feverishly to collect the evidence. The poor guy had an enormous task ahead of him that brisk morning.

Alex turned and looked away, slowly walking back down the snow- and ice-covered cobblestone walkway. Halfway to the exit of the park, he noticed a familiar person off in the distance.

Topol!

Alex hastened his pace, but carefully so as to not slip and fall. Topol saw Alex rushing towards him and turned around and began walking the opposite direction.

"Topol, stop!" Alex shouted.

The man stopped in his tracks as Alex sprinted towards him. Alex was confused as to why Topol would turn and walk the opposite way, but he was tired of the games that the man was playing with him.

"What the hell? Are you avoiding me?" Alex asked.

"No."

"I've been trying to get ahold of you for weeks now, and suddenly you show up at yet another crime scene?" Alex said. "I think it's time you and I talk—at the station."

"Are you arresting me?" the older man asked.

"If that's what it takes to get you to cooperate. So we can do this the easy way or the hard way; it's your choice," Alex said.

The man threw his hands in the air. "Well, let's do this your way."

NINETEEN

78th Precinct, Brooklyn
December 14, 2005
9:18 A.M.

ALEX STOOD OUTSIDE THE INTERROGATION ROOM
peering through the two-way mirror at a distraught Boris Topol
pacing around the metal table that was centered in the space. It
was always Alex's opinion that guilty people typically didn't act
nervously; they usually gave up and sat calmly or sometimes
even slept.

Figuring he had made the suspect wait long enough, he
flung open the door and entered the interrogation room,
holding two file folders close to his body. Boris retreated to the
metal chair that was pulled out from the table.

Alex threw the folders on top of the table, and the contents
scattered across everywhere. He began clicking the button on

top of his pen repeatedly and moving confidently from side to side. Topol sat down in the chair as Alex grabbed a chair directly across from him and pulled it out, scraping the metal legs against the floor. The sound irritated Alex but he also watched as Topol grew more uncomfortable.

"Boris, Boris, Boris," Alex began. "You've got some explaining to do."

"What you're talking about? Why am I here?" asked Topol.

Alex slammed his hand on the tabletop. "We're here because you've been lying to me from the start."

Alex picked up the first folder from the table as Mr. Topol sat there, motionless. Alex opened the cover of the first folder and began sifting through the papers inside.

"First off, it was you who phoned in the anonymous 911 call back on the morning of November 16th. You tried to say you were just walking your dog, but let's cut the crap—you killed that girl. Didn't you?" Alex asked aggressively.

"I've never killed anyone. I was walking my dog through the park like I already said," he replied, a sense of pleading in his voice.

"Now I find you at yet another crime scene a little over a month apart. How do you explain the coincidence? Because as a detective, I don't believe in them." Alex closed the file folder and picked up the second one.

"Okay, all right. So I saw on the news that we found another body in the park. I came down to check out what was going on. Honestly."

"I see," Alex said as he opened the second folder and plucked out a single photo. "Then explain to me why you never told me about this."

Alex flung the photo from Juliette Cochran's files across the table. Boris Topol reached out to stop the photo from flying away. He picked up the four-by-six picture and studied it thoroughly. His mouth awkwardly trembled and a bead of sweat lined his forehead. Alex observed him, trying his damnest to analyze the man's behavior.

"Where did you get this?" Mr. Topol asked as he set the photo back on the tabletop.

"Doesn't matter. Were you or were you not there at the crime scene of Veronica Park?" Alex asked.

Mr. Topol sighed. "Yes; I was there." He paused. "But I didn't kill none of those girls, I swear."

"Now, you can see my dilemma here. We have you at the homicide of the second victim, the third, and now the sixth. And these are just the ones we're aware of," Alex said.

Mr. Topol's patience was wearing, and he was becoming increasingly more hostile. "People walk through that park every day, yet you're homing in on me. Now I don't appreciate these false accusations, so unless you have some sort of hard proof that I killed these women, I'm out of here," he said, sliding the chair away and standing.

"Sit down. I'm not through yet."

Boris eased back into the chair and stared at Alex who was sifting through more papers.

Alex cleared his throat. "So you didn't kill them you say. Let's say that's true, you're still hiding something from me."

"I'm not hiding anything. I'm just unlucky, I guess," Topol said.

Alex kept his poker face in full force, not willing to give up until he had something more than a flimsy story.

"I know you saw the killer. You had to of. Look, I know you're scared you'll be next, but if you don't help us, I can't guarantee he won't come after you next."

"Damnit! I didn't kill 'em, I didn't see who killed 'em. Now, I'm going to walk out that door unless you are charging me."

"You're free to go, Boris. But don't leave town," Alex said as he picked up the files from the table and stood. "Oh, and Boris, the next time we see each other, you bet your ass I'll have a warrant for your arrest."

Alex walked towards the door, opened it, and motioned that Mr. Topol was free to leave. Topol quickly grabbed his jacket from the back of the chair, flinging it around his back, and stormed out the door.

Alex stepped out into the hallway and watched his sole suspect march angrily down the corridor towards the exit. As Mr. Topol disappeared around the corner, Alex leaned against the door frame.

He probably didn't kill them, but he knows more than he's letting on.

He shook his head, flipped the light switch off and closed the door to interrogation room number two. He walked down the same corridor and back to his desk, which was just at the end.

The interrogation had taken only about an hour, including the time Alex spent making Topol wait. When Alex emerged out into the squad room, his partner was back from the autopsy. He caught sight of him sitting at his desk, flipping through a manila folder. Alex was curious because it wasn't like his partner to read case files; it was usually something more like *The New York Times*.

Carr was so engrossed in reading that he didn't even realize that Alex had returned to his desk. The squad room was nearly empty, so Alex decided to have a little fun at his partner's expense.

He slammed the files onto his desk and plopped down in his chair, making a loud thud. Carr jerked and diverted his attention away from the folder.

"Think you can be any louder?" Carr asked sarcastically.

"What has you so intrigued?" Alex said as Carr turned the folder around.

"Well, doc was able to find a retrievable print from our Jane Doe this morning."

"That man is nothing short of a genius. Did you get an I.D.?" asked Alex.

"You aren't going to believe this but she used to be one of us," Carr said as Alex developed a puzzled look on his face.

"Used to be?" Alex asked.

"Yeah, Jill Goldberg—does the name sound familiar to you?" Carr asked.

"No, I'm not familiar with any Jill Goldberg—why, should I be?" Alex inquired.

"Hmm, well maybe it's been a while since you saw her last. Goldberg is her married name, but I guarantee that the name Jill Bausch will ring a bell instead," Carr said, and the blood in Alex's face drained in a matter of seconds.

"Jill Bausch? The victim this morning was Jill Bausch from the 73rd Precinct?"

"Yeah— Jones, you all right? You look pretty pale, almost like you've seen a ghost," Carr replied.

Alex sat there in shock for a few moments. "Yeah, something like that," Alex said as he slumped back in his chair. "Now I'm more convinced than ever that these bastards are back. And the sad thing is I have no idea what they want from me."

"Why didn't you recognize the name Jill Goldberg if you do know her?"

"Let's just say she and I had a falling out when I took this promotion."

Carr shook his head. He didn't quite understand. "What, were you two up for the same job or something?"

Alex leaned back in his chair, and his facial expression remained mute. It was then that Carr nodded and it all finally made sense to him.

"I got you, that's some heavy shit," Carr said.

TWENTY

Bridge Park Drive, Brooklyn
December 16, 2005
9:38 A.M.

ALEX SAT AT THE EDGE OF HIS BED, fidgeting with the watch on his wrist. The clasp of the timepiece clicked into place, and he heaved a sigh of relief. With one frustration down, Alex returned to making sure his dress uniform looked flawless. He finished fastening the final two buttons and placed a black cloth across his badge. Just that little task was enough to fill his eyes with tears once again.

I'm not ready to say goodbye.

Alex had met Jill at the academy back in 2001, and from the moment they met, they were inseparable. Things changed for their relationship after Alex's promotion. It was the same promotion Jill was up for also. A jealous rift had slowly developed between the two. Alex barely saw her anymore after that, even though he never quite understood why their friendship collapsed the way it did.

Mike was in the living room, rushing around trying to finish getting ready. As he passed the opened bedroom door, he noticed Alex sitting at the edge of the bed, lost in his thoughts. He peered into the bedroom and compassionately gazed at Alex. He took a step into the dimly lit room, the curtains pulled closed with only a small ribbon of light filling the room.

Mike understood the pain and anguish that Alex was suffering; given that he had buried his friend Marianne only a month ago. But Mike realized this was hitting Alex even harder. He sensed the emotions in Alex's facial expression; it was the same expression he had when he buried his mother years ago. Unsure of how to go ahead, he did the only thing he could do: bring some lightheartedness to the atmosphere.

"So, how do I look?" Mike asked as he twirled around.

Alex lifted his head. His eyes were bloodshot, the skin beneath his eyes was puffy; he looked like a big ball of hell. But who looks good when they're crying off and on for three days?

"You look like great," Alex replied as he wiped the moisture from his eyes and stood.

Walking towards the corner of the bedroom where a full-length mirror stood, Alex tugged and smoothed out his navy-blue jacket. He straightened his tie, but he just couldn't seem to get it right, and that was annoying him.

Mike walked up behind him and wrapped both arms around Alex's chest. He wrestled with the tie. Things had gotten a little better between the two since Mike returned from San Diego, but not everything was back to being picture-perfect just yet.

Mike pulled Alex closer towards him, "I love you, just remember that."

"I love you too," Alex said as he closed his eyes and took in the warmth of Mike's body being next to his.

"You about ready? Service starts at eleven, and I don't want us to be late," Mike said as he released his tight hold.

"Yeah, I'm ready."

The two exited the bedroom, walking past the television which blared the local news channel. The name Jill Goldberg echoed through the apartment, and Mike broke away and turned it off. Alex continued, walking towards the door in a daze. Mike caught up and grabbed for Alex's hand. He squeezed it as Alex stopped and turned back towards his fiancé.

"We're going to get through this; you realize this, right?" Mike asked.

"I do. And once I'm done grieving, it's time to kick this investigation into full throttle."

Mike shook his head. "You are still hell-bent on continuing this investigation yourself—can't you see what's happening here? Whoever this person is, they are picking our friends off one by one."

"Even better reason for me to catch this guy."

"If you insist on continuing, I'm going to be there with you," Mike demanded.

"Whatever makes you feel better about this," Alex replied as he hugged Mike and gave him a peck on the cheek.

The trip down the elevator was silent. The two men barely even looked at each other, let alone thought of speaking. As the doors slid open to the underground parking garage, they both stepped out. The air was full of must from dampness, and Alex twitched his nose as he inhaled the funky smelling air.

Mike clicked the remote in his hand, and the doors unlocked, and the car started. Alex grasped the handle and opened his door, stretching upward to sit in the high seat of the SUV.

Mike drove out of the tight parking space and took another glance at Alex, who sat in the passenger seat. The Ray-Ban sunglasses blocked his eyes.

"So, why don't you fill me in on this case?" Mike said as he waited for the garage door to open.

"Well I think you know most of it, but there's one thing I haven't told you, or anyone for that matter, about the killer from the cemetery scene."

"Yeah, what about them?"

"The witness recalled seeing Russian writing beneath the skull and bones. She gave me just enough information for me to do an internet search."

"Go on."

Pulling out his notepad, Alex revealed the letters to Mike. "According to the witness, *this* is what was spelled out across the back of the hoodie: *С-м-и-р-н-о-в*."

"And those letters mean what?"

"Smirnov. It's the last name of the leader of the gang that assassinated my father."

"Shit, I was hoping deep down that all of this was a mistake. After learning that—well, that's just the final nail in the coffin." Mike hung a sharp left onto the freeway onramp.

"So, are you going to help me and Carr capture these bastards or what?" Alex asked.

"Hell, yes."

They arrived at the service around ten thirty and walked inside the church. The place was filled to the max, with most officers from all the Brooklyn precincts in attendance. Mike and Alex stepped into a pew near the back of the church. They sat, listening to the muffled chatter of people nearby.

"I can't believe this happened. My heart goes out to her poor husband," one lady was overheard saying two pews in front of them.

"And her poor daughter too. She's motherless now," the man sitting next to her said.

Alex sat there, numb, eavesdropping on the fears, the stories, and the sadness all around him. He wanted to make all the noise stop, but there wasn't anything he could do except sit there and take it all in.

The service started promptly at eleven and lasted around forty-five minutes. Many people spoke about Jill's life, her career, her dedication to the force. Her captain spoke, breaking down as he talked about how much he would miss seeing her smiling face every day. Alex just sat there, motionless, listening to everything said, but deep down wanting to get the hell out of there as quickly as he possibly could.

Even though Alex became upset and pissed, he also realized that there was a lot that needed to be done if he was going to catch whoever was responsible for taking the life of a fellow officer.

He watched as they folded an American flag and handed it to her young daughter on the altar, the little girl's father standing at her side in tears. And as the pallbearers took away the casket, the eerie sound of bagpipes being playing echoed off the walls of the church. The somber tone sent an unsettling shiver up Alex's spine as they carried his friend down the aisle.

The funeral service ended around noon, and Alex bolted back to the SUV parked only a few blocks away. Mike hurried as quickly as he could to catch up with Alex, but it was no use rushing, as his husband-to-be was too far ahead. He watched Alex take his cell phone from his jacket and hastily dial a number and then rest the phone on his ear.

TWENTY-ONE

78th Precinct
December 16, 2005
1:19 P.M.

ALEX SAT AT HIS DESK WHILE HIS PARTNER and Mike sat across from him. Alex watched the two, none of them making a sound as they all exchanged glares and glances. With each passing minute, the silence grew more awkward than the moment before. Each one of them not knowing what to say to make things better. Alex became enervated by the silence and decided the best thing to do was to get back to work. He reached for his mouse, clicking it to awaken his computer. He pulled his keyboard closer to him and began typing rapidly.

"What are you doing, Jones?" Carr asked.

"Looking up known members of the Smirnov gang here in Brooklyn, if you must know."

"Wait—who's that? Are you working organized crime now?" asked Carr.

Mike poked him. "The Smirnov family are the ones who assassinated his father. What Fort Knox over there has failed to tell you, or anyone if I want to get technical, is that your witness from the Quaker Cemetery saw something written in Russian across the back of a jacket the perp was wearing." "Oh, he told me that—but Grandma Moses didn't give that much information, so how does he know what it said?" Carr asked in a hush.

"Because he's Alex, I guess," Mike whispered back, "plus the witness remembered enough of the word that all he had to do was do a quick google search and it probably popped up."

"You guys are aware that I can hear you," Alex said without looking away from his computer screen. "Ah-ha."

"What 'ah-ha?'" Carr asked.

"There are twenty-six members of the Smirnov family living here in Brooklyn. In my best estimate, I'd say we're looking at a pool of about a hundred associates to narrow down from," Alex replied as he looked away from his screen.

"A hundred! We'll need to call in some reinforcement for that sort of search," Carr said.

"Already on it," Alex said as he lifted the receiver to his desk phone and dialed.

Alex spent the next five minutes on the phone with the NYPD gang unit. Afterward, he hung the receiver back on the hook and glanced smugly towards the two sitting across from him.

"Like I said, all taken care of," Alex said as both of their jaws dropped.

Eventually, his partner snapped back to reality. "So, what do we do now?"

"We wait and see what they shake out. One thing I think we need to do right away is put a unit on Topol's house," Alex replied.

"You're losing your mind. I don't think Boris Topol is involved in this," Mike chimed in finally.

"He knows something. He might not be the killer, but he is hiding something," Alex said as he stood.

Alex walked to the other end of the squad room. He stopped at the printer and tapped his fingers on the top. A few seconds later he snatched the pages that he printed and returned to his desk.

"You guys look so shocked," Alex said.

"What do you have there?" Carr asked.

"I'm getting a warrant so we can arrest Boris Topol. Perhaps it'll scare him just enough and might get us a lead we're so desperately seeking," Alex said.

Carr and Mike looked at each other in astonishment. Alex became fired up, a complete turnaround from where he stood a few weeks earlier.

Alex grabbed his jacket and motioned for the other two to follow him.

"Where are we going?" Mike asked.

"Need a signature," Alex replied as they two grabbed their jackets and followed.

The evidence against Topol was flimsy at best, but Alex had to do something bold and unconventional to shake things up. The three piled into the beat-up car and drove to the courthouse to pay Judge Howe another visit.

***

Home of Boris Topol
59 Prospect Park West, Brooklyn
December 16, 2005
6:27 P.M.

With an arrest warrant in one hand and his weapon in the other, Alex arrived at the front door of Boris Topol's snobbish Prospect Park residence. To his rear stood a few officers from the 78th Precinct, including his partner, Timothy Carr. Each of the each of them ready for any hint of trouble that might arise from the arrest.

Alex stepped forward, knocking hard on the wooden door. The door slowly gaped open as Alex looked on in confusion.

Possibly he forgot to close it all the way.

Alex pushed gently on the door, and it swung open all the way. He stood on the stoop of the home looking inside. The house stood eerily dark and quiet, more so than usual. Alex reached into his pocket for his trusty flashlight and illuminated the darkened foyer.

"Boris Topol—NYPD. We have a warrant for your arrest," Alex shouted as Carr backed up behind him.

"Maybe he's not here?" Carr whispered.

"No, he's here. Old geezer is undoubtedly hiding from us."
Alex flipped on a nearby light switch. The room illuminated
brightly.

Alex cautiously moved farther into the home, his service
weapon drawn as he peered around the corner which led into
the living room; nothing threatening appeared. He positioned
his hand against the wall, running it along as he searched for
another light switch. Alex found it and flipped up the switch.
The room came to life, and without delay, he turned around,
and it became instantly clear why the house was eerily still; their
prime suspect in the killings, Boris Topol, was hanging from the
banister. An orange extension cord wrapped around his neck,
his lifeless body dangled several feet above the floor.

Alex's mouth opened as he ran the palm of his hand across
his face. Just as he turned to retreat, Carr stepped into the
room.

"Jesus—looks like your suspect couldn't handle the heat
anymore," Carr said.

"You think this is a suicide?"

"Pretty open and shut case, Alex," Carr replied.

"I think we'll let the medical examiner make that call." Alex
pulled his cell from his pocket and dialed Dispatch directly. The
phone rang twice.

"This is Detective Jones, I need the medical examiner at 59
Prospect Park West for a possible homicide."

Alex acknowledged a few questions and hung the phone up
as he and his partner stood there, staring at the only suspect

they had. Alex noticed a small white paper sticking out of the shirt pocket of the victim.

"I can't believe you told them a possible homicide. Topol grasped that we were onto him and it distressed him. So it looks like he decided to end it," Carr again repeated, and Alex shook his head.

"No—something about this doesn't feel right. I never thought Topol was the killer, I said I figured he knew more than he let on."

"Well, whatever. I'm almost certain we won't be dealing with any more bloodbaths anytime soon," Carr said as he huffed and walked towards the front door.

After Carr left, Alex made another call to his least favorite person: Aaron Finch. The call was answered almost immediately following the first ring.

"Hey, Jones, what's up?"

"You busy? Have a crime scene I trust only you to handle." Alex tried to sound as nice as possible given the recent spat between them.

"Not busy; where?"

"59 Prospect Park West. It seems that our only suspect either decided to take his own life, or someone took it for him," Alex replied.

"Ah, sounds pretty shady," Finch said.

"Now you see why I need your proficiency."

"Totally. Be there in twenty minutes."

"Yeah, I'll be here waiting for the ME's office—as usual."

Alex hung up the phone and stood to watch over the body. Something surely didn't add up, and Alex had a bothersome impression that this wasn't a suicide. It looked more like a mafia-style hit more than anything.

The house was still—too still, and Alex heard the ticking of the grandfather clock that stood several feet away in the corner of the room. He didn't dare venture too far from where he was. There was nothing worse than contaminating a crime scene.

Eventually, the house sprang to life as Aaron Finch and his techs arrived at the crime scene. Alex twirled around, and he and the young supervisor's eyes locked once again.

"Brought some backup for this one—sounded pretty serious on the phone. Like this one's more significant than usual," Finch replied as he pulled a pair of sterile latex gloves from his case.

"Yeah, thanks for getting here so fast. Carr seems to think this is a suicide. I don't, so if you and your guys can just do an exhaustive search… Leave no stone unturned."

"You got it."

Time passed on, and in typical fashion, the Medical Examiner's office arrived about thirty-five minutes after the first call. The investigators who responded were unknown to Alex. Then again, it was a little after seven in the evening. Bradburn's shift didn't start until ten o'clock.

"You the detective in charge?" a slender, well-built investigator asked.

"I am. Detective Jones, 78th Precinct, and you are?"

"Sorry, I'm Simmons, and this is my apprentice, Stacy Smith," he replied. "It's her second shift with us."

"Nice to meet you both. I've never met you before, but then again, most of my homicides occur at like four in the morning," Alex said.

"Completely understand," Simmons replied as he pointed towards the dangling body. "This must be our guest of honor."

"Meet Boris Topol; he *was* my prime suspect in the Prospect Park Slasher case," Alex said uneasily.

"You don't sound so confident about that, Detective," Smith quietly said.

"It's a long story." Alex sighed. "While you're checking the body, there's a piece of paper sticking out of his shirt pocket. Can you get that to me when you're finished?"

"Absolutely," replied Simmons.

Alex watched as the trainee photographed the overall scene, the extension cord, and a few close-ups of the victim's neck and face. Simmons rolled back indoors with a stretcher and black body bag and positioned it underneath the victim. He ascended the stairs and hollered down to Smith.

"You ready?"

"Do it," she replied.

Simmons pulled a knife from his shirt pocket and in one slice cut the cord that suspended Topol from the banister. The body crashed down on the stretcher as the investigator rushed down the stairs.

The two ME officials bagged the victim's hands in plastic baggies, sealing them both with zip ties. Simmons reached for the paper bulging from the victim's shirt pocket and placed it in an evidence bag. He walked it over to Alex and smiled.

"Here you go, as promised."

"Thanks," Alex said. "So, Carr and I will be over shortly. Please let them know not to start the autopsy until we arrive."

"No problem," Simmons said and went back to aid Smith with zipping up the body bag.

Alex stood there, curious as to what was in the letter. Was it a suicide note? A receipt for something? There was only one way for him to find out and that was to unfold it.

He hollered out, "Carr, can you come in here, please?"

Carr dashed into the living room from the foyer and planted himself next to his partner's side.

"The mysterious paper," Carr joked, "I'm sincerely honored you wanted me to be here when you opened it."

Alex huffed as he pulled the paper from the bag. He was oddly nervous about what the letter might reveal. With the note in hand, he slowly unfolded the corner. The handwritten letter was perfect — a little too perfect.

If you thought this was going to be a suicide note, you were sadly mistaken. Boris Topol was just another innocent pawn, and the only error made on his part was witnessing something he shouldn't have when I murdered Marianne.

Sorry about your luck, but you'll never find me, and I'm going to continue killing everyone you know, and everyone your friends know. I'll never let you forget because I can't forget what your family did to mine.

-M.J.

Alex handed the paper to Carr as he paced back and forth around the living room. His partner began reading the letter, his lips moving with each word he read.

"You were right all along," Carr said. "Let's go back through that list of Smirnov family members and look for anyone with the initials, M.J."

TWENTY-TWO

Sebastian's Nook, Brooklyn
December 21, 2005
9:45 P.M.

ALEX SAT AT THE TABLE, LISTENING TO AMY and Josh fill him in on everything that was going on in the lives since they last met up. For a change, Alex was in high spirits, even though a serial killer terrorized him every night in his dreams.

"So, that's what's been going on with us," Amy said, "Now, I'm acutely aware that you detest discussing your cases, but I must ask how things are going; the slasher has been all over the news the past few nights."

"Eh, not as well as you might think." Alex frowned and lifted his pint glass to his lips, taking a sip of his pilsner. "The slasher is making everything personal, and I hate it. And to make matters worse, my captain finally heard the rumors floating around that the killer was murdering people I'm acquainted with."

"Dude, that sounds terrible," said Josh as Alex set his glass back on the reclaimed wood table.

"Well, wasn't the most pleasant conversation I ever had with the man, but then again, it wasn't the worst."

"What did your captain say exactly?" Amy asked as the server dropped off their bruschetta appetizer.

"He wanted to pull me from the case," Alex passionately said, "but thankfully I was able to talk him out of it."

"How'd you manage that? Seems like a conflict of interest if you ask me," Josh said as Alex chomped on his bruschetta.

"Just informed him that I'm an expert on these cases and that no other detectives would have the insight that I have. That and I promised him that I could remain impartial."

"And he bought that sack of crap from you?" Amy joked.

"I'm still working the case, but he put Carr as the lead instead of me, though."

The beers kept flowing and the more booze that flowed, the more queries Amy asked about the case. The questions were insignificant enough that Alex wouldn't get too annoyed, but detailed enough that she could grasp what exactly was happening.

Eventually, Alex looked at his watch; 11:04 p.m.

"Guys, I really have to wrap this up. I just never know when I might get woken at four in the morning," Alex said as he gulped the remnants of his third pilsner.

"Come on—stay for fifteen more minutes. I barely see you anymore," Amy pleaded.

"How can I say no when you look so pitiful."

As promised, they wrapped the evening up close to 11:30 and the server set the check on the corner of the table. Alex reached out for the check.

"I got it," Josh said as he reached his hand out to snatch the check from Alex's hand.

"Hell, no, you paid last time—I got this." Alex pulled out his credit card and plopped it inside the check holder.

With the check paid they all casually made their way to the front door. It was nearing closing time, and the staff was more than eager to see them leave. They emerged onto a quiet street, the dim streetlight above was flickering.

"Alex, you got a second to chat?" Amy asked.

"Sure," Alex said. Josh nodded and moved away. Alex continued, "What's up?"

"You remember that guy I dated last summer—Max?" she asked.

"Ugh, that loser; can't forget him."

"Well that crazy loser left me a dozen black roses on my doorstep yesterday with this card attached." She reached into her back pocket and pulled out a crumpled-up piece of paper.

Alex took the card from her and scanned it for a few moments.

I want you back—you were my one
true love, the only person who kept
me from going insane and doing

something stupid. I'm totally lost
without you.

Come back to me before I do
something we'll both regret.

"Man, can you pick 'em *or* can you pick 'em," Alex said.
"He's a total psycho."

"I know, I know; the crazy ones are just attracted to me.
What should I do?"

"Other than this letter, which is disturbing, has he verbally
threatened you in any way? Have you seen him stalking you?"
Alex asked.

"I haven't seen him since we broke up last summer—and
no, we haven't exchanged words either since our split. But this
note is borderline harassment though, isn't it?" she asked as
Josh watched on from a few yards away.

"I'll pay him a visit and make sure he doesn't bother you
anymore," Alex promised, "but let's be honest, what probably
happened is he got drunk one night, got all sentimental, and
bam, he's dropping off this gothic looking bouquet of flowers."

"You're right, while it's disturbing to get, I'm sure that
you're right and he just had a drunken night," Amy said as she
embraced Alex. "You really are the best person in my entire
life."

Just as Amy let go of, his phone rang. He looked at the caller
ID; it was Mike. Alex lifted his index finger to motion for Amy
to wait just a few seconds so he could give her a proper
goodbye.

"On my way home now, Mike," Alex said.

"Where have you been? Carr has been trying to reach you for the last hour," Mike blurted out.

"I've been with Amy and Josh over at Sebastian's. Never got any calls from Carr, though."

"Probably no cell service inside the restaurant," he said. "Anyway, just meet him over at the picnic house at the park."

"On my way—guess I won't see you tonight then," Alex said as Amy folded her arms.

"I'll meet you there—can't help you with the case, but at least I'll be able to see you and say goodnight."

"See you there." Alex ended the call and focused his attention back to Amy.

"Don't tell me—another slasher victim in the park."

"Not sure," he replied as he reached out for another hug. "Guess I'll find out when I get there."

Alex and Amy embraced one final time before they said goodnight. Josh returned and reached out to shake Alex's hand; instead, Alex hugged the young journalist.

"We're friends now, we don't shake hands—we hug," Alex said as he released his hold on Josh and patted him on the back.

"Thanks again for tonight," Amy shouted out as interlocked her arms around Josh's.

Alex stood on the sidewalk outside the restaurant as he watched as the two lovebirds ventured off into the shadows. He sighed, slipped his hands into his pockets, and walked the opposite direction towards the subway station.

It was fast approaching midnight, and Alex had a hunch it would be yet another sleepless night. But nowadays, it was a welcome relief from the faceless figure who tormented him every night in his dreams.

TWENTY-THREE

Prospect Park Picnic House, Brooklyn
December 22, 2005
12:05 A.M.

ALEX WALKED ALONG THE DRY PAVED path near the
Seventh Street entrance towards the picnic house. He knew he
was on the doorstep of the scene because of the endless flash
strobes from the SLR cameras and the resonating chatter from
the reporters, which only grew louder with each step he took.

He finally had the reporters in sight as he turned his head
down and to the right, like a celebrity avoiding the paparazzi.
The reporters all shouted questions out to Alex, but he politely
ignored them.

These people need to get a life.

He approached an officer at the yellow crime scene tape,
flashed his credentials, and ducked underneath. Once inside the

cordon, he turned around and asked the officer, "Have you seen Detective Carr around?"

"Yup." The officer pointed towards a group of officers standing around chatting.

"Thanks."

Alex marched faster towards the group, recognizing in the back of his mind that an ass chewing was imminent from his partner. He got closer, and the group of about five officers surrounding Carr noticed and scrambled away, exposing Carr standing there with his arms folded and his usual scowled face.

"Jones, where have you been? I tried to call you like a hundred times," Carr said as he flung his hands up.

"Guess I didn't have cell service where I was," Alex said. "I'm here now, though—so what's up?"

"Slasher is back, err, I think," Carr said.

"Always with this 'I think.' Is it his handiwork or not?"

"Looks to be his work with one small variation: our victim's a male," Carr said, and Alex's brow rose.

"Let's get to it."

The two men walked north about forty yards, passing by the picnic house. Amid the densely wooded area was a clearing. Within this undeveloped area stood a lonesome oak tree. Alex's gaze fixated beneath the tree where a white sheet covered the lifeless body of the slasher's newest victim.

"Can you bring me up to speed, as I'm certain the ME's office is ready to take him away," Alex said.

"Oh, you know Bradburn all too well," Carr joked. "Victim is a thirty-one-year-old white male. New York driver's license in the vic's wallet identified him as Elijah Sideman."

Alex stopped dead in his tracks. "Wait—did you say Elijah Sideman?"

"Yeah—oh, right, you're funny." Carr sighed.

"No, I'm quite serious. He dated my best friend, Amy," Alex said.

Carr placed the palm of his hand on Alex's shoulder. "Well, looks like this time I get to tell you to sit this one out," Carr said as he noticed Mike out of the corner of his eye.

Mike approached them, and a speechless Alex just turned and looked at his lover. Mike smiled and greeted Carr as he wrapped his left arm around Alex's back and escorted him away from the scene.

"Hey, Jones," Carr shouted as Alex turned around, "I'll keep you in the loop though."

Alex nodded and continued back towards the picnic house. The world began spinning all around Alex, and he faltered over his thoughts, thinking of something to say. It took a few minutes, but he finally turned to Mike.

"Were you aware that the vic was Elijah before I hauled my buzzed ass all the way over here?" Alex asked.

"No—I swear to you that I didn't. If I had I wouldn't have even called you," Mike replied.

"All right, fair enough. Let's go home—I'm so exhausted that I don't want to think anymore."

"Agreed."

Alex reached into his pocket for his cell as they continued their walk towards the number two train to set out for their condo.

Alex redialed the last person he called. It was 12:30 in the morning, and he was confident that Amy would still be awake as her usual bedtime was closer to one in the morning.

A groggy voice answered. "Alex, what's wrong?"

"I wish I had a better way to break this news to you, but I have something disturbing to say—again," Alex said.

"Ugh, I'm really dreading answering my phone when you call anymore, you realize that right?" she replied, sounding more awake. "Well, spit it out, man."

"It's about your ex, Elijah. How do I say this—the homicide victim we found was him."

A stillness fell over the phone line, only her barely audible breathing resonated over the line. Alex paused, knowing he needed to give his friend a few moments to process the shock before he began to talk again.

She cleared her throat, "Are you sure?"

"Carr says the ME made the identification from his driver's license," Alex said, "are you going to be all right?"

"Oh, me...yeah, I'll be fine. I got Josh with me, so if I need anything, I'll have some support."

"Good. If you need me, I'm just a phone call and a train ride away," Alex said.

"Thanks, Alex. Is it all right if I inform his employer in the morning?" she asked.

"Who's his employer?"

"Sip Coffeehouse. I see him every morning."

Alex coughed. "I'm sorry—you did say Sip, didn't you?"

"Yeah, he and Myles work the morning shift together."

"Myles, ah yes, the cashier. I didn't catch his last name the other day; do you happen to know it by chance?" Alex asked.

"Yeah, it's Johnson. Why?"

A lightbulb went off in Alex's head. The initials M.J. Was Myles the Slasher? He paused to think how to phrase the question he was about to ask.

"Do you think Myles is capable of murder?" he finally asked.

"Myles? A murderer? No, I don't think that's possible," she replied as she chuckled at the pure silliness of the question.

"What about your other ex, Max," Alex said. "What was his last name again?"

"Janco, why?"

"No reason, just want to keep an eye on him for you," he replied, and she laughed.

"You're always looking out for me. This is one of the many reasons I love you."

"All right, well go back to sleep, and I'll see you soon." Alex ended the call and looked over at Mike, who was still walking alongside him.

"What was with all of the questions?" Mike asked.

Alex grinned. "We need to make a pit stop at the station before we head home."

Mike shook his head, but knowing the expression upon Alex's face, whatever was stirring around in his brilliant mind was something worth the detour.

The couple briskly walked north along the edge of the park down Prospect Park West towards Flatbush Avenue. Alex completely forgot about being exhausted and now was on a mission.

"I'm not even going to ask why we're running at a million miles a minute," Mike joked. "Some lightbulb has gone off in your head, something important, and right now that's the most important thing."

"I think I figured out who the slasher is," Alex said as he picked up his pace a little.

"Okay, care to share your thoughts?"

"Max Janco," Alex replied.

"Who's he?"

"Remember that weird guy Amy dated last summer?" Alex asked.

"She's dated her share of weirdos." Mike snickered. "Think you can narrow down my choices a little?"

"Tall, pale, the guy from Belarus. The one with the slicked-back jet-black hair."

"Ah, him." Mike recollected the face in his mind. "You think that jerkwater is the Slasher?"

"His initials are M.J., which fits with the information I gathered from Juliette Cochran's planner. And he fits the psychological profile of someone capable of this."

"Hold up, when exactly did you have a psych profile done on the Slasher?"

"I didn't have an *official* one done, I've just been keeping annotations on individual traits," Alex said as they arrived at the Grand Army Plaza.

Alex walked a few steps ahead of his fiancé, and Mike yelled out, "You never fail to amaze me, every day."

The rest of the walk was silent. Mike left Alex to ponder over what it was he had planned. It was closing in on one in the morning, and the derelicts were out in force on this unusually cold evening. Christmas was a mere three days away, but for Alex, each year without his mother for the holidays was turning him into a bitter old man, quickly.

They arrived at the precinct doors, and Alex burst in like he owned the joint. Mike could hardly keep up with his overexcited fiancé, but he was doing the best he could. Alex dashed up the stairs and into the squad room. He made it to his desk, where he feverishly pulled his desk chair out and dropped down in the unsteady piece of crap.

"Whoa, slow it down. Remember precinct rules, 'if you break it, you buy it,'" Mike joked but Alex paid no attention to him.

Alex sat at his computer, typing away feverishly, his mind focused on finding out as much information as possible on Max Janco. He pulled up the guy's criminal history, put in a request for his immigration status, and did a quick internet search on him, all in a matter of minutes. With each page he visited, he clicked the print button and gathered as much intel together as humanly possible.

"Alex, you've lost it. How are you even confident that this is your guy?" Mike asked.

"It has to be him. Who else could it be?"

Mike sighed. "You got me, but I'm sure there are plenty of other suspects you may've missed. Besides, it's almost one in the morning, and I don't know how things work around here, but I can't be late to work tomorrow. You think we can wrap this up for the night?"

Alex stopped dead in his tracks and glared at Mike.

"If you're tired, go home. I have a lot of work left to do," Alex replied as lifted a stack of papers and tapped it against the top of the desk to organize them better.

Mike shook his head dishearteningly, gave Alex a hug and kiss on the forehead, and grabbed his jacket from the back of the wobbly chair he'd sat in for the past hour.

Mike stood at the threshold of the door. His hand propped up against the wood trim as he turned his head slightly towards Alex.

"Make sure you don't overdo it tonight, and you really should get some rest; you look like shit."

TWENTY-FOUR

Bridge Park Drive, Brooklyn
December 22, 2005
7:05 A.M.

THE SUN WAS JUST BEGINNING TO SHINE through his large bedroom windows when Alex awoke to the ringing of his cell.

He rubbed his eyes and flopped his hand blindly against the nightstand, searching for the phone. He grasped it just in time and flipped the telephone open.

"Hell-o," he said exhaustedly.

"Alex, oh thank God you answered," Amy frantically said.

"What's wrong? Did that Janco character show up again?"

"No, it's much worse," she said.

"What's wrong?"

"It's Josh."

"What about Josh? Is he all right?" Alex asked.

"I'm not sure. He's, well —he's gone missing."

"Amy, come on now. What makes you think he's missing?"

"I'm not joking. Can you come over here as soon as possible?" she asked.

Alex rolled over and looked at his alarm clock. 7:08. He groaned. "Let me get dressed, and I'll be over shortly."

"Okay, thanks. I'll be waiting here for you."

Alex crawled out of his queen-sized bed and planted both feet on the hardwood floor. The floor was cold, and it made him shake to his core. He stood, stretching his arms out and letting out one last yawn.

He didn't get as much sleep as he wanted. He spent the better part of the overnight hours in the precinct compiling information on Janco, leaving around 2:45 a.m. After grabbing a taxi home, he stepped into his loft around three in the morning to find Mike fast asleep on the couch.

Alex was keenly aware that Mike worried about him and figured this was his way of showing how much he cared. Alex had picked up a white blanket which usually stayed slung over the armrest of the couch and covered Mike with it. He'd leaned in and kissed him on the cheek and quietly retreated to the bedroom.

Alex snapped back to his current situation as he looked around the living room. Mike was nowhere in sight. He then remembered that roll call started at seven so he barely missed him. Alex stepped into the bathroom and flipped the switch on. He stood there looking at himself in the mirror. The dark circles under his eyes were growing ghastlier as the days passed on.

I have got to catch this guy for my own sanity.

He quickly showered and struggled to pull himself together. He reached for his keys and walked towards the door.

He stepped into the elevator and pressed the button for the ground floor. The subway trip to Amy's apartment would take him 35 minutes, so he decided to just hail a cab instead. The weather outside wasn't conducive to walking and spending so much time outdoors.

He stood on Furman Street and watched several taxis speed by without even stopping. Eventually, after ten minutes of trying, a taxi squealed on the brakes. Alex ran towards the awaiting car and jumped into the back seat.

"Where to, buddy?" the driver asked.

"The 300 block of Washington Avenue, please," Alex replied as the cabbie sped away towards Atlantic Avenue.

Alex arrived at Amy's doorstep close to eight and stood on the stoop, searching through the list of faded name plates on the call box for hers. As many times as he'd been there, he never for the life of him remembered which buzzer was hers.

He finally found it, pressed the button, and was buzzed inside the building almost immediately. He raced up stairs to her apartment on the third floor. As he turned the corner to take the last flight, he saw Amy standing at her door, pacing back and forth.

"You look like hell," Alex said as he walked a little slower towards her.

"Thanks, I try."

Alex reached out his arms and embraced her as she squeezed him tightly.

"So, let's talk inside," Alex said.

She nodded and motioned for Alex to come in. She glanced around the empty hallway before closing the door. She felt uneasy living in her own apartment now knowing that her ex had access to her building.

Alex walked about halfway into the living room before spinning around to focus his attention on her. She stood next to the door, fidgeting with the door locks.

"Calm down," Alex said, "no one is going to get you."

Amy stopped and turned to look at him, standing six feet away from her. She really did look like hell, as if she hadn't slept a wink the night before.

"Sorry, it's just my nerves, ya know."

"Yes, I understand how you get. So, start at the beginning; why do you think Josh is missing?"

"Yeah, he went out for a walk last night around two, said he'd be right back. He does that from time to time when he can't sleep."

Alex nodded as he watched her begin pacing again.

"Come here, sit."

She cautiously walked towards the sofa and sat down in her usual spot. She slumped over, placing both hands on her face. Alex reached over and brushed his hand against her shoulder.

"It's going to be all right," he said. "We'll find him."

"I hope so."

Amy picked her cell phone from the coffee table and opened her call history. "See, I've tried to call him like seventy times since he left."

"Give me his number, and I'll see if I can get ahold of him," Alex said as he opened his contact list.

Amy fumbled with her phone and pulled up his contact information, "It's 718-929-2750."

Alex typed the number into his phone and clicked save. He slipped it back into his jacket. "Which route does he typically use when he takes these late-night walks?"

"It's usually just around the block, he's typically gone maybe fifteen minutes, max."

"I'm sure he is all right, please don't stress."

"I'll try not to, but now I'm worried that my psycho ex has something to do with this." she said as she stood up and started pacing again.

"Where does Josh live again?"

"In Queens. Long Island City."

"Street and house number?"

"He's in a new apartment building on 49th Street in Long Island City. I believe the address is 3 49th Street to be exact."

"Perfect. Not my jurisdiction, but I can make a house call this afternoon if I don't reach him by phone." Alex closed his notepad and stood.

"That's it?"

"What else is there for me to do from here?" Alex asked.

"I mean you're the police, you can't call in favors or something?" Tears welled in her eyes.

"That's not how it works; we've been through this before. Remember that time you tried to get me to fix your old boyfriend's parking tickets?" Alex joked, trying to lighten her tension.

"I thought you were just making that up," she said.

"I wasn't," he said as he reached out again to embrace her. "I should go, but I'll keep you informed as I always do."

She wiped away the tears that had begun to flow and gave a half-smile.

"One last thing; why do you think your ex-boyfriend has something do with this?" Alex asked.

"He's a complete loon," she said. "When we broke up he told me he'd never let me be."

Alex eyeballed her, perplexed; why had he never heard about this before?

"Hold up, you told me that things ended amicably with him," Alex said, "so, you weren't completely honest with me about him?"

"I didn't want you to worry. But, yeah, I don't trust that freak further than I could throw him."

"All right, I'll take care of this."

Alex marched towards the door. He wasn't happy that his best friend kept the information from him. If she had informed him last year, Alex could have nipped this in the bud before it got to this point. The two stood at the door, and Alex reassured her that he'd call in a few hours with an update. She tried to smile, but given her emotional state, the smile never came.

Alex descended the stairs and walked back out onto Washington Avenue. He pulled out his cell phone and dialed Josh's number. After a half ring, the call went straight to voicemail.

Phone's off.

He hung up and called Carr. It rang once, and his partner answered.

"Are you coming in today?"

"And good morning to you, too; I'll be in later. I have a small errand to run for Amy," he said.

He continued his walk towards the Clinton-Washington Avenue subway station to catch the G train to Long Island City.

"Is she in trouble?" Carr asked.

"She's okay; her boyfriend, on the other hand, has gone missing," Alex said as he reached the corner of Washington and Lafayette Avenue.

"Not good. You need any backup?" Carr asked.

"I can meet you at the Clinton-Washington Avenue station," Alex replied.

"Gonna take me about fifteen minutes to get there."

"I'll wait, I can probably use some backup," Alex said. "I feel a bad omen about this one."

"Well whenever you have that sense, it typically means we're heading to another crime scene," Carr said as he scoffed.

"Let's hope not; for all of us."

Alex hung up the phone. He was only a few hundred feet from the subway station. He stood outside the entrance to the subway, walking around in circles while he waited for Carr to show up. The walk from the 78th precinct wasn't far away, but Alex also realized that Carr was lazy and that his fifteen minutes really meant twenty-five.

About five minutes passed by and his phone began ringing in his pocket. He pulled it out and looked at the caller ID display; it was Mike.

"Good morning," Alex answered.

"Hey, sorry I didn't say goodbye earlier; figured you got in late."

"I did. How did you sleep? I can't imagine that hard couch was comfortable to sleep on. Were you worried about me or something?" Alex asked.

A slight laugh filled the line. "I was just so tired when I got back, I kicked off my shoes, plopped down on the sofa, and the next thing you were covering me up with a blanket. So, what are you up to right now?"

"Right now I'm just standing at the subway station; Carr is meeting me here. We have to go up to Long Island City to check on Josh."

"What? Why? Is something wrong with Josh?" Mike asked.

"Amy is convinced that he's gone missing. I'm gonna check it out, though, for her to call says it's serious," Alex said.

"Yeah, she only tells you stuff when she's worried; what time did he go missing?"

"Around two in the morning. Amy says Josh left for a walk and never came back," Alex said.

"Curious," Mike said as Alex heard commotion on the other end of the line. "Hate to run, duty calls. Keep me informed on what's up."

"I'll call you later."

Alex hung up and scanned the area. A wrought-iron park bench sat empty across the street from the subway station, so he took the opportunity and strolled across the street to rest. There was no telling how long his partner would take to arrive, and he was so tired from his lack of sleep the past few weeks.

He sat down on the cold metal, and a cold sensation crawled up his body. He rubbed his hands together and blew the warm air from his body into them. Not even a minute passed by before his cell phone rang again.

This had better be Carr.

"Carr, where the hell are you?"

"Good morning, Marshall," the distorted voice said.

Alex pulled the phone away from his ear and checked the Caller ID: Unknown Caller.

"Who is this?" he asked.

"Take a guess."

Alex huffed. "I'm going to go with M.J."

"You are smarter than you look."

"Much. I could have this call traced, you are aware of that, right? So since I got you on the line, why are you calling me? Do you want to get caught?" Alex asked.

"You won't catch me. You can't find a ghost," M.J. replied.

"Watch me."

The line sat silent for a few seconds. "I'm calling to tell you that I have a surprise for you."

"More riddles, huh? Cut the crap, man—what do you want?" Alex asked in a disdainful tone.

"I have something you want. Go to 38 Adelphi Street. Be here in thirty minutes and come alone," M.J. demanded.

"But—"

"No excuses—do it, or your friend dies."

M.J. hung up, and the call line went dead. Alex closed and re-opened his phone and dialed Carr. He sat back down on the bench, his leg bouncing nonstop as he began chewing on his fingernails. His adrenaline was kicking in fiercely. Carr answered the phone after a few rings.

"Jones, I'm almost there—calm down."

"Okay, there's been a development—how far away are you?" Alex asked.

"Two blocks."

"Well, pick up the pace a little, huh," Alex joked to ease his tension, "this is big news."

"It's always big news when I work with you."

"No, this time it's real news. Like huge news."

"I'm sure it is," Carr said sarcastically. "See you in a minute."

Pacing back and forth along the sidewalk, Alex gripped his cell phone, tapping the antennae against his teeth every few seconds. He felt uneasy about going to this location by himself. What if it was a trap? Who would help him if M.J. decided to take him hostage, or worse yet, kill him also?

Just as Alex turned around, he caught sight of Carr hauling along the sidewalk across the street. He was rushing so fast that his coattails were blowing behind him.

"Look, let's walk and talk," Alex said as Carr arrived.

"And hello to you, too," Carr said, "now what in the hell is so critical that you caused me to sweat up a storm?"

They walked north along Clinton Avenue. The northwest wind was blowing frigid air against their faces as the sun disappeared in a sea of thick, black, snow squall clouds which were rolling in. Alex was moving quickly down the street as Carr struggled to keep up.

Carr reached out and grabbed Alex's jacket collar. "Stop," he demanded.

"We don't have time to stop. I'm on a timeline here," Alex replied.

"What in the hell is going on," Carr said as he stopped in the middle of the sidewalk.

"I got a call from M.J. a few minutes before you arrived," Alex began. "He says I have to meet him on Adelphi Street in thirty minutes. I'm supposed to come alone or 'my friend' will die."

"Wait -- what? You talked to the slasher?" Carr asked.

Alex looked blankly at his partner. "He referred to himself as M.J. He didn't refer to himself as the slasher."

"You have completely lost your mind, you do know that, right?" Carr asked.

"My faculties are in check, sir. Now when we get closer I need you to hang back," Alex said.

"Hell no! You think I'm going to let you go into this alone?" Carr said.

"This isn't negotiable. If he sees cops there's no telling what he'll do."

"I don't like this. I don't like any of this one bit. But hey, you do your thing," Carr said as Alex stopped.

"Tell you what; give me twenty minutes and if I'm not back, send in backup. Deal?"

"I don't like this, but I'll go along with it," Carr said, and Alex smiled.

Alex nodded and walked farther down Clinton Street towards Park Avenue. All Carr could do was watch as his partner walked away. Carr checked his watch and noted what time he needed to call in backup.

TWENTY-FIVE
38 Adelphi Street, Brooklyn
December 22, 2005
10:45 A.M.

ALEX WALKED FOR FIVE MINUTES ALONG dilapidated
streets full of empty row homes and deserted businesses.
Vinegar Hill wasn't the most prominent area, instead it was the
most rundown portion of Brooklyn.

He walked along Park Avenue until he arrived at Adelphi
Street. Once there he took a right and walked beneath the
Interstate 278 overpass. He was edgy. His heart was racing a
mile a minute. What would he find when he arrived? Was the
person they were holding Josh? There were so many questions
rattling around his brain as he moved closer to the spot.

He reached the house. First, he scrutinized his setting, more
particularly the house; every window was boarded up with

rotted plywood, all except one on the second floor. The broken window drew Alex's eyes upward, and he felt a heaviness fall upon him as if someone's eyes were following his every move. He squinted, but it was broad daylight, which made it difficult to see if anyone was watching him.

The weight was overwhelming as he glanced about the eerily deserted street. A few seconds of scanning and he returned his attention back to the house. He took a step forward, planting his black Gucci dress shoe onto the crumbling concrete steps. The unstable structure shifted beneath his feet as he grasped the spider-web encrusted handrail.

That was close.

He brushed his hands free of any spiders and continued up the final two stairs. He made it safely to the landing and stared at the faded red front door before him. He sighed, closed his eyes, and tried to take his mind off the danger he was about to walk into. He tried to imagine what the house may have looked like years ago in its prime.

He opened his eyes, took in a deep breath of chilly air, and pounded loudly on the door; it moved slightly inward.

Guess they were expecting me.

After all the suspect was waiting for him. He pressed on the door, it creaked as it swung wider open. A blast of mildew slapped Alex in the face. He quickly turned his head and coughed. What in the world was he doing here?

He cautiously entered the building. He checked the floor for possible weak spots while simultaneously checking for hidden assailants. He hollered out.

"I'm here. Come out."

His voice echoed off the four walls that surrounded him in the barren rowhome. He stood still. The home creeped him out. Each subsequent second he stood there, the more uneasy he became. There weren't many situations in his short life that scared Alex, but if anyone were keeping track of fear levels, then his current predicament would surely be at the top of his lease favorite situations.

"Max Janco, show yourself."

There was still no response to his request. He rotated around in the middle of what Alex suspected was once the living room. He heard a loud moan echoing throughout the home. He jumped and without delay reached inside his Hugo Boss suit jacket and retrieved his service weapon from the holster.

He scanned more of the room and spotted a wooden staircase out of the corner of his eye. Time was ticking, and he took some comfort in knowing that Carr was standing by, probably with his stopwatch out clocking the minutes as they passed. He moved quickly towards the stairs and ascended.

Fifteen steps.

He made sure he counted before even taking the first step. He kept his 9mm held close to his chest as he pressed his back against the dirty wall.

Step one…step two… The whimpering grew louder with each one he took. After a few seconds, he was standing firmly on the twelfth step which gave him an improved assessment of the second floor.

Four doors.

He climbed two more steps and stood in the darkened, wide hallway. He pulled his flashlight out, clicked the rubber button, and held it in his left hand while he gripped his weapon with his right. The stream of light pierced through the darkness as he stood still, waiting for the groaning sounds to resume.

It took a minute, but eventually, the sounds of pain continued, and Alex finally determined which room the sounds were coming from. He approached the door guardedly, not sure what to anticipate once he flung the door open.

He stood unwearyingly at the door, reaching out his hand to clinch the doorknob. He joggled it; locked. He stepped away from the door, giving himself enough space to get a running start. He clung firmly to his weapon and rushed the door. He hit it with his right shoulder near the jamb. The door violently crashed inward and the hallway filled with light.

He got his bearings and there sat Josh. His body sat motionless, zip-tied to a wooden chair with a large piece of silver duct tape affixed to his lips. Alex checked him over; a large purplish bruise covered his left cheek, and he was bleeding from his forehead. Alex checked behind him before rushing to the young journalist's side.

"You all right?" he asked as he ripped the duct tape from his mouth.

"I'm as good as I can be," Josh murmured. "Thank God you found me."

"Yeah, me too."

"Are you alone?" asked Alex.

"I've been alone for about an hour now."

"Did you see who did this to you?"

"I've never seen the guy before," said Josh. "Tall, weird accent, and jet-black hair."

"Christ."

"What? You know this guy?"

"Yeah, unfortunately. Your girlfriend's psychotic ex," Alex replied.

Alex knelt in front of Josh and set the flashlight on the floor. He reached into the front pocket of his slacks and retrieved his Swiss Army knife. He flipped the knife open and began cutting the plastic ties which bound Josh.

The first tie came off quickly as he threw it to the side. Just as he reached over to start cutting the second link, Josh let out a gurgling gasp.

"Behind you."

Alex swung his head to his left, just as the full force of a 2x4 smashed against the side of his face. The force knocked him onto his side a few feet away from Josh's chair. His limp body lay there, still, as Josh squirmed and moaned loudly in his restraints.

Alex's body sprawled out on the floor, the impact was so great that it left him unconscious, and bleeding profusely from a gaping wound on his forehead. The masked assailant hoisted him with ease from the ground and dropped him onto a chair next to Josh. The man pulled out six zip-ties from his back pocket and began strapping the detective's extremities to it.

Everything happened quickly, and after a few minutes, Alex began coming around from his assault. He leaned his head gently forward and watched as a large blood drop dripped onto his white shirt and light green tie.

He instantly had a case of déjà vu and flashed back to the fateful night which forever changed his life in Colorado. Everything felt the same, from the way the zip-ties cut into his wrists to the blood dripping from his head onto his clothes.

He blinked, hoping it would shake the repressed memory from flashing before his eyes, but it wasn't helping. He kept hearing the same phrases over and over in his mind.

Alex, stop trying to get out. It's impossible. I've been trying, and it's not working.

Those were the words uttered by Amy that Alex remembered vividly from the moment he awoke in the cabin in Colorado. However, this time, there wasn't a chance in hell that he wasn't going to fight his way out. He was stronger now, even a little wiser.

Alex tried to move his arms and legs to free himself, but it was no use. The assailant had tied them down solidly. He turned his head to his right and saw Josh still immobilized with a new piece of silver duct tape across his mouth. The fear flowed through his body. A horror so intense that even irrepressible Alex now had to face the truth: he was a prisoner. He didn't see the attacker until he refocused his attention straight ahead. There before him, he stood. He towered about 6'4", his face covered with a white hockey mask, something you'd expect to see in a *Halloween* movie. The man stood still, speaking no words at all, which made Alex even more uneasy.

All the masked figure did was tap his fingers together as if plotting something sinister.

The only thing to do now was relax and accept the outcome. Alex told himself to not fight, to save up all the energy possible because he'd probably need it. Also, in the back of his woozy mind, he was aware that Carr would show up any minute with backup. Alex, the guy who wouldn't let well enough alone, began spewing out insults at the man.

"You're a stupid idiot, you really are," Alex said. "You messed with the wrong guy."

The man still didn't speak, he just inched closer to Alex, and in one quick swoop the man yanked out a large folding knife from his pocket. Alex knew something bad was about to happen and he closed his eyes. The silence surrounding him allowed his mind to clear and another memory entered his mind.

I'm not going to sit here and just die. If I'm going to die tonight, I'm going out with a fight.

Those words were like his mantra lately as he seemed to always find himself in a disaster he'd rather not be in. He opened his eyes quickly, and when he did, he now faced Janco, and he was even more ruthless than Heather or Brandy ever were.

As Alex spoke, his voice crackled from fear. "Max, look, man, we can work something out."

The man finally spoke as he unfolded the knife. He was distorting his voice somehow, Alex was certain the person before him was indeed Max Janco.

"No, Marshall, there is nothing to work out. I finally have you right where I want you. You're trapped, and I have all the power now. It's time for a little fun."

"Wait—you don't have to do this. Just let us go, and we'll forget this ever happened."

"Not a chance. You're playing with the big boys now. Those fools in Colorado were nothing compared to my team and me."

Janco lifted the knife to his face, and his eyes lit up as he studied the knife.

"This knife holds the blood of everyone I've slaughtered, and now it'll be covered in the blood of the man we all hate," Janco said.

Alex comprehended something bad was coming so he squeezed his eyelids tightly closed and clenched his teeth. The beat of his heart picked up, soon he heard the beats in his inner ear. His hands grew clammy, and he felt an intense and warm oozy feeling against his leg. It had only taken a split second and Janco had slashed the knife across his upper thigh. The pain was instantaneous as Alex moaned in excruciating pain.

Josh began squirming in his seat. He looked away from Alex's leg and stared at Janco, and saw the determination in his eyes; Janco was hell-bent on snuffing out Alex's life.

Josh closed his eyes and began sobbing as he pondered his own fate. He couldn't take any more.

All he thought was if it was his time to go, he wanted it done quickly and as painless as possible. There was no way he was going to sit idly by and watch as his girlfriend's best friend was butchered to death before his eyes.

Janco swung the knife back over his head, ready to finish what he started, and a loud crash radiated from downstairs. Josh slightly opened his eyes, just enough to see what was happening around him. The voice grew stronger, and he heard the thudding of footsteps against the wooden stairs.

Alex opened his eyes at the exact same time to find Janco had disappeared. He gazed towards the window to find it wide open and the chilly gusts of wind penetrating the room.

Shit! He escaped.

Two familiar faces appeared in the room; Carr and Captain Thompson.

"Where is he?" Carr asked.

"He took off out the window," Alex said as he writhed in pain.

Carr reached for his radio while Captain Thompson began cutting Alex loose from the restraints. Once he finished with Alex, he started cutting Josh loose. Thompson looked at Alex with a mix of disappointment and relief.

"What in the hell were you thinking, Jones?" he asked.

"I guess I wasn't."

"You're damn right you weren't. Help is on the way, and we'll get you both fixed up," Thompson said as he yelled for someone to bring up a first aid kit.

"Captain, I'm all right—take care of Josh first, okay."

Thompson obliged and tended to Josh, who was in worse shape than Alex was. Alex took Josh's hand, squeezing it gently as a gesture of reassurance that everything was going to be all right. Josh pressed back and wiped away the tears from his face.

"Thanks for coming to my rescue and putting your life on the line like that," Josh said.

"Anytime."

Four paramedics rushed into the room bringing along two stretchers along with them.

"Take care of him first." Thompson pointed at Josh.

The first group of medics assessed Josh for a few minutes before deciding it was safe to transport him away. The medics lifted him onto the stretcher and hauled him away towards the staircase.

With one victim rescued, the other medics began focusing their attention on Alex. He sat limply and Captain Thompson stepped aside to allow the rescue team to do their job. They covered the deep laceration on his thigh with gauze and a tourniquet. Alex moaned just as Carr poked his head through the door.

"Everything all right in here, Captain?"

"Everything is good; right, guys?" Thompson asked the medics.

"Yup. Just about to get him to the hospital."

Alex objected. "I don't need the hospital. I have to catch this guy."

Captain Thompson knelt beside Alex and turned his head to look at Carr. He shook his head, disapprovingly, as he turned back around and looked at Alex.

"No, what you need is to get stitched up and get better. We'll get this guy, don't worry."

A medic spoke up, "Captain, we're ready to transport him."

"Do it and keep an eye on this one. He tends to run."

They lifted Alex onto the stretcher and moved towards the exit. Just as they wheeled him through the door, Aaron Finch arrived at the scene.

He gasped. "Jesus, Alex, are you all right?"

"I'll be okay; just get me some evidence to put this guy away," Alex said. The stretcher continued moving swiftly towards the staircase.

"I won't let you down," Finch hollered as the rescue team descended the stairs.

They reached the street and loaded Alex into the back of the ambulance. Carr and Thompson stood at the entrance to the abandoned shithole and watched as the vehicle drove away.

"Carr, how in the hell did you let this happen?"

"I couldn't stop him, Captain. He does what he wants, but he's a good cop with good intentions."

"I just can't allow him to continue working this case. He's getting reckless, and that worries me," Thompson said.

"No, keep him as the lead on the case. I promise I'll keep a better eye on him and slow him down. He needs to finish this one for closure."

The captain ran his palms across his face. "I can tell I'm going to regret doing this, but, and this is a huge *but*, if this shit happens again, you're both off the case."

TWENTY-SIX

Bridge Park Drive, Brooklyn
December 27, 2005
3:55 P.M.

ALEX FIDDLED WITH THE BLANKET across his
abdomen and reached for the remote control lying next to him
on the couch. He smoothed out the covering and adjusted his
flannel pajama top.

The doctor had confined Alex to the house, and that didn't
make him very happy. Overly cautious doctors placed him on
medical leave for a week, and he was only halfway through it.
The wait to return to work was driving his anxiety slowly up.
Yet, Alex tried his best to ignore it.

But that urge to get back out on the streets kept itching at
him. The compulsion to catch Max Janco at whatever cost.
When it all came down to it, though, Alex realized it was
pointless to break protocol and that he wouldn't even be any

use if they did catch Janco. He'd more than likely be the weakest link and be the first to die.

He clicked on the channel up button and flipped through the channels. All he did all day was watch a few minutes of a show, flip it to another show, and repeat the same cycle.

He sighed, realizing that things might have turned out far worse, but after they stitched him up at the hospital with twenty-seven stitches.

He dropped the remote, stopping his constant surfing when he landed on his favorite channel: Cartoon Network. What better way to pass the time than by laughing to the same rerun cartoons he had already seen a million times.

He picked up the bag of barbecue potato chips off the floor and stuffed a handful into his mouth. It was closing in on the time for him to take his afternoon painkiller.

He reached for his water, just as a knocking at the front door interrupted him.

Who would be here?

He flung the blanket off and reached for the single crutch leaning against the coffee table. He hobbled to his feet and painfully made his way across the living room to the front door.

He squinted one eye closed and peeked through the hole. It was Aaron Finch. He slowly unlocked the deadbolt and opened the door.

He stood there, looking more handsome than ever in his civilian clothing, holding an evidence bag with a laptop inside.

Alex cleared his throat. "Finch? Everything all right?"

"I came to check on you. Haven't heard much from you the past few days and I wanted to make sure everything was good," the supervisor said.

Alex pointed to his crutch. "If you call this *good*, then, yeah I'm okay."

"So, I was hoping we could talk for a few minutes?" Finch asked.

"Oh, yeah, sorry, where are my manners —come in," Alex said as he stepped clear of the door.

The two made their way inside and sat down on the edge of the couch. Alex threw his blanket to the other end to make more room.

Finch set the unsealed evidence bag on the coffee table, and Alex studied it with intrigue.

"Um—why are you bringing evidence to my house?"

"There's something on here you need to see," Finch replied.

"You're aware that you're breaking protocols, right?"

Finch smiled. "I haven't logged it in as evidence yet, so it's all right."

"Seriously? It's been three days, and you haven't logged it? Where have you been keeping it?" Alex asked.

"I did this for you, so don't get all high and mighty with me," Finch snapped back. "Do you want to see what's on it or not?"

Alex contemplated the severity of what was happening for a second. Never once in his career had he ever broken the rules like this, but in the end, his curiosity about what evidence the laptop held quickly outweighed the consequences. The adrenaline pulsed through his body, and he grinned slightly.

"So, what is so damning that you went rogue and broke the chain of command?" Alex asked.

Finch slipped the gray HP laptop from the bag, flipped open the cover, and powered the device up. It took a few moments, but once everything was ready to go, Finch opened the file directory. The only thing on the entire laptop other than the operating system were nine video clips. Each one labeled with a name.

Alex's facial expression grew more anxious until Finch double-clicked on the video titled "Rutchel." The video started out with a black screen, but quickly the heavy breathing of the videographer could be heard faintly in the background. Finch reached down and made the volume louder.

Thirty seconds had passed by, and the heavy breathing continued, until suddenly, the petite figure of the first victim, Rutchel Cox, came into view.

She strolled along the familiar path that Alex vividly remembered. The camera moved closer and closer as each second of the clip passed by until the assailant was right behind the victim.

Alex watched Rutchel first realize her attacker was near. She screamed as he flashed his knife.

She began running. It was no use though.

The camera dropped to the ground, and Alex scrutinized every move on the video. It was over almost as quickly as it began as the killer walked back and retrieved the camera. He turned it on himself and left one terrifying message.

"And so it begins again. I'm sure you thought after Anja and Dina —oh wait, Heather and Brandy—died, that your father's past died right along with them; but it didn't. Think of me as revenge, version 2.0."

The screen went black, and Alex flopped back against the couch. He sat still, almost shell-shocked, as Finch glanced at him.

"Jones, you all right? You don't look so good," Finch said.

"I'm — um, where do I even begin. Go ahead and start the next video."

"Sure, in a minute. You mind if I get a bottle of water?"

"Yeah, sure, I'd get it for you, but I shouldn't —" Alex began.

"No, you just sit there and take it easy. I think I can manage to find your fridge."

Finch returned after a minute with two bottles of water. He set one bottle in front of Alex and the other in front of himself. He returned to the task at hand and loaded up the next video in the queue. They sat in the same spot for the next forty-five minutes watching each homicide that was committed, up to the latest victim, Elijah. At the end of each video, there was another message for Alex about his father.

The final video clip ended, and Finch closed the video player. He waited, unsure what to do next. He just stared at Alex who seemed dazed. Out of nowhere, Alex snapped to and pointed to the screen.

"Let's get this over with, Finch. Go ahead and play the one labeled 'For Marshall'."

Finch did as he was instructed and the screen went black.

Soon a scrolling message appeared on the screen with a

distorted voice narrating.

Hello, Marshall. I hope you've enjoyed the presentation I put
together for you. Murdering all of those people was certainly
thrilling.
I'm very saddened that I didn't get the opportunity to finish you
off when I had the chance, but you broke the rules and don't think
I'm going to forget that.

You may believe that you have figured out who I am, but you're
wrong. You'll never have enough evidence to ever catch me, let
alone prosecute me. Our organization is too big and good for that
to ever happen.
But I have some good news for you. This can all end peacefully,
and no one else must die. It's simple: bring back what your father
stole from us.
I'm giving you two weeks to pull yourself together, figure out what
I'm talking about. There will be no more murders in this time so
you can focus all your attention on retrieving us what we want.

I'll give further instructions after the two weeks have passed.
Don't screw this one up or you'll be the next one living six feet
under.

The words stopped scrolling, and the video clip ended.

Finch stared at Alex in disbelief.

"Who's Marshall?"

Alex sighed. "Me. I'm Marshall, or I used to be a long time

ago. The stories too long to get into right now, but one day

when we have more time I'll tell you, Aaron—for now, tell me

you've got something — anything on this guy," Alex said.

"I'm not going to sugarcoat it; he's really good. In fact, he's so methodical that we haven't found any a speck of DNA evidence, no fingerprints, nothing," Finch replied.

Alex shook his head harder. His frustration was building by the second now by the lack of proof, and Finch's words, "he's really good," sent Alex flying over the edge. He had reached a point where he couldn't keep his emotions to himself any longer. He suddenly burst out into tears.

"Alex— Hey, hey…you don't need to cry. We're gonna catch this son of a bitch—I can promise you that much." Finch leaned in closer to Alex and wrapped his arms around his shoulders.

Finch, so focused on getting Alex calmed down, didn't hear the creaky front door swing open, or Mike's heavy footsteps as he walked farther into the condo. Mike got to the end of the short hallway, looked around briefly, and stopped dead in his tracks. He clenched his fists as he stared intensely at how Finch was up on his man.

Mike felt the anger flow through his veins. He stepped closer to the unsuspecting duo. As quietly as he moved, however, the floor beneath him creaked and blew his cover. With nothing else to do, he finally spoke up.

"What the hell is going on in here?" he jealously asked.

Finch twisted his head back and sat in silence for what seemed like forever, but was only a few milliseconds.

"Temple, hey—Alex is just a little upset, that's all."

Mike crossed his arms. "Alex, you all right?"

Alex lifted his head and turned his bright red face towards his fiancé. It was clear that something had upset him, and Mike was acutely aware that his boyfriend was in such a fragile state already. He unfolded his arms and moved towards the couch.

"I think it's best you leave."

The crime scene supervisor grimaced. "Can't you see we're working on the case here? I need just a few more minutes, and then I'll be gone."

"I said go — now," Mike demanded in a harsher tone. "Don't make me forcefully remove you from my home."

Finch huffed, reached for the laptop, and closed the lid. As he stood, he slid the evidence back inside the transparent plastic bag. He sealed the bag, turned to look at Alex, who had finally stopped crying, and then back at Mike who stood towering over him.

"Have it your way," Finch said as he blew past Mike, stepping on his foot as he worked his way towards the front door.

The stinging pain of the heavy boot squashing his foot caused Mike to wince. He shook it off, and quickly gave chase to Finch, following closely behind him to make sure he left. Mike stopped halfway down the hallway and watched as the younger man opened the door, flashed an evil grin, and then quickly slammed the door closed behind him.

Mike stood at the door, his arm propped against it, as he leaned in. He closed his eyes, took a deep breath, and exhaled loudly. He stood back upright and walked back down the hallway.

He emerged into the condo and found Alex lying back down on the couch with the blanket draped across his body.

He sat down, the anger still bubbled beneath his skin, but he also couldn't look at Alex's face and stay mad very long. Mike cleared his throat and turned towards Alex.

"I'm not going to get mad," he began. "I promised myself that much. But if something is going on between you and Aaron, do me a favor and just come clean about it before things get deeper."

Alex turned off the television and dropped the remote control on his lap. He knew that he had to come clean about what happened that night at Flux between him and Finch.

He sighed.

Alex finally looked over at Mike, who sat patiently, leaning forward with his chin resting on his hands. His body language said it all; he was uncomfortable and he really wasn't sure that he wanted to hear the nitty-gritty of everything.

Alex cleared his throat and sat straight up to face Mike.

"First thing I have to say is that I love you. The second thing is there isn't anything going on between us. Aaron made a pass at me a few weeks ago when I went to grab a drink with him. He kissed me, I didn't kiss him back, and I ended up storming out of there."

Mike exhaled as if he had been holding his breath the entire time Alex spoke.

"That's all?"

"I'm telling you the truth, I swear," Alex said.

Mike relaxed his posture and leaned back against the backrest of the couch. The two sat there in silence. Mike lifted his fingers to his mouth and began biting, hard, at his typically perfect nails. He took a chunk out of his right index fingernail and spit the shrapnel out onto the floor. He looked over at Alex, who was watching him like a hawk. "I think I need some time to myself to think this over. I'll be out for a walk. I gotta clear my head."

Alex sat speechlessly and nodded gingerly, as he typically did in these situations when they fought. Alex watched as Mike grabbed his black leather gloves and moved towards the hallway which led to the front door. The broad-shouldered man disappeared into the darkened hallway and soon after the front door thumped closed.

Alex tossed the blanket aside and sat upright on the couch. He grabbed for his crutch and stood slowly. He hobbled around in a tight circle around the coffee table. His head was spinning, his eyes scanned the room for something to do to take his mind off the incoming panic attack.

He limped over to a dark wooden buffet where a photo of his parents sat in a gray wooden frame. He lifted the photo in his left hand and balanced his body with the crutch in his right.

He began crying again. How had his life turned out so different from what he always thought it would have been? The tears started flowing faster down his cheeks. He coughed and spoke aloud.

"I miss you guys so much. I'm certain you're watching over me, but right now I need you more than ever to help me get through this insanity. Give me a sign, anything, to help me put an end to this carnage and get back the life I was supposed to have."

He kissed the picture frame and set it back down right in the same exact spot. He looked closer at the photo and noticed the extravagant necklace around his mother's neck. The thought had never even crossed his mind before until that moment.

How could my parents afford something like that?

He turned around and made his way back towards the couch. He had to sit down and try to put things together in his head.

Just as he reached the couch, his cell phone blared. Amy Williams flashed across the screen, and he quickly answered the phone.

"Hey, was wondering when I'd hear from you," Alex said.

"Well I thought I'd give you a few days to recover before I laid this in your lap," she said.

He sighed; his adrenaline now flew into overdrive. "Your ex-boyfriend reached out to you again — didn't he?"

"No, not this time. Can Josh and I swing by the apartment say in thirty minutes?"

"Of course. I'll be in the same spot that I've been for the past three days."

She laughed a little, but at the same time, his sarcasm worried her. She'd known Alex for close to fifteen years, and she also recognized that when he used humor, he was also trying to mask his fear.

"See you in a bit," she said as they ended the call.

Alex tossed the phone lightly back onto the coffee table and leaned his head back against the couch. He closed his eyes and took a few deep breaths.

Half an hour passed by, and a pounding at his front door startled him awake. He was woozy and took a second to look around the room. Outside the large windows in the kitchen, he saw the sun slowly fading behind the skyscrapers, and then it dawned on him that he had fallen asleep.

These painkillers are no joke.

He rushed to his feet and limped to the front door as quickly as his body would allow him. He hollered down the hallway.

"I'm coming, I'm coming — give me a second, I am an injured soul."

He peeked through the viewfinder in the door and standing anxiously at his door were Amy and Josh. He grasped the door handled and swung the door inward.

"Christ, Alex, we've been here for like five minutes," she scolded. "You fell asleep, didn't you?"

"It's these meds they have me on, I can't help it," he said. "Come in, come in and make yourselves comfortable."

The two walked through the doorway, and Alex looked down at a package Amy was clutching close to her body. He didn't bring it up right away; he figured that was the reason for their visit.

The three sat on the couch, and Amy looked around. "Where's Mike? Shouldn't his shift be over yet?"

"We fought, and he stormed off to get some air."

"This is sort of getting old, Alex. Either the two of you need to call it quits, or you need to take the step to make things right," she said as she set the small package on the table.

"I'm working on it. So, Josh, you're looking much better than the last time I saw you," Alex nervously said.

"A little, but I'd be lying if I said everything was fantastic."

"Touché."

The room sat silent for a moment, and Amy reached for the package. "So, this arrived at my apartment door two days ago. However, given your physical and emotional condition, I knew it was best to wait a few days before I brought this to your attention."

She tapped her fingers atop the box and waited.

"Well, don't keep me in suspense, woman. What is it? And you had better not say it's a bomb or something," Alex joked.

Amy squinted and puckered her face. "You can knock off the sarcasm; I can see right through you. I can sense the fear in your crackly voice."

Alex's mood shifted dramatically, and it didn't take long before he returned to his serious manner.

Amy unfolded the flaps of the package and retrieved a DVD from inside. The case was black, with a plain white paper slipped into the plastic coating with "MARSHALL" written in large block lettering across it.

Amy stood up and walked over towards the entertainment center and opened the DVD player. She dropped the DVD into the player and quickly closed the flap. Alex fidgeted with the remote control and flipped the source to AUX. Amy returned to her seat next to Josh. She reached out, and the two interlocked hands as the video queued up.

Images began popping up on the screen of diamond rings, emerald necklaces; if it was high end, it was there. Alex felt a sinking in his gut, and that's the moment that he had the epiphany. Everything he had just realized was growing more irrefutable as the seconds ticked by.

Suddenly, the flashy jewelry disappeared, and a shadowy figure appeared on the screen. Except this time, something about it felt different. Alex had just spent an hour and a half watching videos of Max Janco, listening to his heavy breathing and his voice as he slaughtered each of his victims. However, the man who appeared on the screen was the polar opposite of Max Janco.

A hush fell over the room as the man began speaking.

"I bet you didn't see this one coming. As you can tell by now, I'm not the same person from the earlier videos.

Alex ran his hands up and down his arms. The voice gave him chills. Even though the hooded and masked figure distorted their voice, something about it felt familiar to Alex, but in his drug-induced state, he couldn't quite pin down what about the monotone voice made it feel so recognizable. He returned his focus back to the video.

"This will be the final video you will receive from us, and it's also the last clue that we will give you about what we want. Now, close your eyes, think back to the last time you saw your mother — picture her clothes, what was she wearing?

Alex closed his eyes as the masked man instructed him. He imagined his mother on the final day he saw her. She stood in the kitchen as he and Amy sat across from her on a set of barstools. Alex recalled that he had his arms folded across his chest, and Amy flung her arms out across the marble counter. The image in his mind evoked the voices as he and Amy took turns begging her to let them stay home from school that day.

Her outfit on that precise day was poignant.

He heard the voice continue talking on the screen, but he decided to ignore it for just a second as he took a deep breath and held it in for a moment. The action triggered a memory of a sweet-smelling perfume, and he grinned sweetly as Amy and Josh watched in disbelief.

The memory of his mother would always be etched in his mind, and there was nothing or nobody that could ever take that away from him. He remembered it was a pristine white Chanel blouse, a black skirt which ended just shy of her kneecaps, and the one thing that stood out in his mind was she was wearing her favorite pearl necklace, which dangled loosely across the front of her shirt.

He kept his eyes closed as the silence grew more ominous. Finally, the voice spoke again.

"Let's just say, it's not money we're looking for, but we are looking for where the money went. We know you're smart and you'll be able to figure this out. Instructions will follow on where to return the goods to us, and once you do, I promise you that this nightmare will finally, and you can get back to your normal life; if you can call your life routine."

The screen went black, and the room became overly quiet. Alex opened his eyes and looked over at his friends, who were in a state of shock at what they had just seen. He pressed the rewind button and paused it on the outline of the man. He muted the TV and pressed play. Wasn't any need to go through the same speech twice.

Josh broke the silence. "Amy—remember beginning to tell me a story about how you and Alex almost died together in Colorado?"

"Yeah," she replied.

"You never did finish the story…would any of what's going on be a part of this story, that, I don't know, you could have possibly shared with me weeks ago?"

Amy bowed her head in embarrassment. Josh was right, they never did warn him about any of this. Maybe if she had, he would have been more guarded, more attentive to his surroundings, and the kidnapping and torture he endured would have never happened.

"I'm sorry for not telling you."

Josh's usual quiet personality quickly changed as he raised his voice. "You mind telling me now what the fuck is going on around here lately?"

Alex paused the video and nodded at Amy.

"We really should tell him the entire story, from the beginning—maybe he can offer us some insight that the both of us are overlooking," Alex began, "but I have a question before we spend the next hour getting him up to speed. Do you think my mother wore a lot of expensive jewelry when we were younger?"

Amy cocked her head to the side and took a few minutes to seriously think back over the years. She finally had it.

"Alex, your mother was well-known around town for being showy. So, yes, she was always wearing expensive jewelry. But then again, it was Ridgewood Hills, everyone was like that— why would either of us think that was abnormal?"

"Suppose you're right."

Alex turned off the TV, and just as he did, the front door swung open and in came Mike. He barged in and didn't even notice the three of them on the couch.

He pulled his gloves, jackets, and black beanie cap from his head and chucked them onto the dining room table. He looked up and jumped back a few inches. He wasn't expecting to find them all there glaring at him.

"Everything all right?" he asked.

"Depends on your definition of *all right*," Amy said.

She stood and rushed up to Mike to give him a hug.

"Perfect timing, you're back just in time to fill Josh in on what happened to all of us back in Colorado," Alex said.

Mike heaved a deep breath and swallowed hard. "You sure you're ready to hear all of this?" Mike asked Josh.

"I'm not sure, but if you think I should know, then bring me up to speed."

"All right, before I start, do you guys need anything? Beer? Wine? Maybe even a shot of something? Because to be honest, I know *I* need something strong, as shit is about to get deep," Mike said.

They put in their requests, and Mike took a few minutes gathering things in the kitchen. Alex looked over at Amy. No words exchanged between the two, but just by looking at Alex's eyes, she knew the future conversation was one Alex really wish he didn't have to re-experience.

Mike returned with two beers, a glass of red wine for Amy, and bottled water for Alex. He passed out the drinks and sat down between Amy and Alex on the couch.

"Sit back and get comfortable," Mike said.

He began telling the story of that horrific night. He didn't want to leave any stone unturned when filling Josh in on exactly what happened during those three days of pure hell.

TWENTY-SEVEN

Bridge Park Drive, Brooklyn
December 31, 2005
4:30 A.M.

ALEX SAT STRAIGHT UP IN BED, gasping for air. The past few days, ever since he had to relive that terrifying snowy night in the Rocky Mountains, his nightmares were growing more disturbing, so real. It was as if he were truly in that fantasy world his broken mind had created.

He sat there on the bed, his back propped up against the upholstered headboard, and took several deep breaths to try and regain control. He reached across the bed sheets for anything to bring him a sense of comfort and felt the outline of a familiar body lying next to him.

His breathing slowed to an average pace, and he flung the sheets away and soundlessly slipped out of bed. He didn't want to disturb Mike, who was sleeping so peacefully.

Alex had given up using the crutches the previous day, but his limp was still noticeable as he tiptoed across the floor, eventually reaching the bedroom door. He cracked it open just enough to squeeze his thin body through. After a second of struggling, he stood outside the bedroom. He peeked back in and watched as Mike rolled his arm across the empty, warm spot in the bed. He smiled and chuckled at the same time at the sheer cuteness of what he had just witnessed. He closed the door and felt his way towards the bathroom.

He found the door frame of the bathroom and emerged inside the dimly lit room. He shut the door partially, and flipped on the small overhead light.

He wanted to sneak a glimpse of what years of fighting his emotional demons were turning him into. All he wanted was some cold, hard proof that his life, as everyone around him reminded him always, had become an emotional train wreck. The thing was, Alex couldn't snap out of the somber mood. It was never his intention to be a passenger on this careening train for this long. He thought about it all the time: how could he derail this out-of-control train and finally board another train with some direction?

He rubbed his eyes, trying to adjust to the light which illuminated the room, then stared into the mirror, and what he saw there forced him to jump back, banging loudly against the wall.

He gasped, covering his mouth with his left hand as he slid against the wall towards the exit. Just as he made his way back into the living room, an arm gripped his forearm. His immediate instinct was to fight. He swung around, ready to start whaling, but to his relief, it was just Mike.

"Alex, what's wrong?"

Alex couldn't even speak, all he could do was point towards the bathroom with his index finger. Mike freed his grip on Alex's forearm and moved catlike in the direction Alex pointed.

Once he reached the door, he slid his arm inside to flip the light switch on, and he ventured inside. His head moved side to side as he searched the room, but just as quickly as he began, he stopped and slowly backed out of the bathroom back towards Alex.

"Get dressed; I'm calling Carr," Mike said.

Alex nodded and finally unfroze from the paralyzed position he had been in. He stammered towards the bedroom, flipping up every light switch he came across along his journey on the way to the closet. The find he made, in his own home even, hit a nerve, but the one good thing about it was that it snapped him out of the self-pity party he had felt for the last week.

He quickly pulled out a black suit, French blue shirt, and striped tie, and flung it onto the bed. He immediately began dressing, deciding that perhaps he could go just one day without a shower. The very thought of returning to that room made his stomach churn.

He finished buttoning the final button on his dress shirt and slipped his jacket on. He plopped on the edge of the bed, reaching for his black dress shoes which he kept just slightly hidden underneath the bed. Just as he finished tying the final bow on his shoe, in walked Mike with a concerned look on his face.

"Finally reached Carr and he's on his way."

Alex finally spoke up. "Was he pissed? I mean it is almost five in the morning, and we both know his old ass doesn't roll out of bed until at least seven."

"He's more concerned about our safety than being upset, Alex. What are we going to do now?" Mike asked.

"Let's look around and see if anything is missing. Doubtful since it appears all they wanted to do was leave me a message, but still good to check," Alex replied.

"I really wish you'd listen to me about recusing yourself from this case."

"I'm not going to do that, Mike."

Mike tossed his hands in the air. "I know you're not, I just don't understand why."

"The reason why is clear. We're going to fight and put an end to this chapter of our lives," Alex said, "I think I know what they're looking for, but they'll never retrieve any of it."

Mike looked puzzled as he sat down next to Alex on the bed.

"What are you talking about?"

"I spent some time last night after Amy and Josh left, and you had retired to bed, sifting through my mother's tax and bank records. I added everything up, and guess what; the numbers don't make any sense," Alex said as he stole a quick gasp of air. "It appears that my father did do what they said. He took their money, and used my mother to cover up the unexpected windfall."

Mike's eye twitched as he tried hard to take in what he just heard. "Are you sure?"

"I'm more than sure, I'm absolutely certain."

"So, let's just give everything back to them and get back to planning our wedding," Mike said.

"Absolutely not. That stuff doesn't belong to me, but it doesn't belong to them either. It's illegal merchandise bought with drug money. The people it really belongs to is the FBI," Alex said as he stood up and began pacing around the bedroom. "I will not and cannot negotiate with these terrorists."

Seeing his lover in the beginning stages of a panic attack, Mike stood up and approached Alex to try to calm his anxiety. He wrapped his muscular arms around him and rocked him back and forth. Alex quit resisting the embrace as he began weeping.

Alex had shed more tears in the past two months than he had in the previous two years. And it wasn't from being sad, it was all the built-up guilt, anger, and frustration that had finally reached its tipping point. Now he had to add into the mix the disappointment of finding out that the perfect life he thought he had was nothing more than lies and greed.

Mike loosened his hold on Alex and pulled away slightly so he could look him in the eyes.

"We'll get through this together, I always promised you that."

Alex sniffled and wiped the warm tears from his face. "If I could go back in time and fix any of this, I would have done it a long time ago, before you and I ever met. We should not have to live our lives this way," Alex said, and Mike nodded.

"You were a kid when all of this happened. There was nothing you could have done to prevent any of this," Mike said. "You hold onto so much anger because you want to keep blaming yourself for this when the blame falls solely on your father, not you."

Twenty minutes passed by and the conversation between the two faded out. A loud knock at the front door caused Alex to jump in his skin as Mike walked out of the bedroom casually to answer the knock.

A minute later, Mike and Carr appeared in the doorway. The two men towered over Alex as he had returned to sitting on the bed.

"Jones, are you all right?"

"I'm okay, just a little shaken up."

"You want to show me what dragged my ass out of bed so early?" Carr asked, and Mike pointed towards the bathroom.

The two turned away from the bedroom and walked towards the door. Carr entered and did just as Mike had earlier, and once his eyes fixed on the item in question, he turned his head back towards Mike, who stood just outside the door.

"Did they —" he said, a stutter in his voice.

Mike nodded.

"But how? Why now?" Carr asked.

Mike just shrugged. He didn't have a valid answer to his question.

Carr stared at the mirror and read aloud the phrase scribbled across it.

Do we have your attention yet?

Beneath the posed question was a poorly drawn image of a skull and bones. Carr pulled out his phone and called Dispatch.

He relayed the address to the dispatcher and hung up the phone.

"They'll be here shortly," Carr said. "Welcome back to work, Jones."

"Yeah, some welcome back gift."

It took a while for the police to arrive, and a few minutes later, in walked Finch carrying his toolbox of goodies. The three looked at each other, dumbfounded. Why was Finch there?

Carr approached him. "They call you in on this?"

"Got the dispatch, something about a burglary. I thought the address looked familiar."

"Well, get to it then," Carr said, "and Finch, this is a priority right now. Start in the bathroom."

Finch nodded and worked his way towards the other side of the condo, carrying his toolbox and SLR camera with him.

Carr returned to stand with Alex and Mike who weren't quite sure exactly what to do now.

"Jones, you know it's all right if you want to take another day," he said. "Don't feel like you need to rush back to the office so quickly."

Alex pondered the generous offer. "Thank, but no thanks — I'm going in today. You think I'm going to sit in this house alone all day after some maniac broke in here while we slept? You've lost your mind."

Carr nodded, Alex had a great point. Would it even be safe for him to be alone at this point? The answer that instantly came to mind was no.

"Are you sure?" Carr politely asked.

"Yes. Once Finch finishes up in there, we're heading to the office. I'm taking this guy down."

"I'm not going to argue with you; learned a long time ago that it's no use," Carr joked. "I'll bring you up to speed once we get to the office."

Finch peeked his head out from the bathroom and hollered out. "Guys, I'm almost done collecting the evidence I need. Just gonna dust for some prints around the door and we can get out of here."

Alex sighed in relief. He knew Finch had to collect the evidence, but at the same time, he was raring to go.

TWENTY-EIGHT

78th Precinct, Brooklyn
December 31, 2005
6:48 A.M.

THE ATMOSPHERE AROUND THE PRECINCT was one of happiness as everyone was gearing up for one of the most famous nights in the city — New Year's Eve. As Alex and Carr breezed through the squad room doors, that buzz was infectious. Well, to everyone except Alex.

His life was rapidly changing, and he wished his state of mind would allow him to join in with the festive mood, but life kept beating him down, and his tired body just couldn't handle much more. And now, some psychopath had broken into his home, the home he shared with the love of his life, and threatened him again — how was he ever going to recover his life back when every chance he had for a peaceful life continuously didn't go as he planned?

He pulled out the same rickety desk chair, gazed around his messy desk, and frowned at the overwhelming clutter he left scattered about before his life almost ended. He sat down, the chair squeaking as he arranged his body to a more comfortable position. He picked up a stack of papers and tried hard to arrange his chaotic creativity into something a bit more structured.

Carr grabbed a cup of coffee from the machine and worked his way back to his desk. He set the mug down and watched Alex rearranging the clutter on his desk.

Carr smiled. "Glad to see you're getting that mess cleaned up. Captain has been bitching about it the entire time you were gone."

Alex looked up. "Really?"

"Yeah — really," Carr replied.

"Shocked he even noticed."

"Jones, I'd watch your attitude. Captain has a hard-on for removing you as lead from this case. If it were me in this position, I'd be as sweet and apologetic as you can be if you have any hope of staying involved."

"He and I have talked about this before; he's not going to remove me. Captain and I, well, we understand each other," Alex said, "but then again, I'd still be okay with it if he assigned you as the lead. Maybe I could actually get some rest for a change."

Carr shook his head and frowned. "Just cool it with the negativity for a day, please."

The conversation died out, and Alex returned his attention to his desktop. The workspace remained serene for ten minutes, but then it all changed as Carr heard a ding from an incoming e-mail.

"Hey, come here — you have to see the information I got back from the crime lab about the videos," Carr said.

Alex moved quicker than he had in the past week and rounded the corner of the desks. He stopped just a few inches shy of Carr's chair and leaned in, his face as close to the computer screen as possible.

"What am I looking at?" Alex asked.

"It's the report that the cyber guys sent over. They reviewed the metadata from those videos that Finch found on the laptop. They're legit," Carr said.

"I didn't have any doubt that they weren't real; what else did they find?" Alex asked.

"Well, says here they were shot with a JVC GY-HD-100 Camcorder," Carr read from the screen.

"Wow, they figured that out?"

"Guess so."

"Hey, wait, I recently saw something about this camcorder; that's a high-end camera. It retails for over five thousand dollars — I could never afford that."

Carr huffed, "Shit, even if we pooled our salaries together we still couldn't afford it. Focus, Jones, let's get back to the report."

"Right."

Carr searched deeper into the twenty-six-page report. Finally, he reached the information about the final video labeled "For Marshall." It was different than the earlier videos.

"This is interesting," Carr pointed at the screen.

Alex scanned the details and stood. "That information doesn't match the others."

"Odd — says it was filmed somewhere called Beelitz, Germany."

Alex rushed back around to his desk and pulled his keyboard closer to the edge. He plopped in his seat, pulled up MapQuest, and typed in the name of the town.

The connection was slow but after a minute the screen filled with a map of northern Germany. A red pin marked the spot, and Alex zoomed out to get a broader idea of exactly how this added information fit into the overall big picture.

"Finding anything?" Carr asked from across the desk.

"It's a tiny town just to the southwest of Berlin," Alex said, "I have no idea what it means."

Carr cocked his head to the side and rubbed his chin. "It means something; what exactly, I don't know either. I have more news, and you're gonna love this one."

Alex stood and walked back over to Carr's desk. The final item on the report was the most damning evidence they had received so far.

Latent Evidence:

Upon an internal inspection

of the HP Compaq nx9600

components, Tech Angela Brown found a lone fingerprint on the internal 40GB hard drive. An IAFIS national database search returned a match to a Maximillian Vladimirovich Janco. The last known address for Mr. Janco is 409 Kingston Avenue, Apartment 4A, Brooklyn, New York.

Alex stepped back, and his mouth gaped open in sheer amazement. This was the exact connection he was looking for to finally take Max Janco down for the last time.

"We need to get a warrant, get a team together, and go break in his door," Alex said as he went to grab his jacket.

"No can do," Carr replied.

"What? Why not?"

"Where do I even start? First off, are you one hundred percent sure he even still lives there? Second, you know damn well that's not how warrants work," Carr rattled off. "I'll make you a deal; in a little while you and me, we'll head over there and check things out. Maybe talk to a few neighbors—sound good?"

Alex frowned but accepted the fact that his partner was right. Just because it was a last known address didn't mean he still lived there. Alex dropped down in his chair, his face displaying a grin. On the other hand, that high he was experiencing quickly disappeared as his captain entered the squad room.

"Jones, in my office, now," Captain Thompson barked as he turned his back and walked away.

Alex sighed and stood and began making his way towards the door. He turned and looked back at Carr, who had hung his head.

This can't be good news.

Alex unhurriedly walked up the stairs to the third floor, and when he reached the top step, he paused and looked around.

In his entire time at the 78th Precinct, this was only his fourth time on this floor. The floor was eerily quiet and devoid of any action. He looked at his watch; 7:20 in the morning.

No wonder it's dead up here.

He began walking again down the narrow corridor, finally arriving at the door to his captain's office. A sliver of light leaked through the crack in the door as Alex lightly tapped his knuckles against the wooden door.

"Enter."

Alex pushed the door slightly, and the heavy door eased open. He stood there as his captain signed a form and dropped his pen on the desk.

"Ah, Jones, take a seat," he said as he adjusted himself in his extravagant chair. "Oh, and please close the door behind you."

Alex pushed the door closed and moved towards a set of chairs which sat angled towards the desk. He eased into the chair and sat up straight as his captain just looked at him. No words, just blank stares at one another. All the while, Alex stayed calm and kept a vacant stare on his face.

Finally, Captain Thompson cleared his throat. "Jones, I've asked you here to discuss a situation. A situation which has been growing increasingly out of control as the weeks have passed by. I hate doing this to you, but I'm removing you as the lead detective on the slasher case and putting your partner in charge from this moment forward."

Alex continued sitting very still in the chair. His facial expression never once changed. He knew in the back of his mind that this day would eventually catch up with him, and who could blame his captain from removing him. His behavior actually was getting more unpredictable. He knew deep down that his superior had his best interest at heart.

Alex stood up and extended his hand. "Captain, I completely understand. I do have a question though."

Relieved, Thompson asked, "What's that?"

"While I'm no longer the lead on this, you're not kicking me off the case completely — are you?"

"No, because let's face it, you know more about these shady characters than any of us do. However, I can't have a loose cannon leading an investigation. You do understand this, right?"

"I completely understand, and I promise, we're gonna get these guys," Alex replied as he half smiled.

Thompson walked around the desk and shook Alex's hand again. The two had a good relationship overall. Alex knew his wife, kids, had even been to a barbecue at his house just a few months before. Thompson taking him off as the lead wasn't even unwelcome news. He looked forward to allowing Carr to get some exposure and hopefully bring something significant to the investigation.

Alex exited the office and descended the stairs back to the squad room. He walked in just as Carr was taking a sip of coffee from his mug. The steam was billowing around his face.

Alex sat back down in his chair and shuffled some papers around on his desk.

"So? What did he want you for?"

"Oh, well, you know —" Alex said.

"I know what?"

"So, yeah, he gave you lead on the case," Alex blurted out.

"See, what did I tell you. You're still on the case with me though, yeah?"

"Yeah, that's one bright spot," Alex replied. "So let's go back to the beginning and cover what we know. It's the only way to move forward."

Carr nodded and stood. He walked towards the whiteboard that Alex had begun weeks earlier, but somewhere amidst the chaos of his life, forgot about.

Carr picked up the dry erase marker and started writing facts they knew about the case.

Underneath "Suspects" Carr drew a thick black line through *Boris Topol.* "Well, we can eliminate him."

He also drew a line through *Myles Johnson.*

"I think it's pretty clear we're not looking at him anymore as M.J.," Alex said.

"Right."

The only name lingering on the board was *Max Janco.*

Carr quickly switched from the suspects column to the evidence one, which sat empty. He wrote down the following; *Janco fingerprint on hard drive found at 38 Adelphi Street, Brooklyn, New York,* and several other items of interest.

"Let's go get that warrant."

Alex nodded as the two walked towards their desks and grabbed their jackets.

After spending an hour pleading with a judge and finally obtaining the search warrant for Janco's apartment, the two men returned to their vehicle and headed towards Crown Heights.

The drive over was one of anticipation for Alex. What would they learn? Would they discover some damning evidence against Janco? These questions rolled around inside his mind as the car raced down Eastern Parkway. Alex watched as the building whizzed by. The weather was being cooperative for a change, and just seeing the beams of the sun shining down on the city was enough to warm Alex's heart, but only just a little.

The car came to a shuddering stop just outside the midsized apartment building. Alex sat behind the steering wheel and gazed at his surroundings. He remembered back to his days as a beat cop, walking these streets every night. There was always a sense of uneasiness that bubbled beneath his skin. That feeling went away after he changed precincts, but now being back in the same area, that same bubbling feeling returned.

"I hate this neighborhood," he said to Carr.

"Yeah, this is the side of Brooklyn people like to forget about," Carr replied, "and for a good reason."

The two sat in the car, watching people come and go from the building. But after an hour of watching, there was no sign of Max Janco, and that was making Alex's anxiety levels rise increasingly.

"What time is it?" Carr asked.

"Eleven forty-two, why?" asked Alex.

"I say we go in and knock on some doors. You down with that?"

"I'm down with anything that will get me out of this car."

The two detectives stood out among the residents of the neighborhood, probably because no matter how hard Alex tried to look ordinary, the more he acted like a cop. And in this area of Brooklyn, cops were nobody's friend. And Carr, being a veteran detective, didn't give a rat's ass how he looked.

They arrived at the front door, and Alex reached out to open it. Locked.

"Just start hitting buzzers, someone will let us in," Carr said.

Alex ran his fingers across every bell until he heard the buzzing sound of the door lock disengaging.

Alex tugged at the door, it swung open with ease. The two worked their way into the foyer of the apartment building, which had a pungent smell of urine and body odor. Alex coughed and covered his face with the scarf wrapped around his neck.

"Man, this place is nasty," Alex whispered.

Carr shushed him and grabbed hold of the handrail to ascend the stairs. Carr stepped forward, one footstep at a time, and with each one he took he was met with more creaking beneath his feet. He tried to shift his body weight around, but it was no use — the antique wood of the stairs was unforgiving and only grew louder the farther up he walked.

They kept their pace moving up the stairs. The ear-piercing sounds of babies crying, people arguing, and doors slamming spontaneously reverberated through the paper-thin walls.

Carr was in the lead position, and Alex trailed back slightly to keep a lookout from behind. They finally arrived at the fourth floor and looked around. Four doors; two on the right and two on the left. Carr stepped up to apartment 4D and lightly knocked on the door.

The door cracked open and all Alex could make out was one eyeball peeking through the crack.

Carr flashed his badge. "Ma'am, I'm with the NYPD, I would like to ask you some questions." The door slammed closed, and Alex could hear the occupant removing the chain from the door.

The door swung open and standing before them stood a frail older woman. Alex studied her appearance and assumed she was of Eastern European descent.

"My name is Detective Tim Carr and this my partner, Alexander Jones. May I ask your name?"

The woman stood hunched over; her face said it all: confusion. *"Mówię trochę po angielsku."*

Carr looked at Alex, and he stepped forward. "What is she saying, Jones?"

"It's Polish. I know a little, so basically what I hear is that she only speaks a little bit of English."

"How in the hell do you know Polish?"

"I worked this neighborhood for two years; you pick up a thing or two," Alex replied as the woman just stared at them.

Carr shrugged. "Have a go at it."

"Czy znasz Max Janco?" Alex asked.

She nodded her head and looked frightened.

"I assume you asked her if she knew Janco, yeah?" Carr asked.

"See, even someone like you can learn Polish," Alex joked as he reached out his hand to comfort the woman.

"Kiedy ostatnio widziałeś go?" asked Alex.

"Dwa dni temu, Myślę, że nadal jest w środku," she said as she backed into her apartment.

"You're scaring this poor woman, Jones. What are you asking her?"

"I asked her if she knew Janco and if she had seen him recently. She got scared when she said she saw him two days ago and believes him to still be inside the apartment."

Carr looked behind him at the wooden, four-pane door for apartment 4A. He broke away from Alex and stepped across the hallway.

Alex noticed his partner slipping away, and he quickly ended his conversation with the older lady. *"Dziękuję za Twój czas,"* Alex said, expressing his appreciation for her time.

The woman's facial expression didn't change as she closed her apartment. It thumped shut, and she began fortifying her apartment door by locking every one of her six deadbolts and reaffixing the chain on the door.

Alex stepped up beside Carr, who had his ear pressed against the wall. "What are you doing?"

"Do you hear that? It sounds like someone is in trouble inside," Carr replied.

"Wh—?"

Alex barely got the question out of his mouth as Carr was knocking the door in. The door crashed against the wall, making a loud bang as it hit. Carr reached for his Glock and flattened his body up against the outer wall. He reached out his arm and pushed Alex backward.

"You've lost your mind," Alex said, "A simple knock and announce would have sufficed."

"Shh. You do things your way, I do things different. Sue me."

The room was vacant, there was no sign of Janco inside. Carr kept his gun front and center as he stepped into the run-down studio apartment. Alex felt uneasy about what they were doing but followed along with his partner. Besides, he wasn't the lead on the case anymore, and if shit hit the fan, it wasn't going to fall solely on his shoulders.

Alex entered and looked around the room. The nine-foot walls were covered from top to bottom with photos and newspaper clippings that camouflaged the peeling white paint underneath them. In the southwest corner was a makeshift command center, which included a desktop computer, printer, camcorder, and various other peripherals.

Alex walked closer to the blatantly plastered collage. The closer he got, the more he felt his heart skipping beats. He recognized the faces of the fallen victims, but he also realized that Janco had been following him and Mike for months preceding the first homicide.

He felt tempted to touch the array of photos, but he quickly restrained himself before he contaminated any of the evidence. Instead, he reached into his jacket pocket and pulled out his blackberry. He touched the camera icon and began snapping photos of everything on the walls.

"Jones, check this out," Carr said. Alex stopped snapping photos and walked over towards the computer.

Alex studied the monitor, and the webcam attached to the top. A red light blinked on and off in a predictable manner. Alex jumped back.

"He's watching us," Alex replied.

"Are you serious? What do we do?"

"Cover it with something — anything you can find," Alex demanded as he returned his attention to photographing the evidence.

Carr removed a latex glove from his pocket and covered up the lens. "That better?"

Alex looked over, "Yeah, that'll work for now — but we need to hurry and get CSU here to begin collecting all of this evidence."

Carr reached into his jacket pocket and pulled out his cell. He dialed the dispatcher and informed them of the situation.

"That's right, I need CSU, preferably Aaron Finch if he's on shift today. Oh, and for the love of God, for once, please be sure you send someone competent enough to handle digital evidence," he said.

Alex stood only a few feet away, chuckling to himself at his partner's new level of stress and humor.

Alex finished taking as many photos as he could and then returned his focus to the computer. He reached into his pocket and slipped a pair of blue latex gloves onto his hands. All ready to go, he shook the mouse, and the computer monitor sprang to life.

The computer sat there unlocked, which gave Alex free rein to investigate the device as he saw fit. He moved the mouse around and clicked on the menu button. But just as he clicked it, instead of the menu opening, a word-processing program opened instead, and Alex watched as letters began scrolling across the screen.

I see you finally found me. If I were you, I'd be more worried about getting everyone out of the building instead of collecting another shred of evidence from my studio.

You have one minute…. starting…NOW.

Alex watched as the screen went from NOW to black, and the word-processing program soon became a countdown timer flashing on the screen. It started at 1:00, then 0:59, and so on. Alex grabbed his partner and ran out into the hallway.

"You, pull the fire alarm and I'll knock on as many doors as I can," Alex demanded.

Carr located the fire alarm and pulled down on the bar. Alex knocked on every door on the fourth floor and raced down the stairs, skipping two or three steps as he flew down. This continued until he made his way back to the foyer of the building.

He looked at his watch—about fifteen seconds before whatever was going to occur. He made it to the sidewalk and turned around and nervously waited for his partner to exit the building.

A second later a stream of people rushed from the doomed building and the last person to exit was Carr. Alex waved his arms to grab his attention. Carr noticed and hauled ass towards the sidewalk. He and Alex raced around to the driver's side of the cruiser and shielded themselves.

The one minute mark passed and Alex slowly peeked his head up and looked through the side window towards the building. Everything was calm, but being overzealous and worried, Alex crouched back down and stayed in his shielded position.

"Looks like it's possibly another false alarm," Alex said just as a loud blast rattled the ground.

He reached his arms up, quickly covering his head as glass and debris rained down from the sky and pelted them.

Carr looked at Alex. "You were saying?"

"Whoa, that was a lot bigger than I was expecting," Alex said.

"Yeah, ya think?" Carr sarcastically replied.

Alex stood slowly and dusted off the dirt and debris from his jacket. He turned around to find the building completely in flames. He looked around, noticing three bodies lying motionless a few feet from where the entrance used to be.

Alex rushed to see what he could do. He could hear the onslaught of sirens wailing in the distance.

He arrived at the first body. He knelt beside the younger woman and extended his hand to check for a pulse, but sadly, there was no sign of life left in the innocent victim who found herself caught in the crosshairs of Max Janco.

He searched through the thick black smoke billowing from the building for partner. He made out his outline crouched beside another body which lay motionless. Alex motioned to grab his attention and waved for him to come closer.

"Anybody alive?" Alex asked.

"Those two are gone, you?"

"Same."

"Where are the rescue units?" Carr asked.

"I hear them," Alex said. "You all right though? Are you injured?"

Carr patted his body. "I'm okay — you?"

"I'm all right, a little shaken up, but that'll pass."

Alex stepped away from the smoky scene and moved to an area a little quieter. He pulled his phone out and dialed up Mike.

The phone rang once. "Alex, where are you? I just got word there was an explosion in Crown Heights."

"I'm all right, Mike. Whatever you're doing, put it on hold and meet me in the 400 block of Kingston."

Mike didn't even hesitate. "I'm on my way — stay put."

TWENTY-NINE

78th Precinct, Brooklyn
January 5, 2005
10:05 A.M.

ALEX SAT IN HIS FAVORITE SEAT, tapping his pen on his keyboard. His body was beginning to wear down from the lack of sleep. In the past five nights, he totaled about nine hours of sleep, which was far less than he needed.

It was prime time in the homicide unit, and Alex looked around the half-empty squad room. Most detectives were still on leave for the holidays, and Carr, well the captain and borough commander had swooped him away for an emergency meeting upstairs. With everyone gone and no distractions, this was the best time for Alex to get some soul searching done — alone.

Alex could hear a pin drop through the silence, until he heard the trudging sound of footsteps coming up the staircase.

He dropped his pen and turned around in his chair. He was ready to welcome whoever was paying the 78th a visit that day.

The footsteps grew louder, and a familiar face strolled through the door — Myles Johnson.

"Oh, thank God you're here," Myles exclaimed.

"Hey, what brings you by?"

"I'm here to pass on a message to you," he began, "your friend, M.J., came by and paid me a visit this morning."

Alex pulled a chair out for his visitor to sit in and calm himself down. "Here, please, take a seat." He pointed towards the chair at the end of his desk. "You need anything? Some coffee? Tea?"

"I have to make this quick," Myles blurted out.

"Okay, you gotta get back to work or something?"

"He'll kill me and everyone I know if I stay here too long. He's watching me, you know," Myles said as he nervously scanned the room.

"Who'll kill you?"

"M.J."

"I'm not going to let him hurt you. What's this important message he needs you to pass on to me?" Alex asked.

Myles handed over a quad-folded note to Alex, who unfolded the paper and read the short handwritten sentence aloud.

"Don't try to find me, I'll find you when the time is right. Be sure you have what we want readily available, otherwise, you'll meet your maker."

Alex looked at the young man, kept his silence for a few moments by biting his lip. He finally spoke. "So you're telling me that Max Janco gave you this note, yes?"

Myles nodded. "But I can't help you anymore. He said if I cooperate with you I'll be his next victim. And sorry to say, I have a future ahead of me to think of."

Alex tried to reassure him that he was safe and that the department could offer him a safe place to go. However, Alex's words were not enough to compel the barista to budge.

He stood. "Sorry, Detective Jones, this is all I was told to do and then I was to get out of here. So, good luck."

Myles scooted the chair away from himself and bolted for the door. At the same time, Mike was entering the room and ran smack dab into Myles.

"Whoa, kiddo — slow down just a little," Mike said.

Myles pushed him away and ran down the stairs.

"Who the hell was that?" Mike asked.

"Just another person Janco has bullied into doing his dirty work for him," Alex said. "So, what brings you to this part of town?"

"I haven't seen much of you since the first."

"I've had a lot going on. We're so close to catching Janco, I can just feel it. I need to find him, and then you and I will have all the time in the world together," Alex said.

"Not my point. Do you remember when I said I couldn't spend my life without you?"

"Yeah, you tell me that all the time."

"The other day, when you called me after the explosion, I thought that was it. I thought Carr was calling to tell me that he had your phone because you were dead."

"But I'm not. It'll take a lot more than someone like Max Janco to end my life," Alex tried to reassure his future husband.

Mike sat in the chair Myles had just vacated. He reached out his hands and grabbed hold of Alex's. Alex stopped for a moment and for the first time, in a long time, could see the pain and sorrow in the eyes of his best friend. If a picture could speak a thousand words, well, just the look on Mike's face told two thousand.

"You're too close to this case and I really think you should consider stepping away for a while. How are you going to catch this man when you can't even see straight?" Mike said. "How about you speak with Thompson and have him put another detective on to finish the case out."

Mike grabbed Alex's hands tighter and watched as Alex gave the proposal more thought than he ever had before.

Before Alex had a chance to reply, he could hear Carr, over ringing telephones and the echo of carrying voices in the squad room, coming full speed down the stairs. Alex gazed in his direction, and the expression on his face looked happy.

Mike released his grip on Alex's hands and adjusted his posture in the chair.

"Must have been a good meeting, huh," Alex said.

Carr stepped closer to the desks.

"Captain and the commander finally took your advice and have elevated our psycho to public enemy number one," Carr said.

"Oh, shit; at least now we know this will end very soon. You don't stay in that elevated status very long in New York," Mike said.

Alex sat there shaking his head. "I really wish they had listened when I suggested this about a month ago. Might have saved some innocent lives."

Mike and Carr stood by in an awkward silence.

"You need to get out and get some air, buddy," Carr instructed.

"Yeah, let's go grab lunch at our favorite place," Mike insisted.

Alex smiled and reached for his jacket. The two hadn't spent much time together, and it would do him a world of good to get out of the station for a while and just focus on the two of them.

"I'll be back in a little while," Alex said to Carr.

"Enjoy."

The two walked out of the precinct and into the blustery cold. The walk to Franny's was typically quick, no more than eight minutes away, but with the whipping wind it was more like six.

They small talked and laughed as they rushed along the crowded street. The minutes passed by with ease and finally, for the first time in months, Alex was slowly beginning to feel tranquility penetrate his icy soul.

At the front door to the restaurant Mike held the door open for Alex.

"Let's see if our usual table is open," Alex said.

Alex dashed to claim *their* table, removed his jacket and tossed it into the window booth. Mike slid into the bench seating and smiled.

A familiar face popped over to the table and greeted them ecstatically.

"It's so good to see you guys again," Allison said.

"Hey, you too."

"Yeah, it's been a while, hasn't it," Alex said.

"You guys having the usual?" she asked.

The two looked at each other and smiled. "Yes."

She smiled back and walked to the server station to input the order into the POS system.

Alex cleared his throat. "So, I think you're right. I am going to back off a little more from this case and give my partner some breathing room to take care of the heavy lifting."

Mike's eyes lit up with happiness. "I'm so glad to hear that — I really am."

"Well, I think I've neglected our relationship long enough, and if I let that happen, then all that means is that I've let them win once again."

"I won't give up on you, Alex. But we also have some serious underlying issues that we just can't ignore any longer."

"You're right, you're absolutely right. We're going to retrieve our lives. I promise," Alex said.

"So, now that we have that in the open, I was thinking that maybe you and I could start going to therapy. I believe that it'll help you out and I know I could sure use a neutral source to help us get through this rough patch."

Allison returned to the table at that moment carrying a hot tea, water with lemon, and an Americano.

"All right, fellas, have you decided on what you'll be having for lunch?"

The two gave their orders and watched once again as the young server disappeared. The quickly returned to their conversation.

"So, what about this — I'll swing by the precinct at 5:30 tonight, we'll go have an amazing dinner somewhere nice; just the two of us," Mike said. "How does that sound?"

"Yeah, I think I like the sound of that."

"Perfect. I've missed you these past few months and I just really want us to get back on track. All I want is things to be the way they were before any of this craziness began."

"Me too."

The food finally arrived after a short fifteen-minute wait, and Alex plastered a smile on his face. The two were in no rush to leave, trying their best to stretch the time together out longer.

Finally finishing, Mike motioned for Allison to drop off the check, and before Alex could even grab for it, Mike already handed his card to her.

They wiggled themselves out of the booth, grabbed their jackets, and bundled up better than they had when they walked there.

Alex took the lead, stepping out of the entrance first out onto the busy street. The sunbeams had dimmed as the sun now blocked by thick clouds that had moved in from the west.

Alex looked up into the sky. His mood had improved tremendously from just spending an hour with Mike, and he now felt a renewed faith in his relationship, but more importantly, he had a gut feeling that his battle with his arch-nemesis, Janco, would soon be ending.

Alex looked at Mike, who was now looking towards the sky also.

"Looks like snow is moving in."

Mike turned his view away from the sky and back towards Alex. "You know, I really loathe winter."

"How can you hate winter? We lived in Colorado for most of our lives. Winter is like our thing," Alex replied.

"Yeah, the funny thing is, the older I get, the more I just hate snow and feeling cold all the time."

Alex just shook his head and chuckled to himself. Mike was right, and Alex felt the exact same way.

"Then perhaps it's time for us to consider a new adventure in our lives then," Alex replied.

"Oh? You're getting tired of living in New York?" Mike asked. "Wasn't this like your dream, to come to a place where no one knew you, a place where you could reinvent yourself?"

"I came, I conquered — maybe soon we can just sell the condo and go someplace warm and start anew," Alex said.

"Something to definitely think about, but for now, let's just focus on the here and now and not get carried away with our flights of fancy," said Mike.

"You're probably right."

They rounded the corner of Sixth and Flatbush, and Mike stood there, looking sexier than ever in his black uniform as he said his goodbye to Alex. The two were never much for public affection, but at this moment, Alex reached out his hand and brushed it against Mike's.

"I'll see you at 5:30; don't be late," Alex said.

"I'd never be late when I have someone like you to meet up with."

Alex smiled and watched Mike walk along Sixth Avenue towards the Bergen Street Station, where Mike would likely catch the number four train back to the Utica Avenue Station. Soon Mike disappeared into a sea of people who crowded the street.

He exhaled joyously as he felt a change in his heart. He couldn't explain it, but to Alex, it seemed like he was somehow going through a revolution in his life. And everything somehow was feeling better by the minute, mainly from knowing that he had a goal now — a goal to regain his life and get back on track. He hoped to soon put the dreadfulness of his past behind him, once and for all.

He ventured back into the precinct and walked back up the stairs where he found his partner sitting at his desk sifting through a stack of case files.

"Whatcha doing?"

"I feel like we're missing something somewhere," replied Carr.

"I think we've combed through all of the evidence and if there were some hidden clues, we would have found them by now."

"You're probably right. How was lunch?"

"Good — I think we had a very productive conversation and things can only go up from here," Alex said.

"Good to hear, man. Nothing worse than having relationship issues and at the same time trying to catch some maniac," Carr joked.

"Yeah, we're going to find him — the question is, when?"

"Give it a few days, we'll get him off the street, and we can move onto the next case."

Alex's smile turned into a frown at the very thought of having to go to another case. The only thing he ever wanted to do was help people who couldn't help themselves, but at no point did he ever consider the emotional distress that it would have on him.

"Yeah, onto the next case."

A few hours passed by and even with the two of them double-checking the evidence, they were no closer to figuring out where Janco could be hiding out.

Alex closed the manila folder and tossed it onto his desk. He rubbed his eyes and looked across his desk at his partner, who still had his face buried in a file. Alex began drumming his fingers against his desk.

The distracting noise obliged Carr to look up.

"Everything all right, Jones?"

"Yeah, I'm good, but I think I'm gonna go grab some fresh air. Be back in like five."

Carr acknowledged Alex's request and refocused his attention back to the case file for Juliette Cochran.

Alex walked out the door to the sidewalk and stepped to the side and leaned against the railing. He looked at his watch and realized it was closing in on four in the afternoon.

Where had the day gone?

He looked up at the sky, which was now full of dark black snow clouds. Nightfall was coming in the next hour, and all Alex could think about was spending a lovely quiet evening with Mike.

He studied the strangers as they passed by along the sidewalk and he half smiled as he turned around and walked back inside.

THIRTY

78th Precinct, Brooklyn
January 5, 2006
5:30 P.M.

ALEX LOOKED AT HIS COMPUTER and noticed the time. His day was over, and he knew that Mike would be arriving shortly. He quickly straightened up his desk and tossed a few files into his desk drawer. He grabbed his key, locked the drawer, and stood up.

Another workday passed and still no sign of Janco on their radar. Six days had passed since they raided Max Janco's apartment and almost lost their lives in the process. Public enemy number one was proving to be even more elusive than anyone had ever thought. Two of the sharpest minds at the 78th Precinct were no closer to finding him. Alex's intuition told him that they'd eventually catch him—but what would the cost be? Another innocent life?

Alex looked towards the whiteboard situated near their desks. He pondered upon the different faces of the eight victims, all of them staring back at him; some were smiling in their photos, others were not. Alex felt a heavy burden to not let their deaths be in vain. He couldn't let them down, but at the same time, at this point he was weary and hungry, and all he wanted to do was have a nice meal with Mike and then sleep for an entire day. While Alex thought of himself as superhuman, not even he could function on five hours of sleep in three days.

He rubbed his face. His eyelids felt heavy. He needed food, coffee, and then sleep. He walked towards the coffeemaker for a refill before he left for the evening. A fresh pot had just finished brewing, and he poured the hot liquid to the brim. He worked his way back to his desk, grabbed his jacket and satchel, and quickly turned around.

We'll get him tomorrow, I guess.

A loud, booming voice snuck up behind him. "Where do you think you're going?"

Alex twirled around, visibly shaken. "Carr—Jesus Christ! I got to go. I'm hungry, and Mike is probably outside waiting for me. Oh, and depending on how much sleep I get tonight, I might not come in tomorrow. I'm completely drained, and I think the best thing for me would be to take a mental health day."

"Completely understand. I'm just messing with you anyhow — you seriously look like shit, Jones. So get out of here and let me get back to work. See you when I see you."

"Thanks, Carr. I'll see you soon."

He sluggishly descended the stairs. Reaching the first-floor foyer, he flung open the heavy wooden doors. The scenery that awaited him outside was vastly different than it had been only an hour and a half earlier. It was blustery and depressing as large white snowflakes fell from the sky at an astonishing pace. The fresh coat of snow did have one thing going for it; it was covering up the grunginess of the city.

His cell phone rang out of nowhere. Figuring it was Carr messing with him, he answered without checking the caller ID. "Jones here."

"You look lost," Mike said.

"How would you know?"

"Turn around."

The phone line went dead, and Alex scanned the area for his fiancé. He turned to face the precinct, and there he stood, propped up against the side of the building. Mike leaned forward, removing the side of his body from the structure as Alex advanced towards him. He had the biggest smile on his face as Alex embraced him and squeezed as tight as he could.

"You ready to go have a nice meal?" Alex asked. Mike nodded.

The two hustled along Sixth Avenue; the Bergen Street subway station was just around the corner. Alex was torn between getting a satisfying meal and getting some rest. And he still had that nagging feeling that he should stay and help Carr find Max Janco as quickly as he could.

The past two days he felt deflated and out of touch, but he knew that spending some quality time with Mike would help erase that mood. And his mood had nothing to do with the fact that he never slept, or because dealing with the Smirnov family had brought back so many painful memories. No, it was the fact that so many terrible heartbreaks had occurred in the past two months.

The couple turned the corner onto Bergen Avenue just as the last bit of sunlight illuminated the sky.

The snow continued coming down significantly, and the cold was penetrating through his wool jacket, chilling him to his core. He pulled the loose end of his scarf across his nose and mouth with hopes of blocking out as much of the cold as he could.

It was no use, the stinging from the wind was causing his eyes to swell with tears. He and Mike stopped, Alex braced himself up against a building. He quickly lifted his glove-covered hands across his face and wiped the tears away from the ducts.

"Everything okay?" Mike asked.

"All good, just this wind is stinging my eyes," said Alex.

He rubbed them a few seconds, just enough to regain his sight. He looked around the vicinity, and across the street, a familiar face stood out amongst the crowd; a face he saw every night in his nightmares—it was Max Janco. The same man the entire NYPD were hunting for was now standing no more than fifty feet away. The deflated feeling quickly dissipated and Alex poked Mike, never taking his stare off the suspect.

"You've got to be kidding me. Mike, look who we've got here," Alex whispered as he pointed in Janco's direction.

"I'll be damned. Got to hand it to that SOB, he's pretty cocky to be out for a wintertime stroll when all of New York City is looking for him," Mike said.

Alex pulled his cell from his pocket and dialed Carr. The phone rang twice.

"What'd you forget?"

"Nothing, look Janco is a few blocks away from the precinct. Mike and I are tailing him," said Alex.

"Can you stay on the phone?"

"Yeah," Alex said.

Alex continued studying Janco like a hawk scoping out its prey. The suspect turned his head suddenly, noticing Alex and Mike watching him. He flashed them a shit eating grin and took off running along the slippery sidewalk.

Mike and Alex followed suit, rushing as quickly as they could to catch up with him.

"Carr, he's on the run. We're passing the Berman Street subway station now. I gotta go, I'll call once we get him cornered."

"Jones, no. Stay on the ph—"

The line went silent.

Janco hung a right onto Dean Street followed by a left onto Sixth Avenue. The perp continued checking behind him every chance he got, and when he realized the duo were gaining on him, he picked up his pace.

We're going to end this right here—right now.

It didn't matter to Alex if he ran faster or not because Max Janco wouldn't be hard to miss. The young Russian towered over everyone in the area. Not to mention that he was wearing his trademark black skull-and-bones hoodie with the Russian lettering basically advertising his organizations name beneath. Alex and Mike turned right onto Pacific Street, and suddenly Janco darted through a cut in the fence to an abandoned factory. It was clear that Janco knew this area well, and Alex began to wonder if he and Mike were wandering into a trap. Alex slowed his pace while Mike continued sprinting.

"You all right?" Mike hollered back.

"I'm good, just my leg is hurting a little — you go ahead, and I'll catch up with you," Alex said as Mike ran away.

Alex tipped forward, taking a small number of seconds to catch his breath. He reached into his pocket and dialed Carr.

The phone rang twice. "Where are you?" Carr asked.

"He's in an abandoned factory off of Pacific Street. Send units," Alex said and didn't wait for a reply.

He hung up the phone and dropped it back into his pocket. The pain in his leg was gone as the adrenaline now kicked in harder, and Alex finally restarted the chase. Mike was already far ahead of him, ascending the sole rickety fire escape that Janco had only climbed only a few seconds earlier.

Alex picked up his pace, running as fast as he could towards the ladder. Mike was street smart, and Alex knew he could hold his own, but he also knew that Janco was a conniving bastard and he felt a little on edge letting Mike take the lead on this one.

For all Alex knew Mike's irritation would explode, and he'd
wind up being the ninth victim in all this chaos.

He reached the ladder to the fire escape but soon discovered
it suspended six feet off the ground. He sighed, knowing that
the only way up would force him to leap, grab ahold of the
bottom slat, which was coated in snow and ice, and use his
upper body strength to hoist himself up.

*How did Mike get up there? If he can do it, I can do it. I know I can
do this.*

Alex squatted down, closing his eyes he vaulted upward
swiftly, his right hand barely grasping the slippery metal ladder.
He hung above the ground for a few seconds, doing his best to
shift his weight around and get a better grip before he fell off.
After some finagling, he eventually pulled himself up.

The weather conditions were making the pursuit less than
textbook, but Alex couldn't give up now. Not when he was so
close to taking Max Janco down, and nothing except an act of
God would disrupt that plan.

He climbed and climbed, finally reaching the third-floor
landing. He rested there for a minute, fumbling inside his jacket
and removing his service weapon. He pulled back the slide,
prepared for anything that awaited him at the top.

A hush had fallen around him, but it quickly ended as Mike
hollered out, "Get off me."

He hurried up the final two flights of stairs, eventually
reaching the top. Not sure what scenario would be waiting for

him, he peeked his head slowly above the roofline. It wasn't what he had wanted to see when he got there.

Janco was standing with Mike at the edge of the roof, his right muscular arm wrapped around his lover's neck, and a semi-automatic weapon in his left hand aimed at the side of Mike's face.

Janco shouted from the rooftop, "No need to be coy; come out where I can see you."

Alex cautiously staggered onto the unstable tar-papered roof and quickly trained his weapon on the two men.

"Max Janco, put the gun down and release the hostage," Alex said.

Janco stayed emotionally unmoved and remained motionless, ignoring all orders that Alex shouted out. Mike's calmness persisted, and Alex could see he was trying his best not to agitate Janco in any way. Even through his calm and cool façade, Alex sensed the fear exuberating from Mike's eyes. It didn't matter how much training Alex had in the academy, nothing would have ever prepared him for this type of situation.

Through the blinding snow, Alex strained to figure out if he'd have to shoot, and if he did, how he could avoid killing Mike in the process.

Minutes passed by in silence as Alex and Janco's eyes locked but now the snow was getting heavier. It became clear to Alex that firing his weapon was out of the question now and that he'd need to resort to other options to defuse the situation.

Janco lifted his head disquietingly. His distrusting green eyes pierced through the blinding snow. He gripped his weapon tighter in his hand as he crept closer and closer to Alex.

"Don't take another step! Put the gun down and let's talk about this," Alex repeated in his authoritarian voice.

"You'll never take me alive."

"We can work this out. Don't do anything stupid, Janco," Alex demanded as he set down his weapon on the roof. "See, I put my gun down. No one has to die here today."

Alex could make out the distinctive sound of footsteps thudding against the tar rooftop behind him. He turned his head sharply but stopped when he heard the sound of a gun cocking. Just then a familiar voice spoke.

"Hello, Jones."

Finch.

Alex lifted his hands slowly and turned his head around; his instinct was right. There stood Aaron Finch waving a gun around in the air. Alex's mouth sank with shock.

"I bet you never saw this one coming, huh?"

"You're working with Janco?" Alex asked.

"Hey, that's what family's for."

"So, you've been in on this the entire time?" asked Alex.

"Yup, and you never even figured that out. What kind of forensic psychologist are you?"

"What about that night at Flux, did it even mean anything to you or was that entire scene just a ruse?" Alex asked.

"Well, I'll admit you're sexy a hell, you have that much going for you at least," Finch laughed, "but your life is even more of a train wreck than mine or Max's."

Finch pointed his 9mm against the side of Alex's head and wrapped his arm around his neck.

Finch inched his nose closer to Alex's neck and took a big whiff. "You smell like fear, the same scent I remember that morning I showed up at your condo to investigate the scene after I broke in and left you that message."

"That was you? So, that's why you knew to show up when you did," he said as he tried to pull himself away. "No one from Dispatch even called you in, did they?"

"You're so smart, Marshall."

"It doesn't make any sense. How'd you get into my house?" Alex asked. "Carr told me there was no forced entry."

"Easy. Remember those waters I grabbed? Well, I swapped out your house key with a proxy while you sat on the couch in the other room all doped up on those painkillers."

Alex thought back to that day. Everything about it was still a little hazy, but a few seconds later he realized the critical error he made by giving Finch full rein of his house.

"You son of a bitch," Alex said as he wriggled.

"Ha, you better calm yourself before you get hurt," Finch said, tightening his grip around Alex's neck.

Alex felt tingles creep quickly up his spine as Finch grabbed Alex's weapon and kicked it away.

Janco stood across the roof with a pleased look on his face. He quickly changed the subject. "Did you put the pieces of my puzzle together yet, or do you need a few more clues?"

"I've seen the tapes that this asshole conveniently provided me. What more do I *need* to know?" Alex asked.

"There's a lot you don't know, Marshall. Quick question though, how badly you miss your father?"

Alex's eyes blazed with anger. "Do not bring my dad into this."

"But why? It's because of your father that we're all here," Janco said. "But had you combed my apartment better before I blew it up, you'd know what I'm talking about."

Alex stood motionless, Finch gripped him closer, pressing the gun harder against his head. "You know, I really hate these games you're playing with me, Janco. Why don't you do us both a favor and just say what you mean, straight out—no more games."

"I have a message for you from Roulette: 'the truth shall set you free,' and now I must set myself free."

Alex's squinted his penetrating blue eyes. "Who's Roulette?"

Janco laughed. "The boss. These are things you should know, Marshall. I mean you certainly looked at all the key players in the organization if you made it this far."

"Stop calling me that, my name is Alex. Alex Jones. Now, just put the gun down, let Mike go, and let's discuss this rationally, okay?" Alex asked.

"Never," Janco said. "You obviously didn't bring what you were supposed to, so now we're all going to die."

He unzipped his black hoodie, exposing a bomb attached to his chest.

Alex squirmed as Finch continued holding him tightly; the vivid LED display revealed two minutes, the red numbers were clear as day through the blinding snowstorm.

Where is Carr with the backup?

"Why are you doing this? I've told you, I told your gang's other cronies years ago—I don't know what you want from me," Alex shouted.

"You're not as smart as you like to think you are," Janco began. "Your father stole money from us—about a half million dollars' worth to be exact."

Finch chimed in, "And your money whore of a mother took all that money and spent it on lavish gifts for herself. Last chance to tell me where it is and then we'll let you and lover boy get back to you boring lives."

"I don't know anything about jewelry... My father never would have taken anything from you. My parents had money because my mother was a doctor," Alex replied. "Your family wants revenge because my father busted them. Everything you've done has been a waste of time. And do you know why? Because I don't have anything that belongs to you or any member of your family."

"Well, suit yourself. You ready for some fireworks, cousin?" Janco pulled a dead man's switch from his pocket.

"Ready as I'll ever be," Finch said as he flashed his creepy smile.

"Hold up—why are you going to take us all out? Isn't it just me you want?" Alex asked.

"I've murdered quite a few people and killed a couple in my apartment building. Do you think the police are just going to let me walk away from this?" Janco asked.

"I won't let any harm come to you, I promise."

"Aaron, you believe this guy? You wanna die too, right cousin?"

"I've got nothing to lose now—a crime scene supervisor going to jail. Not going to happen. Do it," Finch said.

Janco pressed the button to activate the bomb and threw the switch off the side of the building. Alex watched as it fell from the sky and the counter on the bomb began counting backward—1:59, 1:58—and he stood there — paralyzed with fear.

It took a few milliseconds for Alex to fully comprehend what just happened, but it was too late as the bomb was now active. He couldn't just give up and die without a fight. Something distracted Finch, and it was exactly the opportunity Alex was looking for. He grabbed his assailant's right arm, pulling it sharply backward. He bent it back with such force, a loud, cracking sound of the bone breaking echoed in his ear.

Injured and writhing in pain, Finch loosened his grip on Alex. He broke free and retrieved his gun from the ground. It was now or never, and Alex rolled onto his back, aimed the gun at Finch and fired three shots. Each bullet striking him in the chest. Finch dropped his weapon and fell to his knees. Finch grasped at his wounds as he fell over onto his side, his head hitting the rooftop. All Alex could do was focus on the traitor's face as the life drained from it.

Two shots rang out through the still air. One bullet struck Alex in the shoulder and the other missed. Alex returned to his feet, aiming the gun back at Janco. The adrenaline was kicking in full force now, and Alex took a giant step forward. The blood was streaming down his arm and he looked again at the numbers on the bomb; 1:01. Time was running out, and it was now or never for him to make his move.

He continued advancing towards Janco who began moving to his right, his grip on Mike's neck unrelenting. All Alex had to do was pull the trigger, but there was no way to avoid striking Mike in the process.

Janco pointed his weapon. "What, you going to shoot me? We're all going to die up here whether you like it or not."

"You may have come here on a suicide mission, but I have far too much to live for," Alex said as he aimed and fired a shot.

The bullet expelled from the barrel of the gun, a bright flash from the exploding gunpowder ejected. The projectile sped across the rooftop, barely missing Mike and striking Janco in his upper right arm. He flinched from the impact and loosened his grip enough on Mike for him to break free.

Mike ran across the rooftop faster than Alex had ever seen him move before. Janco got his bearings and raised the weapon in his left hand and shot off several rounds, a bullet striking Mike in the thigh. Mike fell to the ground in agony, and Alex looked over towards Janco.

Alex rushed to Mike's side as he looked towards the display on the bomb; 0:14. Time was running out. Alex grabbed his fiancé's jacket collar and pulled his muscular body across the roof with what energy he had left in him.

"Shoot him," Mike cried out.

"I'll get him but I need you to work with me. I know you're in pain, but he's going to blow us up."

Alex popped off two more rounds, the bullets striking Janco in the left shoulder and the abdomen. He fell to his knees and landed face first on the snowy rooftop.

The plan of blowing him off the side of the roof failed miserably, and Alex knew it was only a matter of seconds before the bomb exploded. He pulled Mike towards the ladder, trying to put as much distance between them and the imminent explosion. But time ran out, and the bomb detonated, sending shrapnel, fire, and bodies flying in every direction.

The explosion was powerful enough that it blew a significant hole in the roof of the abandoned building. Alex and Mike toppled through the hole and came to rest two floors below, on the third floor.

The two rested several yards apart, both unconscious as smoke and a smoldering fire thrived through the dry-rotted wood of the building. The smoke was becoming thick and black, and the visibility was slowly shrinking closer to zero.

Alex gradually came to, coughing out the black soot that had built up in his lungs. He could taste the blood in his mouth as he turned his head and spit it out. He strained to move. His legs were numb, and his right arm was pinned beneath a beam that had fallen during the blast.

Through the thick smoke, he could see his lover lying close by. His body was motionless except Alex noticed his shallow breathing.

He's alive.

He managed to move his left arm—his least dominant one—and began patting around the pockets of his jacket in a search for his cell phone.

Where is that damn thing?

The fire was slowly growing in strength, and Alex knew he had to get help as quickly as possible. Otherwise, they would both be burned alive. Alex knew the only person that could save them was his partner.

What seemed like an eternity only took a few seconds, and once Alex could get the phone out of his pocket, he purposely dropped it on his chest.

He was in desperate need of fresh air, but every time he inhaled all he took in was the toxic smoke swirling around him. Each breath was becoming more and more overwhelming. He fumbled with the phone and searched through his contact list for Carr's number. He pressed send and put the call on speakerphone. He laid the phone back on his chest, and after two rings a familiar voice answered.

"Jones?" Carr asked with a concerned tone in his voice.

Alex tried to speak, but no words would come out. All he could do was moan loudly.

"Alex, what's wrong? Are you in trouble? That explosion, you're there, aren't you?" he asked.

"Mmm-hmm," Alex hummed.

"I'm a block away; hang tight," Carr frantically said as he hung up.

The screen went blank, and he dropped the cell phone next to him. He tried to remain as composed as he could. He reached down, feeling for his scarf, which was miraculously still tied around his neck. He yanked it up and pressed the soft cloth against his face. He mustered up as much strength as he could to loosen the hold the beam had on his arm. Success. He began slowly scooting across the floor on his back towards Mike. If he was going to die, he was going to die next to his best friend.

Mike, who only lay fifteen feet away from Alex, was critically injured. Given his proximity to the blast, it was unbelievable that he was even still alive. Those few feet felt like a mile to Alex as he fought across the ramshackle floor. In the distance, the sounds of emergency vehicles approaching grew louder.

After several minutes of crawling, Alex finally reached Mike's side. He reached out his hand slowly, touching the side of Mike's neck for a pulse. In a split second, he lost consciousness again.

THIRTY-ONE

Lutheran Medical Center
55th Street, Brooklyn
January 6, 2006
8:57 A.M.

ALEX SLOWLY AWOKE TO THE SOUND of a door latching closed. A stinging pain shot down his arm, and his mouth was dry from a lack of fluids. Alex blinked his eyes several times, not sure if this was one of his typical nightmares or if this was happening in real-life. After repeating it five or six times, he accepted that he wasn't dreaming. He looked around his surroundings. The IV tube taped to his forearm, the nodes from the EKG machine stuck all over his body, and a blood pressure meter attached to his left index finger.

The exploration of his new environment was interrupted by a soft knocking on the door. He turned his head towards the noise. The distraction gave his body just enough time to forget about the confusion that was floating through his mind. He tried speaking, but the words wouldn't come out. There was another knock, this time a little louder. He wanted to get up and answer the door, but his legs were still numb, and he thought to himself—*I better just stay right here.*

The door creaked open, and two familiar faces poked their heads through the crack. It was Carr and Captain Thompson. Alex lifted his hand and motioned for them to come inside.

They entered the dimly lit hospital room. Captain Thompson carrying a laptop sealed in an evidence bag while Carr was holding a small dry erase board in his left hand and a black dry-erase marker in his right. Alex tried to sit up on the bed but his older partner stopped him.

"No, you lay there and relax. We need you to get better," Carr started, "so for once, I'm calling the shots on this one, pal."

Alex lay back as Carr pulled up a chair and sat down next to him.

"Doctor says you can't speak yet, but I hope that you can write. Do you think you can do that?" Carr asked.

Alex nodded and reached out his shaky hand, taking the black dry-erase marker Carr held out. Carr nestled the board on Alex's stomach.

"I'll try to ask you yes or no questions, and if it gets to be too much just write stop," he said, and Alex nodded in agreement.

Carr sat there with him, asking him basic questions such as how he was feeling, and he even filled Alex in on everything that the doctors had told him so far.

"Well, as you are aware, the blast messed you up, my friend. They say you have a broken arm, a dislocated ankle, lots of lacerations, and you even suffered a nasty concussion and that's on top of the bullethole in your left shoulder," Carr said.

Alex frowned, he already knew he was in bad shape, but there was only one thing on his mind. He took a few seconds and wrote a familiar name on the dry-erase board.

Mike?

Carr shuddered. He wasn't sure how to proceed in answering that question, so he did his best to change the subject. But even in his frail state, Alex was still coherent enough to realize what was happening; and he wasn't having any of it.

Alex grew frustrated. Mostly because he couldn't speak and his partner was now evading his request. He banged the marker against the board, like a small stubborn child demanding an answer.

Captain Thompson stepped in. "Alex, I've got good new and bad news," Thompson said. "Which one do you want first?"

Alex drew a B on the board as he looked into the beady eyes of the captain. No matter what the situation was, Alex always wanted the bad news first. In his mind, it was the most beneficial way to get the shock over with and always ended things on a good note. But even for an optimist like himself, he knew there couldn't be any good news to arise from this situation.

"Well, the bad news is, things aren't looking promising for Mike. He's still in a coma, and the docs aren't sure if he'll ever wake up from it," Thompson explained. "And I guess you can figure out where I was heading with the positive news."

Alex rolled his head away from the two. He didn't want either of them to see him cry. The full aftermath seemed all too surreal now. The Smirnov family had won; he'd let them take everyone who ever meant anything to him. They snuffed their lives out like an old worn-out candle whose wick had reached the end.

Carr stayed seated next to him. He gave Alex space to cope with all that had happened. But there was also even bigger news that Carr needed to share. He cleared his throat, and Alex turned his head back to face him.

"So, there's just one more thing. And this is big," Carr said as he reached down for the plastic evidence bag.

Carr slid the laptop from inside and placed it on the side of the hospital bed. Alex looked onward, not clear as to what his partner was doing.

"We confiscated this during our search of Janco's apartment last week. The computer crimes unit found something of high value to you on here." Carr clicked on a video file. "Now before I press play, I need you to take a deep breath."

Alex closed his eyes and inhaled. He held his breath in for at least ten seconds, and he exhaled slowly. Alex opened his eyes and nodded.

Carr grinned as he pressed the play button and a grainy video started. It came more into focus, and there was an older, salt-and-pepper-haired man tied to a chair. Alex watched as a Smith and Wesson 9mm came into focus, which butted up against the side of the man's head. A current issue of the Berliner Morgenpost newspaper blatantly placed for the viewer of the video to see that the video was current. Alex reached for the whiteboard and wrote down a sentence.

Where did you get this?

"It was emailed directly to me. Got it just this morning," the captain replied. "This is the first we are watching because the email explicitly said to view it with you."

Alex looked dismayed.

"Alex, do you know who this man is?" Carr asked as he paused the video.

Alex inhaled deeply and nodded slowly.

Carr frowned and tapped his large finger against the laptop mouse; the video began playing again. Alex watched as the masked kidnapper ripped away the silver duct tape from the hostage's lips. The older man winced in pain, uttering out more than a few swear words before collecting himself. The silver-haired man spoke.

"Hello, Marshall. It's been a long time since I saw you last and I want you to know that I think about you every day. By now you've probably figured out I'm not dead. After the trial, there was a bounty put on my head, and the bureau staged my death. I fled the United States and headed for Germany to escape the Smirnov family. I was safe until last week when it all finally caught up with me."

Carr pressed pause again.

"Jones, is this your father?" Thompson asked.

Alex wiped the board clean and wrote in large block letters. *YES*.

Carr and Thompson turned their heads, staring at each other in disbelief.

"I think we can take a break for a while. What do you say, Jones? You ready for a break?" Carr inquired.

Alex ignored him. Instead, he reached out and pressed the play button again on the video.

An unfamiliar voice boomed from off camera.

"Tell him what we want."

Mr. Stahl nodded. "I'm getting there. Marshall, they want you here. If you fail to obey these orders, they'll kill me. Now, it's up to you if you want to save me."

The camera panned away from his father and focused onto the man with the deep voice. The camera was out of focus, and Alex watched as it shook back and forth violently. Suddenly, the man came into view. He was dressed in all black with a matching ski mask covering his face.

Alex pressed pause on the video again, he wanted to study the man. The first thing he noticed was a stunning pair of bright blue eyes. Alex felt shivers crawl up his spine as the eyes pierced through his soul. The second thing he saw was a full mouth of jagged teeth, clenched together. The man spoke.

"Don't mess this one up, Marshall. We're surprised that you actually survived the blast, so we'll give you three weeks to get here. Your father's life is depending on you. There will be further instructions to follow in a few days."

The screen went black, and Alex snorted back the mucus that filled his sinuses. A lone tear tumbled down his cheek. So many emotions were stirring around inside his head, and frustration was right at the top of the list.

He couldn't talk, let alone walk. How was he supposed to show up in Germany to save his father? And what about Mike? How could he leave Mike when he was in such a sad state?

Carr removed the computer from Alex's lap and closed the cover.

"Jones, we need to get ahold of INTERPOL and have them work this case. There is no way in hell that I'm letting you leave the country," Carr said.

"Alex, you need to listen to your partner. You're in no shape to try to save your father, as much as I know you want to," Thompson chimed in.

Alex lifted the whiteboard and began scribbling.

I'm going, and I'll do this alone.

Carr and Thompson looked at each other, shaking their heads. Carr knew that it didn't matter how much pleading he tried to do with Alex; the detective would do what he wanted, regardless.

"We'll let you get some rest. And Jones, do nothing crazy like try to leave the hospital," Carr said.

"Yeah, and if you need anything, just shoot me a text message, and I'll be here right away," Thompson replied as he patted Alex's shoulder.

Alex half smiled as the two men began moving towards the door.

"And Alex, one more thing that I'm sure has been racking your brain," Thompson said.

Alex perked up.

"The first two victims had no ties to you or anyone you knew. We found a detailed confession on that laptop from Max Janco. It all started when the first two victims turned Janco down for a date."

"Yeah, he was definitely a sicko," Carr said.

Alex nodded.

The two walked out of the room and closed the door behind them. Alex took a deep sigh, pressed the button for another hit of morphine, and closed his eyes and waited for the medication to kick in.

Not even two minutes later, another knock at the door disturbed his drug-induced state. He opened his heavy eyes and standing in the doorway was Amy.

Alex smiled and motioned with his decent arm for her to come in closer. She moved closer to the bed. Her panicked facial expression spoke more than any words she could express.

Amy stood at his bedside, grasping her shawl close to her chest. Tears filled her eyes as she reached across the bed and grabbed his hand. She sat down in a chair close to his bedside.

Amy stared at him for a few seconds. She had to think of what to say. It came to her as she cleared her throat. "Alex, you look a mess."

Alex grinned and nodded as he attempted to sit up.

Amy stood up, squeezing his hand. "No, you lay back and rest. I had to solemnly swear on my life not to aggravate you in any way just to come visit you."

Alex pressed his back against the pillows, and his tense body relaxed.

Amy spoke about someone close to the both of them.

"I got a call last night from John," she began. "Did you know he joined the Army and moved overseas?"

Alex wrote on the board.

No.

"Well, they stationed him in Germany, just outside of Frankfurt for the next three years. He's doing so good, though."

Alex nodded and smiled the best he could through the pain. And it hit him. It was like all of his cylinders were running on full power.

John. That's my ticket to putting an end to this once and for all.

Alex hadn't seen John since the summer of 1998 when he left for college, joined the army, and moved as far away from Colorado as he could. Alex was mostly to blame for the falling out, but how could he face his former best-friend after everything that happened?

Alex gripped the black marker again and scribbled.

Call him up, I need his help.

Amy reached for her phone and dialed the number and put the call on speaker. She glanced at her watch, it was almost ten in the morning in New York, which meant it was close to three in the afternoon in Germany. Amy knew John better than anyone and suspected he was already back in the barracks and on some crazy YouTube binge. The phone rang twice, and a familiar voice echoed through the room.

"Hey — everything all right? We talked only last night," John answered.

"I'm here with Alex, he wanted me to call you. You're on the speaker by the way, but Alex can't speak, so I'll be doing the speaking for him, all right?"

"Yeah, it's all good. Hey, Alex," John began. "Wait, why can't he speak? Does he have laryngitis or something?"

"It's a bit more complicated than that."

"Then what is it? Why are you so secretive, Amy?" John asked.

Amy looked at Alex as she covered the mouthpiece with her hand. They didn't even need to speak, and Alex nodded.

"Alex has been —— he's in the hospital. Remember those guys from years ago, the same ones that shot you and kidnapped Alex and me? Well, they're back, and this time they tried to kill him and Mike with a bomb."

"What? A bomb. Are you serious?" John asked.

"I don't joke about things like this. I've grown up a lot since I last saw you," she said. "I called at the request of Alex because he needs your help with something."

"Yeah, anything."

"Stand by, he's writing down what he wants me to say," she replied.

Amy made some small talk with John while Alex wrote down what he wanted her to relay to him. A few minutes went by and eventually Alex had written down almost an entire paragraph.

"All right, you ready for this, John?" she asked.

"Fire away."

"Okay, it says: *John, I need your help. The Smirnov family has my father held captive somewhere outside Berlin. I am coming to rescue him when I get better. Are you in? Can you help me?*"

The line sat silent for a few seconds, and soon John's voice echoed across the line.

"Of course, what do you need me to do?"

For the next ten minutes, Alex wrote down his request and Amy delivered the messages to John. By the end of the conversation, poor Amy was caught in the midst of a devious, well-orchestrated plan. A plan that involved murder, mayhem, and from everything she garnered, was downright scary.

Nonetheless, she kept her feelings to herself. She understood Alex's need to regain the one thing he lost in his life, but she also feared for his safety at the same time.

THIRTY-TWO

John F. Kennedy Airport
March 4, 2006
6:45 P.M.

ALEX SAT CLOSE TO THE WINDOW waiting at the departure
gate in Terminal 4 for his overnight flight to Berlin. His body
had healed up well, and the only sign he almost perished in a
stew of thick, toxic smoke and flames was the sling that his arm
rested in. Even his ability to walk without crutches and voice
had returned, but not without several weeks of intensive
physical and speech therapy.

It could have been worse for Alex. His young lifespan
almost snatched by the hand of death, which is the way it ended
for the three others involved.

Alex sat, anxious, scoping out the waiting area. He searched
for any ounce of happiness he could in the stranger's faces he

observed. Before that day on the rooftop, Alex felt he had an opportunity to find his happiness again, but now the possibility of that ever happening were bleak. Without even realizing it, he bounced his leg up and down, shaking the entire section of seats. Annoyed passengers turned and stared at him, but he paid them no attention. He stopped, slouched back in the uncomfortable plastic chair, and closed his eyes. He allowed his mind to drift back to the 12th of January. This day would forever remain frozen in his mind. For that day was the final moments he spent with Mike in the hospital.

He remembered the day well; it was seven days after the explosion. He was changing out of his hospital gown and back into a comfy pair of jeans, button-down shirt, and a sensible pair of tennis shoes that Amy had delivered to him. The doctor had just signed off on his discharge from Lutheran Medical. But there was just one thing; he wasn't leaving Mike alone to die in the hospital.

By now, Alex had regained the ability to speak and made the heart-wrenching call to Mike's family. He'd had to tell parents before that their loved one had passed, but when the loved one is also yours, it tears your insides out. Mike's parents and brother boarded a red-eye flight from San Diego and arrived the morning of the 13th.

He recalled napping, his head lying on the side of the hospital bed when they all rushed into the room. He never left Mike's side.

A loud crash as someone's luggage slammed against the marble floor jogged his mind back to reality for a split second, but he again closed his eyes and focused back to Mike.

He remembered how on the 15th of January the doctors
came in and spoke with him and Mike's parents. God, how Alex
hated them. The doctor delivered the bad news; Mike only had
a less than five percent chance of ever regaining consciousness,
and even if he did, he'd never been the same person as he was
before the explosion.

Alex stood next to Mike's mom, as she broke down in tears
and fell into the arms of her husband, Jacob. He recalled how
he interjected, trying to clarify what the doctor was saying.

Alex pleaded with the Temple family.

"Keep him on the ventilator, he will pull through, I can feel
it."

It didn't matter — Alex's voice didn't make one difference,
and his wishes were overruled by the family's because he and
Mike never made it to their official wedding date. According to
the law, Alex was nobody and didn't get to decide life over
death. It was up to Mike's parents now.

The family took a few days to ponder the pros and cons of
removing their son from life support, and the day arrived, the
17th, and Mike's father pulled the plug.

Alex stayed in the room, watching as they unhooked the
breathing machine from him. He watched as his breathing
slowed with each breath until after fifteen minutes, his chest
stopped rising. The Temples said goodbye first, and after a few
moments, they left Alex alone to say his final farewell to the one
solid figure in his life.

Alex held his cold hand and said a few words as a stream of tears rolled down his face, dripping onto the bedsheet. Alex pulled himself together and kissed his lover on the forehead as he stood. He didn't want to feel anymore, he didn't want to think, all he felt now was revenge pulsing through his veins.

His face leaned in closer to Mike's ear and he whispered, "I love you with all of my heart, and there will be hell to pay for what these bastards did to you."

He walked out of the room and into the sterile corridor, and there stood his best friend in the entire world, Amy. The two just gazed at each other and without even saying a word, she ran up to him and wrapped her arms around his shoulders, pulling him in closer to her.

Alex sobbed. They stood there together until Alex couldn't stand anymore and allowed himself to fall against the wall. His knees gave out next as his tattered body slid down to the cold floor.

Amy knelt down with him and placed her hand under his chin, lifting his head up so she could look at him in the eyes.

"I understand now why you have to go to Germany. If you don't finish this, then who will?" she said as she handed him a tissue.

Alex wiped his face and blew his runny nose. "So, you support my decision?"

"100 percent, yes," she said, "at first I was being selfish. But now we've lost Mike, and someone has to pay for taking him."

"They'll pay. And you better believe I'll be back, stronger than ever."

Amy looked worried. "One thing that still bothers me is that I'm scared if you go, you're not coming back except in a body bag."

She began crying again.

"But, after everything that's happened, make me a promise — promise me you'll take out every single one of them. No one kills the people we love and lives to tell about it."

Alex nodded as the two sat on the floor of the hospital corridor a little while longer.

Alex had to get out. The two left the hospital, and Amy drove him back to his condo a few miles away. His thoughts were working overtime. How was he going to feel walking inside the home they both shared for so long — alone?

If I survive this rescue mission, I'm never returning to this condo again.

She escorted him to the door and unlocked the door for him. They walked inside. It felt odd. He walked along the hallway, eyeballing the pictures hanging on the wall. Each picture told a story of love, determination, and sacrifice.

Happy. Smiling people. That's who they used to be until the Smirnov family destroyed all of it.

They emerged into the living room, and the first thing that caught his eye was a mysterious FedEx envelope with his name on it lying on the coffee table.

How'd this get here?

Alex shook the envelope and determined it posed no threat. He couldn't understand how the package made its way to his coffee table.

Alex ripped the perforated tear strip and inside was just a sheet of paper with instructions typed up.

Your father is waiting for you. On the 4th of March take the overnight flight which departs from JFK at eight in the evening.
The flight will bring you to Berlin.
Go to locker number 242 in the arrivals area, and you will find further instructions located inside.
No surprises—and come alone.

Amy snatched the letter from Alex's hand as he shook the envelope. A small metal key dropped onto the table, and Amy lifted her eyes from the paper.

"Looks like this is it," she said, "we have plenty of time to prepare for the attack."

With those words from Amy bouncing around in his head, his eyes flashed open, and he looked down at his watch. It was 6:55 in the evening and the sun was fading into the horizon. He knew he'd have to board in five minutes and had one final phone call to make before he got on that plane.

Unzipping the small pocket of his backpack, Alex pulled out his Blackberry. Alex searched through his contact list until he got to John Davidson. He pressed send and lifted the phone to his ear, and it rang once.

"You ready to do this?" Alex asked.

Alex nodded as he listened to the response. The gate agent came over the speaker and announced the boarding of the flight.

"I'll meet you at the baggage claim in Berlin. And John, remember, this is just between you and me. No one else can know about our plan."

Alex ended the call. He slipped the phone into his backpack, stood, and flung it across his good shoulder. Alex limped towards the gate. He gazed about and took a deep breath.

Well, this is it.

He stood in line, and once he arrived at the front, he handed his paper boarding pass to the agent. He strolled down the jetway wondering if he'd even make it back to New York alive.

ACKNOWLEDGMENT

Thank you to the following individuals who without their contributions and support this book would not have become a reality:

First, to my husband Jesse for his love and support throughout this process. None of the work would have ever been possible without his constant support and love to help me share this story with the world.

Also, special shout-outs have got to go to my beta-readers: Jennifer Cobleigh, Kelly Milliken, and Heather Bothern. These ladies worked countless hours reading and offering constructive feedback. Their challenging work helped fine tune this book into a finished product.

I must thank my amazing editor Deborah Nemeth for all the hard work and time spent working with me to edit this amazing story and giving it the voice it deserves.

And finally, to my amazing fans who keep me striving to keep writing for you and developing amazing stories.

ABOUT THE AUTHOR

C.L. Brees, the author of the thrillers An Unsettled Past (2016) and Dark Ending (2017), was born and raised in rural northeastern Indiana but always had his sights set on exploring the world. Currently, he and his husband live in Baden-Württemberg, Germany where they will live until 2021.

In his free time, in between work and other obligations, he has his attention focused on completing two future novels: Repressed Memories which will be available in late spring 2018 and the third and final novel in the Alex Jones series, *The Whole Truth*, which will become available in 2019.

C.L. earned his B.S. in Forensic Science, Magna Cum Laude, and his M.S. in Cyber Forensics from the University of Baltimore in 2014 and 2015, respectively, where he also worked as a criminal justice/forensics research assistant for two years.

For more information, you can reach C.L. Brees via:
Facebook -CLBrees
Twitter – CLBreesAuthor
Instagram - c_l_brees_author
Goodreads – C.L. Brees

www.ingramcontent.com/pod-product-compliance
Lightning Source LLC
Chambersburg PA
CBHW070645180626
46817CB00006B/2247